BODY
IN THE
WOODS

Dawn Brookes

Body
In the
Woods
Carlos Jacobi PI

Large Print Edition

Dawn Brookes

Oakwood Publishing

Paperback Edition 2020

Kindle Edition 2020

Paperback ISBN: 978-1-913065-24-9

Hardback: 978-1-913065-25-6

Large Print: 978-1-913065-29-4
Cover Images: Dog AdobeStockImages/© Даша Швецова Man: AdobeStockImages/© sanderstock

Cover Design: Janet Dado

Be Strong

Chapter 1

Fifty-five years of marriage and he'd not once been late for a meal. Meg stared wearily through the window. The streetlights blinked on the pavement and the darkening sky now reflected her mood.

She paced the floor for the umpteenth time, finding herself once more at the back of the lounge-dining room. Her trembling hands hovered over the two cold dinners neatly placed on decorated table mats. *Should I clear them away?* What would he say if he found cold food on the table? She shook, not knowing what to do.

'Where are you, Harold?' The empty walls ignored her quietly spoken, tremulous words.

Seven, and the cuckoo burst from her husband's clock, screaming loud and incessant, making her jump. Tears burned the back of her eyes. Anxiety threatened to overwhelm her.

'Don't cry, Meg. Crying gets us nowhere.' She imagined her husband's sharp voice chastising her as he always did whenever she showed a trace of emotion. But where was he? If only he would chastise her now. She snatched at the phone for the second time, desperate to call the police, but then remembered the dismissive voice of the desk sergeant she had spoken to earlier. Was it only two hours since she'd placed hot dinners on the table? Only one hour since she had called the police?

Harold Sissons was never late. She had explained this to the sergeant after insisting she was put through to someone in authority following a conversation with a girl whose disinterest had caused Meg to raise her voice. Something she never did.

The sergeant had responded with the same degree of condescension as the girl who answered before him.

'Look, madam. He's only been missing for an hour, that hardly counts as late in my book.' To make matters worse, he'd laughed, clearly not understanding her distress. When she hadn't responded to his inappropriate attempt at humour, he had sighed and continued. 'He's probably stopped by the shops, gone to the pub, dropped in at the bookies.'

'We live in a village, and my husband doesn't gamble, Sergeant. And he wouldn't go to the pub without letting me know, or to the shops, for that matter.' *Or would he?* she thought.

'You keep him on a tight leash, then?' The sergeant's tone infuriated Meg.

'Sergeant, my husband is missing. Do. You. Hear. Me? He hasn't come home, his dinner's gone cold on the table, and I'm telling you again. HE IS NEVER LATE!'

'Have you tried calling him?'

'Of course I have.' *You stupid man*, remained unsaid. The tension in her hand as she gripped the phone tighter translated into her voice and her head ached as she fought to remain calm. 'He's left his mobile phone behind; he must have forgotten it.'

'And is that out of character?'

'Yes, it is, as a matter of fact.' Meg tried to control a cold chill sitting on her stomach.

'There you are, then. He's having an out of character day. He'll be home soon, I'm sure.' Meg detected the smug tone in his triumphant explanation and wasn't sure whether she could also hear a girl giggling in the background.

'HE WILL NOT!' She was shouting for the second time in a matter of minutes. The anger caused her to shake. *I mustn't lose control; Harold wouldn't like that.*

The sergeant had briefly hesitated; she imagined him weighing up whether she was a lunatic or whether to take her seriously.

'Madam, why don't you ring round his friends and ask if they know where he is? Someone will have seen him. Do you have any family you can call?'

'I am not acquainted with my husband's friends. He would have been at the community centre this afternoon for their weekly lecture, and then he would come straight home. As for my daughter and son-in-law, they have a lot on their plates presently. I can't call them.'

She neglected to say that her daughter hadn't spoken to her father in twenty years.

'The only other thing I can suggest for now is that you phone the local hospitals in case he's been involved in an accident. If he doesn't come home later, give me a call back and I'll send someone round to get a description. I'm sure he'll turn up.' The sergeant's tone had turned more serious and she was grateful that he'd finally got the message.

After ending the call, she had phoned all the local hospitals, but her husband had not been admitted to any of them. She deliberated walking up to the village church to find the vicar, who would have seen Harold that afternoon, but she knew Harold wouldn't like that. He'd think she was checking up on him. Should she call the vicar's wife? She was always kind.

As Meg stared again at the telephone in her hand, she wondered if an hour constituted 'later'. What the heck? She dialled the number, asking to be put through to the desk sergeant.

While she was waiting for the police to arrive, a feeling of dread caused her to go lightheaded as she sat beside the window, staring out into the dark wintry night once more.

Chapter 2

The queues of traffic sprawling across all three lanes of the motorway finally moved, and within minutes, the car was back up to seventy miles per hour. Seeing no obvious reason for the delay, Carlos Jacobi was just happy to be making headway. Inexplicable delays were not unusual on the M1 motorway, but that didn't make them any less frustrating. The traffic had been snarled up for over forty minutes.

A huge ball of late afternoon sun produced an unwelcome glare, making it difficult to see clearly as he continued northwards. He was already running late. Darkness soon replaced daylight and he kept his distance behind a stack of taillights, finally arriving at his turnoff and heading northwest into the Derbyshire countryside. Thirty minutes later, he pulled up on to a large gravelled driveway as the sound of rain tapped out a melody on the roof of his pride and joy, an ancient refurbished Ford Capri.

'Wake up, Lady, we're here.' His three-year-old liver-and-white English Springer Spaniel immediately leapt up and whined. He stroked her head before opening the car door. She didn't wait to be let out the passenger side, but flew after him, diving through the driver's door and, with one swift movement, she stood by his side, tail wagging furiously.

'Looks like you're as pleased to get out of the car as I am, girl.' Carlos bent down and rubbed her head.

The dog let out a small bark before bounding around the car to find a patch of lawn off to one side of the low-walled front garden where she relieved herself.

The front door of the cottage flew open and Sophie rushed out.

'Where have you been? I expected you hours ago.' His younger sister looked well, a five-foot-six rounded bundle of energy. Light from the hallway shone on to the now soaking wet drive where heavy rain bounced off the gravel. He rushed over to embrace her and kissed her on both cheeks.

'Sorry, I was late leaving London and got stuck in traffic three times, the worst lot south of Derby.' Following the greeting, he raced back out to the car and pulled his suitcase from the boot. As he was locking the boot by hand, he almost jumped at the figure of an anxious older woman, her face drawn with tension, staring through the bay window from the cottage next door. Recovering, he smiled, but she didn't smile back. Her haunting stare sent a shiver down his spine.

Carlos broke eye contact and headed indoors with Lady close to his heels. His lively companion soon made herself at home, running enthusiastically around the living room, excitement overwhelming her.

He stopped to admire his sister. As her big brown eyes looked at him affectionately and her round face broke into a huge grin, his heart melted.

'You're looking good, Sophie, and wow! What about this?' His arm extended to envelop the large open-plan lounge-diner. 'A bit bigger than your last place.' Carlos took in his surroundings. Sophie had married in the spring and she and her husband, Gary, had moved six months ago into their first owned home: a large detached cottage on the edge of the village. It was the first time Carlos had visited their new place in Peak Hollow.

'Thank you. We love it here. The cottage is just what I've always wanted; plenty of space and room for a family.'

Carlos's mouth dropped open.

'No, Carlos. I'm not pregnant. Yet. But we would like children in a few years' time. You know I love kids.'

'When they come along, I'm sure they'll be wonderful. I can't wait to see little Sophies running around the place. By the way, where's Gary?'

'Working late as usual,' she sighed. 'You men are all the same.'

'Whoa! That's so sexist, Sophie. And as you well know, in this particular man's case, Rachel works as much, if not more than I do.'

'I stand corrected. Just a figure of speech; he'll be home soon, anyway.'

His sister walked through to the kitchen and put the coffee percolator on. Carlos followed. The interior contrasted with the property's age and was tastefully decorated with fashionable ash-grey paint and smart laminate flooring, now covered in muddy pawprints. He grimaced.

The expansive tile-floored kitchen was dominated by an island in the centre with a table in a recess. He parked himself on a stool at the island while his sister made coffee, feeling at home immediately. He and Sophie had always been close. It didn't matter that they lived a hundred and sixty miles apart, he would make the effort to see her. They were the only two of their family still living in England. Their parents and older brothers had moved back to Florence in Italy while Sophie was at university, and Carlos felt responsible for his baby sister, even though she was only a few years younger than him at twenty-six. Now she was married it was different, but he had promised his parents he would always take care of her, and this duty – albeit more of a pleasure – he took seriously.

'How is Rachel? It's such a shame she can't join us.' Sophie's voice pulled him from his reverie.

'She's good. Working too hard, as usual. On nights right up to New Year. After that, she moves to London, so I'm not complaining. I'm hoping to nip up to Leeds while I'm here to take her out for a Christmas celebration before one of her shifts.'

Carlos's heart pounded as it always did when he thought about the woman he'd been dating for just over a year. Sometimes the love he felt for her threatened to overwhelm him. Rachel worked as police officer and they had met on a cruise ship when he was working two cases. Rachel's beauty had distracted him from the moment they met, and as it turned out, she was the one who had saved the elderly woman he was supposed to be protecting.

He reached into his rucksack and brought out a dog bowl. 'Would you mind filling this? Lady needs a drink.'

Sophie took the bowl and filled it before setting it down on the floor. Lady gulped the water down as if she hadn't drunk in days and almost finished the bowl, dribbling water on to the pristine white tiles.

'Yuck! Is she always this messy?'

'Only when she's thirsty,' he laughed. 'Dogs are always thirstier after car travel, it seems; either that or she's showing off.' Carlos unpacked another bowl from his rucksack and pulled a bag of dried dog food from his suitcase before filling that too and laying it on the floor. 'Sorry about the mucky pawprints.'

They were interrupted by the front door opening. Sophie's eyes lit up again as she ran through to the lounge. Carlos followed.

'About time too!' She hugged the tall, wiry Gary who leaned down to kiss her. His sister was a whirlwind and was well and truly besotted with this most unlikely of matches.

'Sorry, Soph. We have to finish the project before the Christmas break.' He smiled down at her.

Carlos coughed.

'Hello, Carlos, I saw the Capri. She's looking good. Welcome to Peaks Hollow. How do you like our new home?' Gary shook Carlos's hand. He was the exact opposite of Sophie: a reserved Englishman, tall and lanky compared to her, but it was obvious the man adored his wife as much as she did him.

'Love it. I approve of the choice. Almost on the edge of the village, too. It beats London flats, that's for sure.'

'And this must be Lady.' Gary bent down to stroke the excited dog who was running circles around him, flicking his legs with her tail.

'That's her, and she likes you, so that's a good sign.' Carlos laughed as Gary cautiously stroked her belly while she rolled on to her back, keeping enough distance not to allow dog hairs to meet his neatly pressed trousers, Carlos noticed.

The happy trio retired to the kitchen and chatted excitedly. Lady settled down at Carlos's feet.

'What are you working on that's so urgent it can't wait until after the festive season?' Carlos asked.

'Come on, Carlos, you know better than to ask him about his work,' Sophie scolded.

Gary worked for Rolls Royce in Derby as a scientific development manager and Carlos knew his work was highly confidential, but that wouldn't stop him asking. Industrial espionage was a real threat in big business, according to his brother-in-law. 'All I can say is it's something very exciting and we have to finish stage one by Christmas Eve.'

Carlos raised an eyebrow. 'Electric cars are old news, you know.'

Gary jumped. 'No-one has seen the likes of this project. It's groundbreaking, and I didn't say it was a car.'

Carlos grinned widely and shot a smug look Sophie's way.

'Don't be irritating, Carlos, and don't imagine for one minute you know what my husband's working on.' Sophie frowned. 'Anyway, what about you? Any exciting cases lately?'

'Not exactly, but I am still wrapping one up – another reason I chose Derbyshire for Christmas.'

'That's so flattering, brother. Did you hear that, Lady? He's going to make you work over Christmas.' Sophie appeared to be warming to having a dog around and knelt to stroke Lady's ears. The spaniel's eyes were as big and brown as

Sophie's; it brought a smile to Carlos's face seeing the two girls gazing adoringly at each other. 'That's the real reason you're not in Leeds.' It was his sister's turn to look smug. The easy banter came automatically whenever they were together.

'Life's never dull for a private detective; you understand that, Sophie. I miss your help, to be honest, so I've had to take on a new guy.'

'Remind me I need to speak to you about something important later.'

Carlos raised his eyebrows quizzically, but Sophie's attention was now taken up with chopping vegetables.

'Anything we can help you with, bro?' asked Gary, pouring himself a coffee from the percolator.

Did you just call me bro? Carlos's eyebrows hit the ceiling. Although a geeky scientist, his brother-in-law showed a keen interest in Carlos's work. Gary wouldn't have the stamina or the stomach to deal with the things he got involved with, though.

'I'll let you know if I need anything, but I'm hoping it will be over in a few days so we can enjoy Christmas.'

Gary kissed Sophie on the head. 'I'll take a quick shower, then I can help you.'

'No need, it's all under control.'

Chapter 3

Sophie cooked spaghetti alle vongole, knowing it was one of Carlos's favourite dishes. They shared a bottle of Santa Margherita Pinot Grigio, a famous white wine from the Valdadige region of northern Italy. Carlos had produced a case from his car shortly after Gary arrived home – it was his brother-in-law's preferred Italian wine. They talked easily during and after dinner, and Carlos relaxed from his hectic day.

'I'd better take Lady out for a walk before it gets any later; the poor girl's been cooped up all day. I took her to the office today so we could head straight up here after work.' Carlos checked his watch: ten-thirty. 'Where do you recommend?'

'There's a green close by. I'll come with you,' said Gary. 'We can take torches.'

'What about the woods?' asked Sophie.

'That sounds good. Lady loves woodland – is it near?'

'Yep, just across from the green. Would you rather go there? There's a circular path we can take, runs for about three miles. We might even hear some owls now the rain's stopped lashing.'

The rain had turned out to be a heavy downpour with strong winds that battered the building for the first few hours after Carlos arrived. Now it was eerily quiet, the calm after the Derbyshire storm.

Carlos nodded. He and Lady often went for late-night walks in London, as his job frequently meant burning the midnight oil and he preferred the solitude the dark offered. He picked up the dog's lead, which caused her to leap up and race round in circles, tail wagging like a helicopter rotor blade.

'I sometimes think she's going to take off,' he laughed while waiting for her to settle. Eventually she sat and allowed him to apply the lead. Carlos exited first with Lady and subconsciously turned to look to where he'd seen the old lady earlier.

He was disturbed to see the gaunt shadow still at the window, staring out into the darkness from an unlit room.

'What's with your neighbour? She's been staring out of her window since I got here, I think.'

'That's Mrs Sissons. Her husband went missing a week ago. She's more or less sat by the window ever since. The police think he's done a runner, she tells us. It's odd, because they seemed such a devoted couple; a little eccentric, but decent and welcoming when we first moved in. Soph pops in most days to make sure the old dear's had something to eat, but other than that—'

Before Gary launched into one of his long-winded explanations, Carlos cut in. 'Why do the police think her husband's left her?'

'I'm not sure, Soph knows the details better than I do. In fact, she's going to ask you to investigate his disappearance. Mrs Sissons has convinced her there's something sinister going on, but don't tell Sophie I told you or I'll be in the doghouse. Sorry, Lady – no offence.'

Carlos's interest was piqued; Sophie wasn't easily taken in, so if she thought there was more to the story than a wayward husband, there probably was.

They crossed the field in the dark as drizzle started to fall again, making him wet.

'Do you still want to go into the woods?' asked Gary, not appearing quite so keen now.

'I'm game if you are.'

'Why not?' Gary shrugged. 'It's just across the road there.'

They crossed a dimly lit road and entered a clearing through a kissing gate. Carlos shone his torch and noticed the path went in both directions.

'Which way?'

'Either. It's a circular, so you choose.'

'Looks like Lady's chosen for us.' Lady had her nose to the ground, taking the path to the left. Going clockwise, she raced ahead, clearly delighted by the new smells. She dashed in and out of the woods, always coming back to check that Carlos was where she thought he should be.

Gary laughed. 'She's enjoying this.'

'I expect she can smell other dog scents and squirrels; she has a great nose. She's an ex-police dog, belonged to a friend of mine. He emigrated to Australia.'

'Why isn't she still a police dog?'

'Seems she has some quirks that make her difficult to work with. Barry told me she wouldn't work with the guy who was supposed to take her on. Refused to do his bidding, so they decided she was too unpredictable for a police dog. Can't say I'm complaining, though. She's been a great help with my investigations. I've taught her some new skills; she's a fast learner. She obviously likes your woods.'

'This is a dog walker's paradise, so I'm not surprised.'

The two men walked along the path with Carlos training his torch to light the way ahead. The path was wet and muddy from the earlier rain and the drizzle fell a little more heavily, although the larger tree branches and evergreens provided some shelter.

'I bet this is beautiful in the summer,' Carlos remarked.

'It is. Once the leaves are on the trees, they form a canopy. They've taken a lot of the trees out to let some light in. It's called Shady Woods because it used to be exceptionally dark. Now, it's just dark. The woods are a wildlife haven with many varieties of birds nesting in the spring. We're looking forward to that. The locals tell me they often get a pair of green woodpeckers. There are bats, badger setts and fox dens.'

'Sophie spends a lot of time here, then.' It was a statement rather than a question. Carlos was aware his sister loved bird watching and he imagined her out with binoculars and camera.

'She's started to. At first, we were too busy doing up the house and arranging furniture how she likes it. You know what your sister's like; has a real eye for interior design. Wait until you see what she's done upstairs, I think you'll be impressed. Her new job's time-consuming as well, but she loves it.'

Carlos smiled at the pride in Gary's voice, feeling as much pride himself. He was pleased that the man next to him loved his sister. It made him easier to get along with despite his nerdy ways.

As children, Carlos and Sophie were sometimes teased for their Italian accents. Sophie had been a sensitive little girl who never saw bad in anyone. She took it badly. Carlos dealt with boys who teased his sister, but he couldn't do anything about the girls, as he had been taught to treat girls with courtesy and respect. The teasing only lasted a few months. Sophie toned her accent down, told people to call her Sophie rather than Sofia and adapted so much, she sounded English until she got excited. Carlos hung on to a slight Italian accent more by stubbornness than necessity. He was proud of his heritage, but could sound as English as anyone when necessary.

He and Gary had been strolling around the woods for twenty minutes when Carlos realised Lady hadn't checked in on them for a while. They stopped walking and he listened to a tawny owl's familiar hunting call: a sound that could be frightening on a dark night. He sensed Gary's unease at the spooky sound as the owl obviously dived towards its prey, then he heard barking in the distance.

'That's Lady. I bet she's found a foxes' den. LADY!' he called, but she didn't appear. The barking continued.

'Good job we put boots on; it's coming from the woods through there,' moaned Gary. 'Perhaps we should get her and go home; the rain's getting heavier.'

Carlos puffed out his cheeks in despair, but led the way, shining his torch to light the route ahead of him, calling his dog as he went.

'Sorry about this, she doesn't normally run off, but it's a new place and I guess she's found something interesting.'

Finally, Lady appeared from nowhere, paws covered in wet mud.

'Am I glad to see you, you filthy mutt. Come on, Lady, it's wet. Let's go home, girl.' Carlos turned to go back in the direction they'd come from, but Lady barked and dashed back into the dense part of the woods again.

'I think she wants us to follow her,' he said and walked faster, taking the direction his dog had gone. Carlos felt the damp seeping through his trousers and muttered, 'If this is a fox den, she's getting no supper.'

Gary slowed down; Carlos could hear his footsteps cautiously following. He turned and checked on his brother-in-law who was now using a mobile phone as a torch.

Lady's barking drew Carlos off to the right. As he turned, he tripped over a raised tree root and stumbled headlong into a holly bush. He cursed. The torch hit a large stone and stopped working. He felt the pain in his palms as holly leaves pierced his skin.

'Are you all right?' Gary arrived and shone his mobile on Carlos's face.

'Fine, just a few prickles, and feeling like a bit of an idiot. Torch's stopped working now; I'm afraid my girl is being a nuisance tonight.'

'If I were a dog in these woods, I'd be running around like a headless ape, too! You might want to take a shower or a bath when we get back, though. How do we clean her up?'

Gary was clearly concerned about the hall carpet. Carlos ignored the question for now, looking down at his hands under the illumination of the torch from Gary's phone. They were grazed and prickled. Spots of blood mixed with dirt trickled down his palms, his clothes were covered in mud, but getting Lady back was his main priority.

'I just hope it's only mud I've fallen in.' He grimaced as he picked up his torch, shaking it a few times. The light came back on and they walked another hundred yards towards Lady's barking. Carlos saw his dog, who quieted as they arrived at a small clearing.

Lady sat still, head in the air, exactly how his friend had taught her to, and Carlos's heart sank. This was not a good sign. He looked at the ground in front of her where she had carefully dug down through the soft earth.

Gary gasped as Carlos shone his torch on where she sat. Carlos immediately recognised the remains of a human hand, exposed by her digging. As Gary turned and walked quickly away to the edge of the clearing, Carlos empathised slightly before rolling his eyes as he heard his brother-in-law heaving up the dinner he'd eaten earlier. Meanwhile, Lady continued to sit stock-still and barked, waiting for a meaty treat. Lady had initially trained as a cadaver dog.

Chapter 4

Carlos shone his torch, trying to analyse the scene while waiting for Gary to return with the police. There was no phone signal in this part of the woods, but Gary had been pleased to get away to make the call; his brother-in-law had never seen a dead body. Carlos suggested Lady accompany him as she would be able to retrace her steps and lead the police back to the exact spot; he didn't trust Gary in his state to remember where the body was and didn't want to spend a wet night in the woods.

Lady had been meticulous in her digging, revealing just enough to show the bloated hand. A man's wristwatch was buried deep within the flesh that bacteria and gases had caused to swell. There wasn't much else for his torch to reveal.

The hand protruding from the mound of wet earth where Lady had dug a small hole was that of a male Caucasian. It was a left hand, no wedding ring. Older men didn't always wear them, Carlos mused. Maggots had already begun their work of moving through flesh and the stench of the bacteria, which had been released along with the hand, now assaulted Carlos's nostrils. He had come across this smell before in Afghanistan and more recently as a PI, but he took a deep breath, nonetheless.

'Anaerobes,' he muttered. This, and the state of decay, pointed to the body being buried in recent days or weeks. Forensics would be able to provide a more accurate estimate.

The body appeared to have been carefully buried and well-hidden. Carlos sorely wanted to move more earth and investigate, but knew he shouldn't disturb the scene. He realised it was a lucky find: only a canny fox or a dog such as Lady, trained in searching for cadavers, would have been able to dig this one up. The earth was soft, but well-camouflaged with rocks, twigs and leaves. Anyone crazy enough to be walking this deep inside the woods would have walked right over the burial site without noticing anything was amiss.

It wasn't easy searching around with a torch in the drizzly black night, but he picked up a piece of cloth from the hole Lady had dug and pocketed it. He argued with himself about doing this, but shook his head, on instinct refusing to listen to his conscience.

Carlos was relieved to hear Lady's barking, shortly followed by torchlight and the sound of a man's voice as the police finally arrived. He was cold, wet and tired. Lady came bounding into the clearing and brought herself to a halt, sitting stock-still in front of the exposed hand just as she had done after she revealed the body.

'Good girl.' Carlos gave her another meat treat from his pocket.

The dog wagged her tail vigorously in response.

A burly uniformed officer arrived, brusquely insisting Carlos move away before taping off the scene around the body.

'I hope you haven't touched anything,' he growled.

'Not a thing. My dog exposed the hand you can see over there, that's all. She was a trained cadaver dog before I had her.'

'Yeah, right,' the officer grumbled, ignoring Carlos and Lady, continuing to set up the required cordon with striped tape.

'Totally unnecessary,' Carlos muttered to himself, particularly annoyed as it had taken all his willpower to resist unearthing the body and looking for more clues.

'You can go now. CID is on the way.'

'Don't you want to take a statement, Officer?' Sarcasm flowed through Carlos's voice.

'We have your details from the man who called us. Someone will be in touch.' His tone remained gruff, but Carlos saw no need to argue so shrugged his shoulders.

'What have you done with my brother-in-law?'

'He's waiting on the path at the edge of the woods, didn't want to come in, said the dog would lead the way, and he did.'

'She.'

'What?'

'She. The dog is a she.'

The officer shrugged his shoulders. 'Well, whatever the sex, it shouldn't have been digging. Might have destroyed a crime scene.'

Carlos raised his eyes at the man's ridiculous comments. 'I can assure you, she hasn't destroyed anything. She used to be a police cadaver dog, as I just said. I'm sure my brother-in-law would have mentioned it as well!'

'He did say something about the animal. Difficult to hear in these woods.'

Carlos clenched his fists in his pockets. 'Yeah, although I heard you coming long before you arrived, but perhaps your hearing's less acute than mine, PC Brandon.'

The officer stopped what he was doing. 'How did you know my name?'

Carlos swung his torch over the officer's shoulder. 'It's on your epaulette.'

'Can you shine that thing elsewhere?' Brandon growled. 'Anyway, as you can see, I need to get on.'

'No problem, Officer. Come on, Lady. Good girl, time to go.' Carlos gave her more treats, praising her as they left the scene. He very much doubted PC Brandon would get on with anything other than wait for senior officers to arrive, but was glad to see the back of him. He would try to find out more about the cause of death when whoever was in charge interviewed him.

Lady relaxed now she was released from duty and bounded ahead towards Gary, who they found pacing back and forth along the path.

'Sorry, Carlos. I couldn't face that sight again.'

'I get that. Not pretty.'

On the way out of the woods, they noticed torch lights approaching from a different direction, cutting through the undergrowth rather than taking the path. They veered off out of sight.

'I don't think that copper liked coming out on his own. Complained the whole time he was with me that he should have someone with him and how he'd only just cleaned and polished his shoes. Then he moaned about cutbacks before trudging after Lady. I'm not sure he believed there was a body at all.'

'He gave me much the same impression, a true professional.'

Carlos couldn't keep the sarcasm or his annoyance at the officer's attitude back any longer. 'He's in for a long night once forensics is on the scene.'

Gary didn't say anything else until they were almost at his house. The drizzle continued to add to the macabre atmosphere following their discovery. Carlos knew his brother-in-law was shocked by the experience.

Carlos spoke first. 'I have a sinking feeling that might be your neighbour's missing husband.'

'What makes you say that?'

'Too much of a coincidence not to be. Obviously, we won't know until the body has been identified, but how likely is it to be someone else when a man goes missing and a body in the right state of decay turns up a week later, hardly a mile from his home? I had a closer look while you were away. The hand was that of an elderly white male, so unless you've got a geriatric serial killer in the neighbourhood, my money's on it being him.'

'Poor Mrs Sissons.'

Carlos felt relieved when he noted she was no longer sitting in the window. 'Get some sleep while you can,' he whispered.

***

It was well after midnight when Sophie suggested they go to bed having been brought up to speed with the grisly find. She had taken the information in her stride as she always did, except for the part about the probable identity of the body.

Carlos hugged her goodnight and she looked up, tears welling.

'Poor Meg. I do hope it's not Harold – she'll be devastated, you know. They doted on each other; she hardly ever went out without him. She's been completely lost since he went missing. I was going to talk to you about his disappearance. When I told her what you did for a living, she suggested she could hire you to trace him. The police told her he'd done a bunk. They haven't been helpful at all, she tells me.'

'That's the bit I don't get. Why did the police think that? It seems an odd conclusion unless they have evidence she doesn't know about.'

'I'm not sure; you'll need to ask them if it does turn out to be Harold.'

'I will, and from the sounds of the racket outside, I won't have to wait too long. You go up to bed, Gary needs the rest. I suspect he won't want to relive the scene again tonight, delicate man that he is. I'll deal with the police.'

'You're right, he hates anything gory. The only TV he ever watches are scientific documentaries and football. I have to record my crime programmes and watch them when he's working in his study or at a Mensa evening.'

Carlos hadn't realised Gary was a member of Mensa, but it figured. 'That must be challenging. The crime thing, rather than the Mensa. I know how much you like a good thriller.'

Sophie smiled up at him. 'It's no hardship, Gary's a wonderful husband.'

Carlos opened the front door before any more noise woke the old lady next door. He was about to tell the police to be quiet until he saw the brawny man with the familiar snake tattoo on the right side of his neck, poking its head above his loose shirt collar and overcoat. Carlos scowled, hoping this was a bad dream. His night had just got a whole lot worse.

'Jacobi. I heard that a guy going by your name had found a body in my neck of the woods. Not many people with that, erm... surname in these parts.'

Any hope that the man in front of him might have changed evaporated when the lightly veiled anti-Semitism surfaced.

'Masters, I didn't know you worked in these parts.' The man had aged a bit, but looked the same arrogant idiot he'd always been. No wonder the poor woman next door had been told her husband was AWOL. This explained everything.

'Well, I do. DCI Masters now. Shall we do this outside or are you going to invite me in?'

Carlos stood to one side while Terry Masters brushed past, bursting into his sister's lounge followed by a smaller round guy, also in plain clothes, who Carlos assumed was his detective sergeant. Carlos closed the front door and the door to the hallway and followed the men. Lady sensed Carlos's distaste for Masters and stayed put, emitting a low warning growl while the insensitive man threw himself down on an armchair.

'Jacobi, McDonald.' A slight tilt of the head. That was all the introduction he was going to get.

Carlos and McDonald eyed each other cautiously, giving swift nods of greeting.

'I was just telling McDonald on the way here how I'd served with a man by the name of Carlos Jacobi in the specials. Didn't imagine it would be the same one, though. Last I heard you were working in London as some sort of pretend investigator.'

Carlos had wondered how long it would take before the next snipe came. 'I'm just visiting my sister for the Christmas break. This is her house. Her husband and I found a body in the woods. I assume that's what you're here about?' Carlos was growing impatient with the dancing around, but Masters clearly wasn't finished.

'Good, so you won't be staying long, then? I don't want amateurs poking their nose where it doesn't belong. Know what I mean?'

'Are you here to interview me about the body I discovered in the woods? Because if not, I've had a long day and would like to get to bed.' Carlos knew from experience the sparring had only just begun and Masters would box for ages until he felt he'd won. He was doing his best to stay calm. The worst thing he could do would be to nudge Masters into a place where he might be seen to lose face, particularly in front of someone he was doing his best to impress.

'Sergeant,' Masters nodded at the overweight man accompanying him.

Sergeant McDonald was late forties, moustache, nicotine-stained fingers, ill-fitting clothes and dirty shoes. Probably divorced or never married, weighed up Carlos. McDonald pulled a notebook from his pocket, but couldn't find a pen. Carlos raised an eyebrow while Masters tutted and handed one to the flushing sergeant. Poor man was probably confused at his boss's behaviour, unless Masters always spoke to witnesses like this.

'Yes, sir. Perhaps you could walk me through what happened this evening, Mr Jacobi.'

Carlos sighed. 'My brother-in-law and I were taking a walk in the woods on the other side of the village with my dog when she disappeared. We heard her barking, followed her into the denser part of the trees, and she led us to the body.'

Carlos was weighing up whether DS McDonald was like his boss or had been thrown by his attitude. His tone was flat, not aggressive, but there was an edge.

'Could you tell me what you were doing in the woods so late, Mr Jacobi?'

No-one from the police force had impressed Carlos so far this evening, which didn't bode well for finding the killer of the next-door neighbour's husband. If that was who Lady had found in the woods. He ran through the little he could tell them.

'As I said just now, Sergeant, we were walking the dog. I arrived up here late from London, had dinner and the dog needed exercise. My sister suggested the woods.'

'Fine dog, that,' said Masters, looking over at Lady who had settled herself at Carlos's feet, keeping one eye on Masters the whole time.

'Yes, she is, belonged to a friend of mine. Barry Tate, I'm sure you remember him.' Carlos couldn't resist the challenge.

A brief flicker of fear filled Masters's eyes. 'Yeah. Brute of a man, and a bully, McDonald. Be thankful you never met him.'

Nothing could have been further from the truth, but Carlos resisted retaliating. Instead, he took a different tack.

'I take it you believe the body's that of the neighbour's husband. The one who had done a bunk according to the local police?'

Masters's head shot up, 'Don't get smart with me, Jacobi. Just stay out of my way or—'

'Or what?' Carlos raised his eyebrows quizzically.

'Or I'll have to arrest you for obstruction. We don't know who the body belongs to yet. In the police force, we don't make assumptions; we wait for the evidence, and then make conclusions based on fact.'

'Touché,' answered Carlos, smiling for the first time.

Masters stood abruptly. He had the winning hand. 'Right, McDonald, I think we've got enough from Jacobi here. We may need to interview the sister and brother-in-law tomorrow. We'll need to know their whereabouts once we establish time of death.' He smirked.

'Leave them out of this, Masters. Whatever gripe you have with me doesn't involve them.'

'I don't know what you mean. It's for me to decide who does and does not have anything to do with my investigation.' Masters smirked again. 'Goodnight, Jacobi. We'll be in touch if we need anything else from you. Good dog,' Masters reached down to stroke Lady, but she let out a low growl and he withdrew the hand quickly.

Carlos would have slammed the door after them if it weren't for Sophie and Gary being in bed and it not being his own home. He felt the familiar rage that Masters always managed to bring out in him. He was furious with himself for taking the bait about Sophie and Gary; now he'd put them firmly on the man's radar as a weak spot.

Lady snuffled his hand and he ruffled the fur on her head. 'You didn't like him, either. Good girl. Shows you have taste. Why did it have to be him of all people? I thought I'd never have to see his face again. At least he didn't wake the old lady next door, that's something.'

Carlos sat for a while, reliving the memories of a day in Basra a few years earlier. Then he rubbed his dog's ears.

'Nope, Lady, he hasn't changed one little bit. Looks like it's down to us now.'

Chapter 5

Carlos slipped out of the house at 6am. He'd heard Gary get up and turn on the shower. Sophie was more of a night person, so he assumed she would be fast asleep. The morning was still and fresh, with frost turning the previous night's rain to ice patches.

'Come on, girl. Let's see what we can find.' He removed Lady's lead once they were at the edge of the woods and broke into a jog with

Lady running in and out of the trees like she had the night before. It was still dark, but he wore a head torch. He had hardly slept, mulling over his meeting with Masters all night, but now he had a plan of action.

When they got about halfway round the circuit path, Carlos stopped, waiting for Lady to join him. He put the piece of old cloth he'd removed from the crime scene the previous night to her nose.

'I knew it was right to keep this. Lady, find.'

Lady barked and hurtled off the main path into the denser part of the woods. He followed at a brisk walking pace, not wanting to trip over again. He still had grazed hands from the night before.

It didn't take long to arrive at the now cordoned-off area. It was just as he'd expected: police tape surrounding the scene, but no-one had been left to guard it. There was a forensics tent over to one side where someone could be sleeping, although he doubted it. Masters was living up to expectation.

Carlos approached the spot where Lady sat. His army training helped when stealth was required; he carefully avoided snapping any twigs on approach. Thankfully the ground underfoot was still damp under the canopy of trees where the frost hadn't managed to get through. This made his task easier.

'Good girl,' he whispered. 'Stay.'

The body had been removed. He made out five sets of footprints around the area where the digging had taken place. He suspected the forensics team would be back this morning to search for anything they may have missed under floodlight in the early hours. Masters was unlikely to put the team under pressure unless his senior officer was more diligent than he was.

Carlos decided to move away from the taped-off area. Concluding it would have been thoroughly searched, he started examining the perimeter. This part of the woods didn't appear well-used; Sophie had said that apart from kids and nature lovers, most people stuck to the main path. Even the adventurous would be more likely to venture into the denser areas during the spring when birds built their nests, attracted by the woodland and nest boxes strategically placed on trees at appropriate intervals.

Carlos called Lady softly with a low hooting sound and put the cloth to her nose again.

'Good girl. Find.' After turning her head back towards the cordoned-off area, she understood that he wanted her to look elsewhere, so she put her busy nose to the ground and snuffled, heading off a few metres away from where they stood. He followed cautiously. After a couple of minutes, they came to another small clearing and Lady stopped in front of a pile of leaves.

'Good girl, but shush. You deserve mega treats now and a big breakfast. Here, girl.' He handed her a few meat treats.

Carlos found a stick and moved the leaves slowly, using the stick to separate them. They were stiff from the frost which had reached them and moved in clumps. Underneath a large cluster, he stopped prodding as he spied something black protruding out of the soil. Carlos's heartbeat quickened as he looked around to make sure no-one was there, knowing he shouldn't be doing this. He donned a pair of gloves and pulled gently at the soil.

'Look at this, Lady. A wallet.'

He carefully opened it to find fifty pounds in ten-pound notes. There were a few coins in the zipper part, but more interesting were the credit cards and photo driving licence. An elderly man's face stared back at him. The name Harold Edward Sissons sent grim shock waves through his body. Even though he had been convinced the body would turn out to be that of Sophie's neighbour, he'd hoped not, for his sister's sake. And for the sake of the frail-looking old lady whose image he couldn't shake. Her staring out of the window of her picturesque country cottage haunted him.

Light broke through the trees and Carlos worried the police or forensics team might turn up any minute. After a quick shuffle around to see if anything else was hidden, he took a few photos and returned the wallet to where he'd found it, covering it again with the leaves. Any other time, he would have taken it to the lead investigating officer, but knowing Masters as he did, he knew the man would be furious. It was not an option.

'Come on, Lady. Time to go. Any forensics team or detective worth their salt should find it.' He hoped he was right. If not, he would have to accidentally stumble across the wallet at a later date and hand it in.

He and Lady finished running the circuit of the woods, something they hadn't got to do the previous night.

***

Carlos passed the time of day with a couple of dog walkers on the green he crossed on the way out of the woods. A few people defrosting their cars waved as he passed through the village. Most of them called out, 'Good morning.' Gary's car was no longer on the drive when he got back to their place.

He was still scrolling through the photos on his phone of the crime scene and the area where he'd found the wallet when he let himself in with the key Sophie had given him the night before. Lady ran in ahead. Sophie was up, buried in a long, fluffy purple dressing gown, and she greeted them both.

'Nice run?'

'Enlightening. We went back to your Shady Woods.'

'I bet Gary told you the story behind the name. Some people round here won't go in at all. They believe the name refers to odd goings-on. There's always folklore in village life. You'd better tell me what you found over a strong coffee. Gary hardly slept; he still felt sick this morning, you know. You could have told him not to come near once you found that body, Carlos. You know how sensitive he is.'

Carlos rolled his eyes. 'Seriously? He only got a brief glance before he ran off to throw up.'

Sophie laughed. 'It's not his thing. He's a scientist. Good at putting parts together, but not good with bodies. Anyway, he said it was the smell that made him sick. Says he could still smell it this morning.'

'It was rather rancid. But if it was the smell, what was I supposed to do? Ask the Good Lord to direct the wind in the opposite direction? He can only have got a whiff. Perhaps next time we go out, I'll make sure he brings a mask and dark goggles.' Carlos was more amused than irritated.

'If you could arrange that, I might get some sleep. Sorry, I'm a bit crotchety this morning. You know what I'm like if I don't get my eight hours.'

'In that case, I'll get the coffee. I need to give Lady breakfast anyway.'

He could already smell the percolated coffee coming from the kitchen. He poured two mugs, gave Lady some fresh water and food, and joined Sophie on a seat at the breakfast bar.

'So, tell me, why did you go back to the woods? Presumably to take another look at the scene.'

'I wouldn't have felt the need if I hadn't met the man in charge of the investigation last night. He's bad news, Sophie.'

'I thought I heard an edge to your voice when you answered the door. I was trying to listen, but Gary was telling me how ill he felt so we ended up watching an episode of

Gilmore Girls to get him calm enough to sleep.'

Carlos's eyebrows shot up. 'You're kidding?'

Sophie gave him a mock glare, daring him to continue, so he elected to say no more.

'So why is the detective bad news and what did you find at the crime scene?'

'How do you know I found anything?' he teased.

'The smug look on your face. You used to do that as a boy when you uncovered some secret.'

Carlos laughed. 'You obviously know me too well. To start with, I'll tell you about Terry Masters – he's the DCI leading this investigation. We were on the same team in Afghanistan.' Carlos sighed heavily, knowing it was going to hurt to recount events from that time. These were things that most ex-servicemen tucked away in the recesses of their brain like a Pandora's box, never to be opened.

'Go on,' Sophie encouraged, pouring them both more coffee.

Sophie's doorbell prevented him saying anything else.

'Who the heck's that? Can you get it? I'm not yet the housewife that answers the door in her dressing gown.'

'Working on it, though,' Carlos teased. He obediently went to the front door, hoping it wasn't Masters carrying out the threat to interview his sister. Lady accompanied him and he could see from the shadow through the frosted glass that it was not the burly DCI.

He opened the door and immediately recognised the frail, thin face looking up at him. Meg Sissons was enveloped in a large brown coat and he noticed she was trembling.

Carlos smiled down at her. 'Good morning. I'm Carlos, Sophie's brother, she's in the kitchen. Would you like to come in?'

'No, thank you. Please could you tell her the police found my Harold.' Her bottom lip trembled as she stoically tried to hold herself together. 'He's dead. I'm expecting a chief inspector at ten. I was wondering if you and your sister could be with me. I get a little forgetful these days and...'

'I understand. I'm sure Sophie will be there. I, erm... need to work this morning, I'm afraid.'

'Oh? I thought you were coming up for the holidays.' She stopped herself. 'Sorry, that's none of my business. I'll see Sophie at ten. Tell her thank you.' Mrs Sissons turned abruptly and marched with surprising vigour for one so small back down the drive and right towards her house.

Lady whined.

'I know, girl. She didn't notice you, but she has a lot on her mind. Come on.'

Carlos was gutted he couldn't agree to the neighbour's request. He told Sophie who the caller was and what she wanted, which sent his sister into frenzied activity.

'I can't go like this!' She raced upstairs to get ready, much to Carlos's amusement. Sophie might be dumpy, but she was always immaculately turned out and had exquisite dress sense. Plus, layers of makeup would need to be applied and the wavy dark hair combed into submission before she would consider leaving the house.

He sighed heavily, wishing he could go next door, but he knew how much that would rile Masters. He'd be bad enough with Sophie present, but that he might understand. Carlos's presence would be regarded as interference.

He felt disappointment and relief in the same measure at not finishing the conversation with Sophie. He realised it was time to open up. His sister had long suspected he had suffered severe trauma during his last tour – he could tell that from the sympathetic looks whenever anyone mentioned Afghanistan, but she knew him better than to press, knowing he would tell her when he was ready, and he loved her for it.

He poured another coffee and looked into his dog's adoring eyes.

'Didn't even bother to tell Mrs Sissons face-to-face, Lady. I hope he's more sympathetic when they meet.'

Chapter 6

Sophie flew down the stairs, satisfied her makeup was in place and she was dressed just smartly enough to come across as professional, but casually enough to put her neighbour at ease.

'I wish you were coming.'

Her brother stood to see her out.

'Me too, but you'll be less threatening alone. Trust me, Masters won't want me anywhere near. Try not to tell him what you do for a living.' Carlos kissed her cheek.

'Unless he asks.'

'He won't. He's not one for detail, and experience tells me his only interest is himself. I'm going out for the morning to chase up some leads on the case I'm working on. Should be back around two. Is it all right if I leave Lady here? She won't be any trouble.'

'No problem. I'd better go, Carlos.' Sophie ruffled Lady's fur before departing.

As soon as she arrived at her neighbour's, the door opened. Meg must have been looking out for her; she appeared years older and much frailer than she had been just a few days ago.

'Hello, Meg. I'm so sorry to hear about Harold.' Sophie knew better than to try to hug her, as an attempt in the past had turned awkward, the older woman going stiff as a board. She and Gary had laughed later that day when she told him. He had explained that some older people just don't like being hugged.

'Thank you, Sophie. Do come in. I've made a pot of tea.'

Sophie scanned the familiar room as she followed Meg into the lounge. Everything was in exactly the right place, just as it always was. She'd only been in the house half a dozen times, but nothing ever changed. There was not a grain of dust, as far as she could see; the polished dining room sideboard held a fruit bowl placed dead centre on a doily that, although ancient, was clean.

The sterility of the lounge always struck Sophie as lacking personality, particularly as the place had no photos. Most elderly people she knew displayed family photos, often a youthful wedding photo to remind themselves of times past, but there were none. She knew Meg had a daughter called Caroline, but when she had asked about her, a faraway look had appeared on the older woman's face. Now that she thought of it, Sophie didn't know her neighbour at all. They passed the time of day, spoke about mundane things like the weather in the typical British way, but Meg and Harold had always answered questions with automatic responses.

'How are you?'

'Fine, and you?'

Since Harold Sissons's disappearance, Sophie had managed to get a little more information out of Meg, but not much.

'How are you?' Out of habit, Sophie asked the ridiculous question.

'Holding up.' Meg looked behind Sophie as if expecting someone else. The police were due any minute; perhaps she was looking for them.

'I can't believe he's gone.'

Was that a sense of relief Sophie detected in Meg's usually expressionless eyes? *Of course not, she's in shock.*

'Have you told Caroline?'

Sophie noticed the immediate stiffening of the old woman's body as she stopped in front of the tea tray she'd neatly prepared for her arrival. A vacant confusion crossed her face.

'Who?'

Sophie's mouth dropped open. She wondered if the woman's shock was more serious than she'd realised.

'Here, let me bring that through.' Sophie lifted the tray and laid it on the coffee table in the lounge part of the room. Meg followed, like a puppy.

'Harold usually does that.'

Sophie nodded, understanding. 'Shall I pour?'

'No!' Meg snapped. 'I do that. Harold wouldn't like it.'

Sophie was glad she'd put the tray down or she might have dropped it. Gary teased her about how clumsy she was, and the sudden sharpness in Meg's usually meek tone had made her jump. She withdrew her hand and smiled. The routine she had previously thought quirky now struck her as verging on obsessive.

Why didn't I notice it before?

'Please take a seat.' Meg recovered, taking over the pouring, but not before moving the tray to the exact central position on the table. Sophie sat down, and almost straight away she heard car doors slamming outside, followed by a loud male voice.

That must be the DCI Carlos mentioned, the reason he's not here.

Meg remained seated, pouring tea as if she hadn't heard anything and not looking up when the door knocker banged. Sophie surreptitiously glanced to check whether her neighbour wore a hearing aid.

'Milk, no sugar, isn't it?'

'Yes, please. Meg, I think the police are here. Should I answer the door?'

'No. We don't answer the door at this time. Harold doesn't like to be disturbed when having tea.'

'Meg,' said Sophie gently. 'The police are here to talk about Harold. I think we should answer.'

Meg gazed up from pouring her own tea. The vacant mask and confused eyes appeared once more. The pause lasted forever as the door knocker banged again, louder this time. Then, as if a light had been switched on, the older lady rose from her seat and hurried to the door.

'Mrs Sissons, I'm DCI Masters and this is DS Cook. I believe Sergeant

McDonald called earlier to arrange an appointment.'

'Yes, Chief Inspector. Do come in, I've made tea.'

Sophie remained seated as a burly man in his mid-thirties stomped into the room, followed by a scruffy female wearing a pale blue plastic mac. DCI Masters was handsome in a rugged sort of way and obviously kept himself in shape. He was dressed more smartly than his DS in a brown suit with an immaculately positioned tie. His hair screamed ex-army as if he wanted to let people know where he came from. She noticed the head of a snake tattoo peering from the right-side of his neck, above the collar of his shirt.

DS Cook was mid-forties, obese and the opposite of her boss. She wore a loose-fitting pink floral dress that had seen better days underneath the unbuttoned mac. Her lipstick was smudged, but her face was radiant and kind. Sophie liked her immediately.

'And who might you be?' The DCI addressed Sophie.

'This is my neighbour, Mrs Cole. I asked her to be here, Inspector. I don't want to miss anything with my memory not being what it was.'

'I see.' He shrugged.

'Shall we sit down?' DS Cook motioned to the remaining two armchairs and the DCI sat down heavily on the one nearest the fireplace.

Meg let out an audible gasp. DCI Masters missed the reaction, but DS Cook was on it in an instant.

'It's all right,' she said. 'It will be easier to talk if we all sit.' Her voice was low and reassuring.

Meg returned to the sofa, sitting next to Sophie while anxiously keeping the other chair in sight.

DS Cook fetched a dining chair from the far end of the room. 'Sir, why don't you sit over there while I sit here and take notes?' She directed her boss to the other armchair.

'Why?'

'I think it would be better, sir. You would be able to see Mrs Sissons better.'

The DCI, clearly oblivious to the distress he was causing Meg, let out a deep, impatient sigh and moved his heavy frame from one chair to the other. Meg visibly relaxed and poured two more teas, not asking if either of the police officers wanted milk or sugar.

'If we're quite ready?' DCI Masters stared pointedly at his DS. 'Sergeant.'

'Mrs Sissons, we understand Detective Sergeant McDonald called you this morning to inform you that a body had been found in Shady Woods last night?'

'Harold.'

'We believe it is your husband, as the clothes fit the description on file, but we need to await confirmation. I was wondering, do you have a recent photo of your husband?'

'Harold didn't like having his photo taken.'

'I see.' DS Cook looked at her boss, obviously not wanting to proceed without permission. He nodded for her to continue. 'Did your husband wear a wedding ring?'

'No. Harold said such things were a needless expense. He didn't like waste.'

DS Cook raised an eyebrow and proceeded gently. 'Are you certain there are no photos? A driving licence or passport perhaps?'

Meg thought for a moment. 'Harold did renew his passport last year. Just a moment.'

Sophie couldn't understand why the police couldn't just check the DVLA records for themselves, but didn't say anything. She was here as an observer.

'Show her the photos,' DCI Masters hissed while Meg was out of the room.

DS Cook shook her head.

Meg returned with a purple passport and passed it to DS Cook. Sophie realised it was a good move, bringing DS Cook along. Perhaps the DCI wasn't as bad as her brother thought he was.

DS Cook handed the passport to the senior officer before continuing. 'We'll show this to the coroner for confirmation. Would you be happy to look at some photos of the clothes we found?'

Meg nodded before glancing at the photos briefly. 'That's the tie he always wears on a Thursday. The jacket's his favourite.' She looked away. 'He went missing on a Thursday. You told me he left me.' Meg's head shot round to DCI Masters, who swallowed hard.

'I don't think that's exactly what I said, Mrs Sissons. I said there was no evidence that any harm had come to your husband and that he could have gone away for a while.'

Sophie noticed the disbelief briefly cross the sergeant's face before she reined it in.

'Mrs Sissons, perhaps we could go over the day your husband went missing again another time, but I think for now you've had a lot to take in. You should prepare yourself that it is almost certainly your husband we've found.' DS Cook looked at Sophie. 'Is there anyone else we can contact?'

'Meg has a daughter, Caroline.' Sophie glanced towards Meg. 'I don't think Meg wanted to worry her; she hasn't been told her father is missing.'

If DS Cook was shocked, she didn't show it. 'Mrs Sissons, could we have your daughter's contact details, please?'

Meg got up again. This time she went upstairs.

'Do you know why her daughter hasn't been told?' whispered DS Cook.

'Not entirely. From the brief snippets I've been able to gather, they weren't on speaking terms. Harold and Caroline, that is. They haven't seen each other in years.'

'Families can be complicated.' DS Cook sighed, and Sophie suspected she had first-hand experience of this.

'Do you know how he died?' Sophie lowered her voice.

'Bashed over the head, from what we can gather,' DCI Masters answered. 'Most likely a mugging gone wrong. We didn't find a wallet, and he had no money on him.'

Meg appeared and handed DS Cook a note with an address and phone number. 'Harold won't be happy about you contacting her, but tell her it would be nice to see her.'

DS Cook nodded.

The two officers stood before DCI Masters stopped abruptly and turned to Sophie. 'A neighbour, you say. Which side?'

Sophie had also stood as the officers made to leave. She pointed to the left.

'There's only one side. Meg's is an end cottage.'

DCI Masters scowled and abruptly marched out with a confused DS Cook following close behind.

'I don't like him,' said Meg.

'She was nice, though.'

'Yes, I like her.'

'Meg, do you think it would be a good idea if you called your daughter before the police do? It will be much better coming from you.'

'I was wondering what should be done. Harold would normally see to such things.'

'But you're the one in touch with Caroline. I thought she and her father weren't the best of friends.'

'Harold doesn't allow me to call her, but I go to the telephone box in the village. He checks the bill, you see. And I write.'

Shocked, Sophie said, 'I'm sure she should know about this even if she and her father weren't, erm—'

'Speaking? I don't know what happened there. Neither of them told me. I'll go into the village.'

'Meg,' Sophie spoke softly, 'I don't think that's necessary; you can use your house phone now. Would you like me to stay with you while you phone?' Sophie wasn't convinced Meg would call at all if she didn't.

'That would be kind of you.'

Meg picked up the telephone after glancing around as if to check Harold wasn't going to appear. She tapped in the number, leaving Sophie wondering why she'd made such a play of going upstairs to find Caroline's contact details. That said, Meg did still appear to be suffering from shock.

'Aiden? Hello, it's Meg. Is Caroline there?... Oh, I see. Yes, of course. Would it be possible to have her work telephone number?... Right. Yes. I'll wait to hear from her, then... Urgent? I'm not sure.' Meg looked towards Sophie who was frantically nodding.

'I have someone with me. Perhaps it would be better if I put her on.'

Meg handed the phone to Sophie and began clearing cups and saucers away into the kitchen.

'Who is this? Is Meg all right?' a concerned male voice asked. 'She never calls from this number.'

'My name is Sophie Cole. I live next door to your mother-in-law.'

'Is something the matter?' Sophie could hear children playing in the background, or perhaps the man was watching television.

'I'm afraid so. I don't know how to tell you this, but your father-in-law has been found dead in the local woods.'

'What? When? How?'

'Last night. I think it would be good if someone could come and be with Meg. She's had a terrible shock. I'm worried about her.' The clattering stopped in the kitchen as Meg awaited the response.

'I see. Of course, but it's Christmas and my parents are arriving up here for the holidays this afternoon. I'll have to discuss it with Caroline. She may want to come down.'

Sophie knew families could be fractured, but she couldn't believe what she was hearing.

'I'm sure she would want to be with her mother at a time like this. Please could you ask her to call Meg as soon as possible?'

'Yes, yes, of course. I'm not being insensitive, but we haven't seen Meg in fifteen years, not since our wedding. Harold didn't come; I never met him.'

'I understand. Nevertheless, Meg would love to see her daughter. By the way, the police will be calling today, too.'

'The police? What have they got to do with it? Wasn't it a heart attack or something?'

'They don't believe Harold died of natural causes, Mr...?' Sophie lowered her voice.

'Winslow. What was it, then?'

'You'll have to ask the police that question.'

Sophie put the phone down and watched the colour drain from Meg's face.

Chapter 7

Carlos arrived back at Sophie's and let himself in using the spare key. Lady threw herself at him as soon as the door opened. He knelt down and gave her the affection she craved before making his way to the kitchen. A note waited for him on the breakfast bar.

'Meeting friends for Christmas shopping.

I'll fill you in on this morning when I get back.

Be home around five, help yourself
to food,

Love Soph xxx'

He sighed, disappointed again that
he hadn't been able to be next door
when the police arrived. He'd found
it difficult to concentrate on the job
he was being paid for after meeting
Masters last night. It had unsettled
him in every way possible – the
deep-seated memories resurfaced,
along with the possibility... no,
probability that Masters would
dismiss the murder of the
neighbour's husband as some
random robbery or any other
simplistic resolution without
following due process. The man was
lazy but ambitious, making it highly
likely he would arrest a poor,
unsuspecting minor criminal and fit

him up for murder. That was Masters's modus operandi.

Lady gazed up at him. 'You're right, girl. I should forget it, but you know what? I just can't. I was a coward last time, but never again. That woman next door deserves justice, and so what if I get revenge at the same time?'

Carlos had decided to investigate whether Masters liked it or not and felt better for having made the decision. He would quietly dig around, even though he had no idea where to start. He needed information, but Sophie would be gone for hours yet.

He smiled, wondering whether the police had managed to find the wallet yet. The hidden wallet puzzled him. The only conclusion he could come to was that it had been hidden to make the murder look like a robbery.

'But why didn't the killer take the wallet and dispose of it later?'

Lady whined in answer.

Deciding there was nothing for it but to wait until his sister came home, Carlos set about transcribing audio notes from the morning's investigation. At least he'd made progress with the case and should be able to close it and contact his client with the evidence that his son was embezzling money from the family firm. His client would not be happy and Carlos hated these kinds of jobs, but they paid the bills. They also gave him time to do his unpaid or low-paid work for those who couldn't afford his fees, but needed help.

He was busy transcribing when he heard a car pull up outside and a door slam. Going to the window to see if it was the police returning to Meg Sissons's house, he saw a familiar figure walking up Sophie's driveway. He raced to the door just as the bell rang and beamed at the woman standing on the step.

'Fiona! Great to see you. I forgot you worked in these parts. Come in.'

He hugged the large-framed woman who kissed him on both cheeks, Italian style.

'Carlos Jacobi, I heard you were here urinating in our pond!' The familiar belly laugh filled him with hope while Lady danced excitedly around the new visitor's legs. She bent to stroke the excited dog. 'And this must be the Lady I've heard so much about.'

'Yes, that's Lady. I'm not deliberately getting in the way, but yes, I guess I am now. Do you work for CID?'

'Yeah. DS Fiona Cook at your service. I've been assigned to work with DCI Masters on this one.'

Carlos couldn't help frowning. 'What about that McDonald chap I met last night?'

'This morning was his last shift. He's on holiday over the Christmas season, on his way to Scotland. Lucky beggar.'

'Wonderful news! I'm really pleased to see you. Come on through, I've got the percolator on. I remember you like it black and strong.'

Fiona followed him through to the kitchen and sat on a barstool with difficulty.

'These things aren't made for people my size.'

Carlos loved the way she could laugh at herself and didn't take life too seriously. Her attitude was the thing that had drawn him to her when they met while he was working a case in London.

'Here, bring your coffee. Let's go through to the lounge where we can both sit comfortably.'

'Working?' Fiona nodded towards the open laptop on the breakfast bar before they moved.

'Just finishing up a case and combining it with a visit to my sister. Rachel's working nights over Christmas.'

'Me too – not nights, but covering the whole festive season. Someone's got to do it. I met your sister Sophie this morning. I like her.'

Carlos smiled, proudly. 'I haven't seen her since I got back so don't have an update. I take it the dead man's the neighbour's husband?'

'Yeah. We have confirmation now. I'm going next door in a bit, I was hoping to take your sister with me. And catch you, of course, once I heard you were here. Be careful. I don't know the history, but the DCI doesn't like you at all.'

'Feeling's mutual.' Carlos glared into his coffee mug. Fiona clearly accepted he didn't want to talk on the topic.

'I have to be loyal; you know that, don't you?'

'I wouldn't expect anything else. Are you happy to tell me where you're at?'

'As far as the boss's concerned, it's an open and shut case of a mugging gone wrong. There was no wallet on the body—'

Carlos laughed. 'What did I say, Lady? Robbery or some such thing.' He stroked Lady's head.

'I assume it was this wonderful Lady who found the body?'

'Yes, she's an ex-police dog.'

Lady walked over to Fiona and lay on her feet. 'Clever girl,' said Fiona, stroking her.

'She likes you.'

'Good with animals, hopeless with men, that's me. Anyway, back to next door. Harold Sissons was killed by a blow to the head with a blunt instrument. The pathologist believes it may have been a spade; he found mud in the wound that he thinks came from the blow, not just the fact he'd been buried. Something to do with the depth.'

Carlos raised an eyebrow.

'I know. How can they tell? The mud in the wound was fertilised topsoil whereas the burial site is, I guess, just mud! Occasionally, according to a PC who lives in these parts, people go metal detecting in the woods and dig up their finds. I need to check whether next door's spade is missing. The boss believes the old boy stumbled across someone in the woods and was hit with his own spade, then robbed. It's plausible.'

'Does your crack DCI have any suspects?'

'Oh yeah. He's on his way to arrest one of the local yobs now while I tell the wife the case is just about solved.' Fiona couldn't hide the disdain in her voice. 'I'm not sure the poor thing has even grasped her husband has been murdered yet.'

'She does appear frail. I take it you don't think the case is quite so simple?'

'I don't know yet, but I do like to investigate and cover every avenue before leaping to an arrest. It makes us look foolish when it turns out to be a false one. His theory is plausible, but by no means proven.'

'Do you have any suspects yourself, Fiona?'

'No, but I'd like to rule a few people out and check alibis. There are half a dozen people who could know something, maybe more.'

She had Carlos's attention. 'Such as?'

'Well clearly we have to look at family. That's just his wife, from what I can gather. As you know, more often than not, the victim is known to the killer. The wife seems muddled and frail, so she doesn't go to the top of my list, but there's an estranged daughter I'd like to talk to. Presumably there's also a son-in-law. We don't know if there's any financial motive yet – other than the fact he had no wallet on him, so that's missing. Then I want to speak to people who saw him in the local community centre before he disappeared. From what I've managed to find out so far, he was a bit of a mystery. Known but not known, if you understand the meaning. Then there's the spade.

Was it his or someone else's? If our local yobbo was involved, he's hardly likely to be walking round the woods carrying a spade.'

'I see. Why the community centre? Where is it?'

'It's on the side of the green where you cross to go into the woods. Harold Sissons had been to the weekly lecture there, so he could have gone to the woods afterwards, either alone or with someone.'

'He couldn't have been metal detecting, then, unless he went home first. His wife told Sophie he didn't go home that afternoon. Have you managed to speak to anyone from the centre yet?'

Fiona sighed. 'I've been told not to, but I will. I'm loyal in that I'm not going to talk about my boss, but

I've still been assigned, so will do my job.'

'Why doesn't he want you to interview people there?'

'He says they were interviewed after Harold Sissons went missing and we shouldn't waste time repeating work that's already been done.'

Carlos rolled his eyes and heaved a sigh. 'Are forensics still working in the woods?'

'They've left the area cordoned off but have finished. Why?'

Carlos gulped his coffee. 'Fiona, I need to tell you something.'

'Why does that fill me with dread?'

Carlos grimaced. 'About the dead man's wallet...'

Fiona listened as Carlos explained his find from this morning's outing and how he had hoped the wallet would be discovered when forensics or the police returned to the crime scene.

'I do hope you've got an alibi for last Thursday, Carlos, or you might find yourself under arrest.'

Carlos pulled out his notebook and traced back to the date. He looked over to Fiona. 'To be honest, I don't, apart from Lady here. We were on a stakeout. Surely, Masters wouldn't think I had anything to do with it. I didn't even know the man.'

'Perhaps not, but something he said in the car after we left next door this morning made me fear for you. I think you'd better tell me where this wallet is, and I'll go and find it after I finish up next door. He won't be happy, but I can come up with some excuse as to why I decided to return to the scene of the crime. It will save him embarrassment later, so I should get away with it.'

'Please don't get into trouble on my account. I'm a big boy.'

'Think of it as a favour to Rachel. We can't have her boyfriend locked away for Christmas, can we?'

Carlos had introduced Rachel to Fiona shortly after he first met her, and the two women had become inseparable when Fiona later moved to Leeds, where Rachel was based. *Complete opposites in that Rachel's a fitness fanatic and health food guru while Fiona's a junk food addict and would swear she's allergic to exercise. Their humour brought them together. That and the fact they both go to church – a rarity in the police force.*

The women had bonded and Rachel was gutted when Fiona moved to take up a DS promotion. Carlos had forgotten it had been Derbyshire Fiona had moved to and wondered why Rachel hadn't reminded him so he could look her up. Surely it wouldn't be jealousy, although Rachel still bore the scars of a broken engagement. Her loss was his good fortune, but the scars ran deep and their relationship, though solid, sometimes felt like walking on broken glass. Convincing her of his love was all he wanted to do, but the man before him had done that, and then betrayed her with another woman.

He sighed. 'Thanks, Fiona. I appreciate it.'

'She does love you. You know that?'

'I hope so. Love isn't something we talk about yet. I need to give her space and time to trust me.'

'She's the most stable woman I know. This hiccup over that pathetic ex of hers will pass. It's all about trust. Hey, listen to me – the one who can't hold a relationship together for longer than a month – giving advice.' The infectious laugh rang out, causing Lady to jump up and wag her tail frantically.

'Thanks again, Fiona. You're a good friend, and your turn will come.'

Fiona turned serious. 'Maybe, but what if I don't really want it to?'

Carlos couldn't tell whether she was joking or not. He liked this woman and had a feeling he might be getting to know her a whole lot more over the Christmas break.

'You're a wonderful person. There's a Mister Right out there looking for you.'

'How do you know it's not a Miss Right?'

Carlos flushed, hoping he hadn't made a dreadful mistake. She thumped him on the arm, laughing.

'No, I'm straight. Shame, really, because I think I'd have much more luck with women.'

They laughed again as he walked her to the door.

'Sorry about the wallet.'

'You're going to owe me. That's enough reward for now. Hey, while the boss isn't here, do you want to join me next door? I know you're gonna stick your oar in, so you might as well.'

Carlos grinned. 'Love to, but do you want to check with the old lady first? I might have offended her this morning when she asked me to join Sophie for her meeting with Masters. I didn't think he'd welcome my presence.'

'Goodness, that would have been a disaster. The right decision, whether she was offended or not. I'll ask and text if she says yes.'

Carlos hurriedly shut down his computer and gave Lady fresh water. Moments later, he got the text message with a thumbs-up sign. He scribbled a note to Sophie letting her know where he would be should she arrive home early and opened the front door, stopping in his tracks when he saw another car approaching the house next door. He recognised the man at the wheel with a face so hot it could melt snow. Closing the door quickly, he fired a text back to Fiona, warning her of Masters's imminent arrival, and let out a huge sigh of relief their paths hadn't crossed again so soon.

'That was close, Lady.' He wondered why Masters looked so angry. Surely it couldn't be anything related to him? Masters couldn't know that Fiona had been to see him, although a few minutes earlier and he would have caught them talking. They would have to be more careful in future. Fiona might have been able to fob her boss off with an excuse that she had come to see if Sophie would join her to deliver the bad news to Mrs Sissons on this occasion, but not if it became a habit.

He put the mugs in the dishwasher, changed the note to Sophie and grabbed Lady's lead.

'Come on, Lady. Let's go visit that community centre.'

Chapter 8

Carlos arrived at the community centre in the village just as a meeting was ending. He tied Lady up outside.

'Stay, girl.'

From the notice on the door, he gleaned it had been a historical society lecture. A general hubbub echoed around the large main hall with groups of people chatting while drinking tea or coffee. Carlos wandered in with no-one challenging him as to why he was there. He noticed a few people engaging in conversation with a man packing away a slide projector, presumably the speaker. Spying a crowd around a kitchenette serving bar, he made his way over. People mingling close by were being served hot drinks and biscuits.

A vicar stopped him in his tracks.

'Hello there. I'm afraid the talk is over, but we are still serving tea and coffee. You're welcome to join us. I'm Barney, Barney Milnthorpe.'

'Carlos Jacobi.' Carlos shook the proffered hand.

'We haven't seen you here before. Are you visiting the area? We have so many delightful villages in the Peaks. In fact, we've just had a talk on the plague of Eyam. I'm sure you've heard of it.'

Carlos didn't know which question to answer first, but realised the vicar wasn't expecting one at all as he waxed lyrical on the afternoon's topic of interest. Carlos had to confess he'd not heard of the Eyam plague.

'Eyam's just up the road from here,' the friendly vicar continued. 'You may have visited it already. The astonishing thing was that while the bubonic plague was running rampant throughout the country, the residents of Eyam, under instruction from the rector, William Mompesson – now famous in these parts – locked themselves in and cut themselves off from the outside world to contain the infection. A selfless act if ever there was one.'

Carlos found himself fascinated by the story despite himself, and momentarily lost the focus of why he was visiting the community centre.

'They showed incredible bravery,' Barney continued. 'Well over half the population died and are buried around here. The village has been a source of local and national interest to historians ever since.'

'My girlfriend studied history at university. She would love the story if she doesn't already know about it. She and her father share the passion. Actually, her father's a vicar in Hertfordshire.'

'How interesting. Perhaps I've met him. We do leave our cloisters every so often and gather for national and international meetings. What's his name? Forgive me for asking, but Jacobi is a Jewish name, isn't it? I'm interested in names; etymology is one of my hobbies.'

Again, Carlos was stumped to know whether an answer was required to either question, but as the ebullient vicar had paused for breath, he decided to answer the first one.

'Brendan Prince is my girlfriend's father.'

Barney shook his head. 'No, not familiar, but I might know his face if I saw him. Prince, now that is an interesting surname—'

'Barney, darling, do let this young man find a drink.'

Carlos was rescued by a tall, slim woman with permed ash-blonde hair. She was around the same age as the vicar, mid-fifties, and presumably his wife. She took Carlos by the arm and directed him to where tea was being served.

'My husband loves to talk to people he hasn't met before,' she apologised.

'He was telling me about today's talk, it sounded fascinating.'

'Oh, it was, although when you live so close, you've heard it so many times, but it is an old favourite among our historical society, particularly when Reggie delivers it.' She turned and waved to the speaker who was leaving the hall. 'Are you visiting the area?'

'Yes, I'm staying with my sister and brother-in-law. Sophie and Gary Cole.

'We've met Gary, but I don't think your sister comes to church, does she?'

'They've not long moved to the area and she's been busy decorating the house. She works long hours, too.'

'I see. What does she do? I know Gary works for Rolls Royce.'

'She's a paralegal for a law firm.' Carlos didn't mention the firm specialised in medical negligence, as he didn't want his sister inundated with questions about potential claims.

'Interesting. Perhaps we'll see both of them at the carol service in church Sunday night. And you, I hope, if you're staying over the Christmas season. I'm Doreen, by the way. Barney's my husband.'

'Pleased to meet you, Doreen. I'm Carlos. I'll mention the carol service when I get back, and I'd love to come, thank you.' Carlos knew from

Rachel's home village how the community often congregated around the church in one way or another, if not for religious services, then for other meetings. The community centre was next door to the church, he'd noticed on his way in. 'You probably know their next-door neighbour, Meg Sissons.'

'Yes, we do. Poor love. I try to visit her most weeks. She hasn't been seen much since her husband went missing. Not that she ever came out without Harold. I expect you've heard about his disappearance. The police told her he'd run away, but I couldn't bring myself to believe that. Now we've had sad news on that front. A body's been found in the local woods. It's sent shock waves through the community, I can tell you.'

Barney appeared behind his wife, clearly not wanting to miss out on what could be the village gossip for some time.

'We don't know for certain it was Harold, Doreen.' Looking back at Carlos, 'I overheard you saying you're staying next door to Meg, Carlos. Perhaps you've heard something.'

'Yes, a body has been found, sadly. My brother-in-law and I stumbled across it last night. Well, it was my dog who found the poor man, really.' Carlos had now drawn a crowd of half a dozen people keen to glean what they could. A woman serving tea craned her neck as she handed him a cup and saucer.

'And was the body that of Harold Sissons?' asked an elderly man with piercing blue eyes and an air of military authority. Others stood aside to let him in closer.

'I believe it was Mr Sissons, yes. Earlier, I met a detective who was about to give Mrs Sissons the tragic news.'

Quiet gasps and a murmuring filled the air, with some people saying, 'I told you so. No way he would have left Peaks Hollow.'

'Heart attack, I suppose?' said Barney.

'Well, death comes to us all eventually. He did tend to be a stress head, I'm not surprised he's snuffed it. Can't say he was popular around here, either.' The military man sniffed.

'Martin, you shouldn't say things like that,' admonished Doreen. 'They were a very solid couple. He donated hundreds to the church restoration fund.'

Martin sniffed again, loudly. 'Only so he could get lead mention in the parish magazine. He never did anything without an ulterior motive.'

Carlos paid attention. The general nods Martin's comment attracted confirmed the late man's lack of popularity. It appeared Harold may not have been the innocuous elderly gentleman Sophie thought he was. Certainly not according to some members of the historical society.

'Was he also a member of your society?' Carlos enquired.

'Yes, he was,' answered another man, smaller than the rest, with a shiny bald head that appeared as though it had been recently polished. 'He was on every committee, for that matter, a member of every club and into everything, whether it concerned him or not.'

Carlos finished his tea in one gulp, trying not to retch at the amount of sugar in it. The woman serving had not asked him whether he took sugar, which he didn't, but he hadn't wanted to halt the conversation.

'What about Meg?'

'Under the thumb. Did as she was told. Too good for him by far,' the man called Martin answered. 'Mind you, I wish there were more women who did as they were told like that.' Carlos watched as Martin glanced at a woman around the Milnthorpes' age. She scowled.

'I heard that, Martin Webb. You watch yourself,' one of the women serving tea protested, but followed it up with a flirtatious smile, taking over from where Martin left off. 'If you ask me, Harold Sissons was one of those male chauvinist "women should do as they're told" types. Meg never went anywhere without him—'

'She comes into my shop,' another woman interrupted. She was younger than most around her, probably sixty rather than in her seventies.

'Well that's the only time, then,' snapped the woman across the counter, clearly not happy at being corrected now she was in the spotlight. 'She was totally dependent on him for everything. It wasn't normal.'

The woman who had scowled at Martin joined in.

'How is Meg?' she asked Carlos

'I'm not sure; my sister was with her this morning when the police went to tell her about the body,' Carlos replied.

'If there's anything I can do, please let me know.'

'Josie's a nurse,' Doreen introduced the woman. 'That's Clara behind the counter and this is Colonel Webb.' She indicated to Martin.

'Is it right he was last seen leaving here on the day he went missing? Was he with anyone in particular that day?' Carlos asked.

'Now you're starting to sound like a policeman, surely there's nothing suspicious?' Martin was on to Carlos in an instant, seizing back control.

'I'm not sure,' Carlos lied. 'I'm not a policeman, but I do work as a private investigator in the day job.

Apologies, but I can't resist asking questions.'

The tension disappeared as quickly as it had arrived, and people returned to the conversations they were having previously. Perhaps they felt they had heard as much as they were going to from their visitor.

'He did leave here a week ago yesterday. That's the day we usually hold these meetings, but there was a memorial service this week, so we moved it to Friday.' Barney was oblivious to the suspicion that the others had displayed a few moments earlier. 'It was odd, as a matter of fact. He left without having tea, which was out of character. He was a rigid man, steeped in ritual and routine. Worse than a vicar in some ways,' Barney laughed at his self-effacing joke. 'Seemed a bit agitated, now I think about it. I've read that people can get like that before having a heart attack, you know.'

'What makes you think he had a heart attack?' asked Carlos.

'I'm not sure, really, but he was the sort of person who was a coronary waiting to happen. Uptight and secretive. It can't make for a happy life. He did create tension with some of the locals and my parishioners.'

'Do you hold confessionals here, Vicar?'

'No, that's more Catholic. Parishioners do share secrets with men and women of the cloth, though. You're not suggesting I share any of Harold Sissons's secrets, I hope? I might talk, Carlos, but I hold my parish duties in high regard.'

'I'm sure you do. No, I was just wondering whether there were any to share. I wouldn't expect to hear what they were.'

Barney stroked his double chin before answering. 'As a matter of fact, no. Harold Sissons, as I inferred, was a secretive man. If he did have anything hidden, it will have gone to the grave with him; sealed tight as a drum, he was. Let that be a lesson. Men should be much more open in my opinion. Women are so much better in that regard than we men.'

Carlos had to admit that, although he considered himself a modern man, he kept far too many things tucked away in the recesses of his mind. The persistent headache since his encounter with Masters the night before was a sure sign of unresolved anxiety, but would it really help to let it all out as so many seemed to do these days? He often joked about the fashion of having a mental health disorder. His army training baulked against the trend.

'Perhaps,' he said. 'But is it always a good thing?'

'You pay for it if you don't, you know.' Barney's voice drew Carlos in as if he could see inside him. Rachel would say it was divine intervention or guidance, but Carlos wasn't convinced.

'Perhaps you're right.' He noticed Barney fixing him in his gaze. It felt uncomfortable all of a sudden.

I'm not here to get counselling, I'm here to investigate the death of Harold Sissons, he told himself. Why was his heart pounding? The headache throbbed and he felt an overwhelming desire to run. What the heck was happening to him?

'As I expect you gathered, Harold wasn't all that popular.' Barney was now back on safer ground and Carlos listened while reining his heart rate in to a normal rhythm. 'Doreen felt sorry for Meg. Clara was right. He did appear to rule the woman.'

'Do you think he was abusive?'

'If you're asking if I think he was violent towards her, no, I don't believe he was, but abuse can come in many forms. Doreen says he was controlling, both at home and in general.'

'Hence his being on every committee and part of every club?' Carlos suggested.

'Yes. That sort of thing. He could be quite difficult if he didn't get his own way. In fact, Colonel Webb would go so far as to say Harold occasionally resorted to bribes.'

'Really? What makes the colonel think that?'

'Votes would change at the last minute. Take this club, for instance. The colonel wanted to invite some of his old pals from the army to speak. He also has contacts in the wider community, extending as far as Chatsworth. The committee was open to it, keen in fact, but as soon as it went to the vote the following week, it was voted down. Word was that Harold had met with members at other meetings during the week and somehow persuaded them to veto any change. He and Colonel Webb didn't get on at all. They didn't speak to each other much, which could make things awkward.'

'Do you think Harold Sissons was capable of bribes?'

'If I was pushed into a corner on the matter, I would have to admit it wouldn't be hard to believe.'

'And Colonel Webb and Harold Sissons didn't speak to each other. For how long?'

Barney stroked his chin again and shook his head as if remembering something significant. 'They rarely did, as a rule, for years, but that last Thursday, they spoke. I noticed them having a hushed disagreement just before I introduced the speaker. The talk was a most interesting one: Missing Peak District Children, or something like that.'

'Any idea what they were arguing about?'

'None at all, I'm afraid. Petty rivalry, I expect.'

'Barney, time to close,' Doreen tugged Barney's shirt sleeve.

'As you can see, I'm not the controlling one in my marriage,' Barney laughed as he moved to shepherd people from the building.

Carlos had much to consider, not least his own personal response and the unpleasant reaction that the earlier comment by Barney had triggered. Could it have been a panic attack?

Chapter 9

Carlos took Lady for a long run to clear his head. Memories assaulted his senses, resurfacing uninvited, causing his headache to pound with every step. He ran faster and faster, up and down hills, until he found himself high above the Peak District landscape. He could see for miles around; Peaks Hollow was just visible in the distance.

Lady sat next to him, panting. Thankfully, he always carried his rucksack when running, and included within was a foldable dog bowl. He poured water into the bowl from his flask and drank the rest.

'I think we must have run around six miles.' He looked at the distance measure on his watch. 'Okay, 5.8 to be exact.' He collapsed down on a carpet of heather as dusk formed and allowed himself to take in what was left of the stunning views from the hill, realising now why Sophie and Gary appreciated their new life away from London. The verdant greens were exceptional, and although a cold north wind blew, the sky had been clear most of the way up. But it would be dark soon, so he packed up his rucksack and reluctantly started a slow jog downhill, putting on his head torch.

'Lead the way, girl.'

Lady ran ahead, stopping every so often to make sure he was still with her. As darkness gathered, so did the chill. He paused to pull a tracksuit top out of his bag, took two paracetamol for the headache and started after his dog again, taking it more slowly as the ground underfoot was still damp from the rains the day before. Now the sun had disappeared, it was more slippery.

The run cleared his focus and the exhilaration from the adrenaline rush felt good. He mulled over what he had discovered from the people in the community centre. Not much, really, other than Harold Sissons was generally unpopular. A man who abused his wife, and others, psychologically. Would either of those things cause someone to want him dead? There was the argument between the dead man and Colonel Webb, witnessed by the vicar, Barney Milnthorpe. What was that all about?

He arrived back just as Sophie's car was pulling up on the drive. She waved before getting out and opening the boot to reveal half a dozen bags from various High Street stores.

'Do you need a hand?'

'No thanks, I can't remember what's in what bag. Anyway, it looks like you need a shower.'

He grinned and saluted. 'Right, Sis.'

The rich coffee aroma reached his nostrils as he headed towards the kitchen half an hour later.

'Mm, that smells good.'

Sophie pushed a mug towards him. 'Your phone's not stopped vibrating since I got here.'

He picked up the phone and saw sixteen missed calls and five messages, all from Fiona, saying he should call her urgently.

'What's up?' asked Sophie.

'I'm not sure. They're from Fiona Cook – she's the DS you met this morning.'

'Oh yes. Nice woman. How does she know your number?'

'We go back a while. I saw her briefly this afternoon. Sorry to tell you, but she was heading next door to let your neighbour know it was her husband they found.'

Sophie's jaw dropped and her eyes threatened tears. 'It had to be, I suppose, but I still held a shred of hope that it might be someone else. What does the DS want?'

'Not sure, but I bet it's not good news. I saw Masters pulling up next door with a stony face before I went out after lunch. I'll call her first, and then we can fill each other in on our day.'

His phone vibrated again, only this time he picked up.

'Hi, Fiona, what's going on?'

'You've given me one hell of a day. Look, why don't you meet me for dinner and we'll discuss it?'

He watched Sophie pulling meat out of the fridge. 'If you haven't cooked already, Sophie, Fiona wants me to meet her for dinner.'

'No problem. I'm just getting started.'

He turned his attention back to the phone. 'Okay, where?'

Fiona gave him directions to a pub *The Miners Arms* in Eyam.

'Small world. I was just hearing about the history of that place today. I went to the community centre.'

'Thought you might go nosing around there. Give me an hour to get away; I'm still at the station.'

'Right, see you in ninety minutes.'

'Be careful when you get there, the pub's reputedly haunted by all those plague victims.'

'I'll take my chances.' After putting the phone down, he shrugged apologetically at Sophie, fed and watered Lady and joined his sister at the breakfast bar.

'Where's Gary?'

'He's got a meeting tonight; that's why I shopped today, so I can get everything hidden before he gets back. Now I don't have to cook, I think I'll settle for a chippy. Our fish & chip shop is the best in the village.'

'You mean the only one in the village.'

Sophie chuckled. 'I know I shouldn't, but I still love everything that's bad for me.'

Carlos knew better than to say she was beautiful as she was. Rachel had warned him it was one of the worst things he could say to a woman who was weight conscious, so he kissed her on her head instead.

'We all need comfort food occasionally.'

She smirked. 'There's always the New Year.'

'When I went to the community centre next to the church this afternoon, the vicar's wife told me she expects to see you at the carol service Sunday night. Nice woman.'

Sophie groaned. 'And what if I have plans for Sunday night?'

'Do you?'

'No, but I'm still Jewish, despite being married to a Christian.'

'Sophie, you're Jewish by birth, same as me. We haven't been near a synagogue in decades. Unless there's one in this village you haven't told me about.'

She thumped his arm. 'That's not the point. These things run deep.'

'You're telling me! Nevertheless, I think we should all go.'

'Is that Rachel rubbing off on you or do you have an ulterior motive? What were you doing at the community centre anyway?'

'Ah, that would be telling. As for my reasons, a bit of both, if you must know. I met a few people who knew Harold, including Barney Milnthorpe, the vicar, and his wife Doreen.'

'I see her occasionally. Meg told me she visits her once a week when Harold's at a meeting.'

'Then there's a Colonel Webb. Sharp man who didn't like your neighbour Harold at all – the two men argued on the day he disappeared.'

'Interesting,' said Sophie.

'There were two women – one was flirting with the colonel and the other – a nurse – seemed to snub him.'

'You probably got to know more people in a few hours than I have in six months. We've been so busy decorating and working we haven't got out and about. Gary's been to the church a couple of times. I'm only just realising, after being with Meg this morning, we don't know our neighbours very well at all. I met your Masters fellow.'

Carlos's face hardened as he checked his watch. 'Tell me about it tomorrow. I'd better get going or I'll be late. Are you happy to—?'

'Look after Lady? Yes. You go and leave us girls to our chippy.'

'She'll love you forever. Bye.' He kissed Sophie on the cheek and headed out with Fiona's directions in his head.

***

Arriving in Eyam ten minutes early, Carlos went straight inside the pub and ordered a pint of draught bitter. It would have to last, because he was driving, so he sipped it slowly.

There was a handful of people at the bar with more sitting around tables eating. The atmosphere was genial; he supposed the lack of interest shown to him as a stranger was due to the village's notoriety as a place of historical interest. He wondered why Fiona had chosen Eyam rather than somewhere nearer to Sophie's, then guessed she didn't want anyone knowing about their meeting.

He was sitting at the bar, compiling a list of persons of interest from his meeting at the community centre, when he felt a tap on the shoulder. He turned to see a big grin, but the wide eyes told him his friend was worried.

He hugged her. Once she'd ordered a pint of lager, they moved away from the bar and found a quiet table where they wouldn't be overheard.

'What's going on, Fiona?'

She took off her mac and gulped back a mouthful of lager while he waited.

'The investigation's up in the air. Masters is furious and you're persona non grata.'

'Why? What have I done? I only went to the community centre to chat to a few people who might have seen Harold Masters on the day he disappeared.'

'It's not that. You can tell me what you found out in a minute, but that isn't why he's so annoyed. By the way, I retrieved the wallet.' She tapped her handbag. 'I haven't dared mention it yet. The problem for DCI Masters is that Caroline Winslow turns out to be some high-powered civil servant working for the Scottish government. She's coming down here tomorrow, by the way.'

'But what's that got to do with me?'

'Well, it turns out, Mrs Winslow phoned her mother before I got there this afternoon. When her mum informed her that her father was dead and how Masters had dismissed her concerns when he went missing, telling her he'd left her – which he did suggest, by the way – Mrs Winslow was livid. Took it all the way to the Chief Super. A formal complaint's gone in and Masters was dispatched to give Mrs Sissons a personal apology, along with his reassurance that the death of her husband would be investigated thoroughly with no stone unturned. He was also told to release the thug he'd arrested, as the man had a perfectly adequate alibi.'

Carlos laughed loudly. 'Now both of those things I would have loved to see.'

Fiona giggled. 'I have to admit, I enjoyed witnessing the attempted apology. It was sort of coughed out. But the best part – or worst, depending how you look at it – is yet to come.'

Carlos took a gulp of bitter. For the first time since his reintroduction to Masters last night, he felt some sense of glee. He knew he shouldn't, but he couldn't help it.

'I'm only sorry I missed it. So, you said there's more?'

'When he got to the part about how we would be investigating thoroughly, Mrs Sissons replied in a hushed but controlled voice – almost rehearsed – that she wouldn't be able to trust him to do his job properly.'

Carlos almost choked on his beer.

'The diminutive Meg Sissons has more about her than I imagined.'

'Not only that, she informed him that when she had explained to her daughter that a highly respected and reputable private investigator was staying with her neighbour, Mrs Winslow suggested she should hire said investigator!'

'Me?'

'You.'

'He looked angry enough when I saw him heading your way this afternoon. I'd give anything to have seen his face on leaving. I hope he didn't shout at Meg.'

'No. He wouldn't have dared after his shakedown from the Chief Super. He gritted his teeth and remained controlled, but firm, explaining to Mrs Sissons this was a police matter and that you would only get in the way. He advised her that it would be better if she left it to the professionals, and his parting shot was that he would discuss it with Mrs Winslow when she arrived tomorrow. He felt sure she would see sense.'

'Then what happened?'

'I was summoned to accompany him outside. By then, his rage was uncontrollable. Thankfully, he doesn't know about our friendship, and even if I wanted to, I wouldn't dare tell him now. Seriously, he was scary. Chilling, almost. He's a dangerous enemy, Carlos.'

Carlos sat back thoughtfully. He knew Fiona was right. Masters had been humiliated, something that would make him more dangerous than ever. Perhaps he should back away now while he had the chance. If he took this case, there was no knowing how difficult it was going to get. Plus, it would dredge up more pain and ill feeling from the past. One thing was certain: Masters would give him no assistance whatsoever, and would likely block his every move. How far would his nemesis go? That's what troubled him.

'Let's eat,' he suggested, picking up the bar menu.

'You're going to take the case, aren't you?'

'I have to, Fiona. For more reasons than I'm prepared to share. Besides,' he grinned, 'I'm a highly respected and reputable private investigator.'

She smirked before shrugging, replying in a serious tone, 'Then I'm going to have to watch your back.'

'Do you think I'm in danger?'

'Looking into that man's eyes today, I'm certain of it. Are you sure you want to do this?'

'Yep. I'm sure.'

Chapter 10

The winter sun formed a bright orb outside in contrast to the room Carlos was standing in. Carlos gazed around Meg Sissons's lounge-diner, absorbing the lack of personalisation or knick-knacks usually present in people's homes. The cottage wouldn't be out of place in a sales brochure had it been on the market, except for the outdated décor. Caroline Winslow had called an hour earlier, not long after he'd noticed a taxi pulling up outside Meg's house to invite him round. Sophie accompanied him, warning him in advance to expect a minimalistic and regimented interior.

Caroline was around forty, with frown lines marking her forehead. She wore a tweed skirt and jacket with a plain Crimplene blouse buttoned tightly up to her thin neck. A heavy gold chain adorned the front of the blouse. He watched as she shuffled through papers, noticing her right knee jerking up and down while she concentrated. Highly strung, he concluded.

Meg called from the kitchen for assistance with the tea tray and Carlos was only too pleased to help. The frail-looking woman smiled appreciatively and followed him back through to the lounge space. Once they were seated and Meg had poured tea – Sophie had warned him about the ritual – Caroline looked up from her papers.

'Mr Jacobi, I understand from my mother you are a private detective.' Not waiting for an answer, she proceeded, 'As you are aware, a body was found in the woods the night before last, and it turns out to be that of my mother's husband.'

Carlos didn't miss the matter-of-fact nature of the announcement, nor the omission of the word "father". Caroline could have been describing a missing piece of jewellery or a stolen car.

'Yes, I am a private investigator, and yes, I was aware of the sad discovery. In fact, it was myself and my brother-in-law who found your, erm... Mr Sissons.'

'Oh, I wasn't informed of that. Mother, you need to tell me all the facts. How else am I supposed to help?'

'I don't think the police mentioned it, did they, Meg?' Sophie cut in protectively.

Caroline Winslow straightened. 'Well, judging by their incompetence so far, that doesn't surprise me. Anyway, Mr Jacobi—'

'Carlos, please. I rarely go by Mr Jacobi.'

'As you wish. Carlos, I have discussed the matter with my mother, and we would like to hire you to find out who killed my mother's husband. I believe she wanted to do so even before you found him.'

'We would be grateful,' agreed Meg.

'I would be happy to help, but there's something I should make clear.'

'What?' Caroline's head shot up, causing her long neck to lengthen further, reminding him of a turkey.

'I will need to ask questions, some of which you may not be happy about. And I must insist that you don't keep anything from me. In my experience, people are rarely murdered randomly, although I don't rule that out. Often, there is a reason behind such a killing. I warn all clients they might not like what I uncover in the course of an investigation.'

Caroline's knee jerk became frenetic as she replied. 'So be it. If it will put my mother's mind at rest so she can move on, we will assist. However, Mr, erm… Carlos, please try to refrain from the modern trend and insatiable lust for digging up dirt for the sake of it. And try not to upset my mother. She's been through enough. Not that you'll uncover any hidden secrets, of that I'm certain.'

The accelerated knee jerking made Carlos think otherwise. Meg blanched as she stared into her teacup, miles away.

Carlos took the veiled warning in his stride. 'Would you like to hire me on a day-by-day basis or for the duration?'

'I would like you to find out who killed Harold.' Meg lifted her gaze to meet his. He noticed the dullness behind the light grey eyes; she spoke quietly, casting a brief glance at her daughter as if to check she hadn't spoken out of turn.

'I will do my best. I must work with the police and report any significant findings to them.'

'Agreed,' said Caroline.

They finished their tea in uncomfortable silence and Carlos felt now was not the time to begin asking questions.

'How long will you be staying in Peaks Hollow, Mrs Winslow?'

'If I'm to call you Carlos then you must call me Caroline.'

He smiled agreement. 'Caroline?'

'I'm not certain. The in-laws have arrived at our house in Edinburgh for Christmas. It's inconvenient at this time of year to have to be dealing with this, but I suppose it can't be helped,' she huffed. 'I can work from here for a few days next week, and will need to fly home on Christmas Eve for Christmas Day and Boxing

Day. Will you be coming with me, Mother?'

Meg clapped her hands together, almost giggling. 'Oh yes. I can't wait to meet the children at last.'

'So, there you have it. We'll fly up on Christmas Eve and return on Saturday if need be.'

'Could the children come back down with us?' asked Meg, still clearly excited.

Carlos viewed the exchange. A complete transformation in Meg was taking place before his eyes. Poor woman hadn't even met her grandchildren.

'We'll have to wait and see, Mother. Aiden's parents are staying now. They haven't told us when they are leaving.'

'Oh,' Meg stared down at her hands. Sophie patted her on the arm, but Meg baulked at the contact.

'Would it be all right if I come back in an hour and look in your room, Mrs Sissons? It would be useful if I could go through your husband's things.'

'Yes. But it's Harold's room you'll need to see. I'm not allowed in there.'

'Why haven't the police already done that?' snapped Caroline.

'They were perhaps allowing your mother time for the news to sink in,' answered Sophie. 'The chief inspector I met thought it might have been a mugging gone wrong.'

'Humph.' Caroline blew out the word. 'The same chief inspector who told my mother he'd left her?'

'Yes, that's the one. A surly man, but I liked the sergeant with him.

She was nice,' Meg chimed in, looking to Sophie for support.

'Yes, Detective Sergeant Cook,' Sophie agreed.

'Has anyone been in the room since your husband disappeared, Mrs Sissons?' asked Carlos, trying to bring the conversation back to the point. He didn't want Caroline to know there was friction between him and the DCI in charge.

'No. I'm not allowed in Harold's bedroom, and Caroline has only just arrived.'

'I won't be going in that room.' The knee jerking, which had eased a little, set off at a pace. 'Please let me know if there are documents I should know about when you do your search. I suppose it could have been a mugging. Did they find any money on him?'

Carlos hoped he didn't redden. 'They didn't find a wallet.' He felt terrible not being up front about it, but he owed it to Fiona to keep it quiet until she made it official. 'I'll let you know if I find anything.' Carlos stood. 'Now, I think we should leave you to catch up with your mother. I'll try not to intrude, but I will need to ask you both some questions. Will tomorrow do?'

'Yes.'

'I'll be back in an hour to check the room.'

'What the heck was that all about?' asked Sophie when they got home. 'Why wasn't Meg allowed into her husband's room?'

'And why won't Caroline go in, or what's worse, even acknowledge him as her father?' asked Carlos, shaking his head. 'I understand from the vicar and the flirty woman I met yesterday that Harold was a stern man, controlling, bordering abusive. Did you ever notice anything?'

'Not when he was alive, no. But, in retrospect, I don't think we knew them at all. They were pleasant neighbours and appeared kind and devoted, but his apparent air of protector and chivalrous husband could have been something else.'

'Harold Sissons had secrets, and despite what Caroline says, she knows something. But what?'

'Perhaps they just didn't get on. Remember, she's not spoken to him in twenty years. I hope you don't find anything sinister, Carlos. Be careful when you go into that bedroom,' said Sophie, shivering.

He laughed. 'Don't let your imagination get the better of you,

Sophie. Lots of people are protective of their own space, particularly men like Sissons who thrived on being in control.'

'I do wish I'd taken more notice.'

'Of what? You were neighbours, that's all, and they may yet turn out to be an ordinary boring couple with no more secrets than the average person. No-one knows what goes on behind other people's closed doors.'

'It's just... what if he was a wife-beater, and I didn't help her?'

'There's no suggestion he hit his wife, but there is most certainly something about him. I don't like all this "Harold wouldn't like... Harold didn't allow..." stuff. Their place has OCD written all over it, but they might both have chosen to live that way. The murder is most likely related to whatever he was up to outside of home – something he kept from his wife. Good old fashioned embezzlement, bribery or even an extramarital affair. The vicar implied Harold Sissons wasn't above offering a bribe to get his own way. I'll dig into his background, but might need help with that. I also want to talk to the colonel I met yesterday. He argued with Sissons, and I'd like to know what that was all about.'

'Now, all that stuff I can deal with,' laughed Sophie.

'Don't worry, Sis, I'll get to the bottom of this.'

He hoped he sounded reassuring, because he too had a bad feeling about the man next door.

Chapter 11

Carlos didn't go next door an hour later because he recognised Masters's unmistakable bright green Audi RS5 Coupe parked on the road outside. He waited impatiently, keeping an eye on the DCI's car. Another hour passed before a red-faced Masters lumbered down Meg's driveway, climbing into his Audi and screeching away. A minute later, Carlos's phone pinged with a message.

'All clear. Come round, Fi X'.

He smiled, relieved that his comrade in arms would be joining him to go through the mysterious Harold Sissons's off-limits bedroom.

Gary's car pulled up on the drive just as Carlos was leaving with Lady on the lead. Gary clambered out of his Citroën DS3 SUV and tapped the side of his nose.

'Off to investigate, are you? Do you need any help?'

'Erm, thanks, Gary, but that won't be necessary.' Noticing the look of disappointment cross his brother-in-law's face, he added, 'Sophie would kill me. She's got a special dinner ready. Something about a "dating" anniversary?'

Gary's hand went to his head. 'Damn! I almost forgot.' He reached into his jacket pocket and pulled out a wrapped gift box, holding it up for Carlos to see. 'I was a boy scout.'

Carlos stared quizzically at the twinkling green eyes.

'I bought this a few weeks ago and tucked it in my jacket pocket just in case I did forget.' Gary brushed one of the curls from the front of his face. Carlos laughed out loud.

'Aren't you full of surprises? You'd better go give it to her, then.'

Fiona was waiting at Meg's door when Carlos arrived, her finger to her lips.

'I've left them to eat after Masters disrupted Meg's regimented mealtime. She got more and more agitated the longer the boss stayed. We arrived at dinnertime and "dinnertime is never delayed", apparently.' Fiona shrugged.

'Don't tell me: Harold wouldn't like it?'

'You guessed it!' Fiona smirked.

'I was going to ask if it was all right to bring Lady in. She might help us find something.'

'Hang on.' Fiona disappeared and returned a moment later with a thumbs-up. 'The bedroom's upstairs, right on to the landing and the last door on the right.'

Carlos followed Fiona up the narrow staircase, noting the dark landing, a stark contrast to his sister's. Sophie and Gary's house had been modernised with a new staircase and restructuring of the rooms upstairs, including additional windows. As he looked around this cottage, he admired what a good job they'd done next door.

He grinned. 'I take it Masters didn't persuade Caroline not to hire me?'

'You're right on that count. In the end, he was asked to leave. He was none too pleased about that, I can tell you.'

'I caught a glimpse of his face when he left. Even if I hadn't, I would have known he was angry when the tyres burnt rubber. How come he let you stay behind?'

'He insisted upon it when they told him you were coming to look in Mr Sissons's bedroom. I'm to make sure you don't find anything without him knowing about it first, hide evidence from you if I come across it and call him if you do find something.'

Carlos couldn't help grinning again, but paused as they arrived at their destination.

'I don't want to get you in trouble, Fiona.'

'You let me worry about that. The less he knows about our friendship, the better. I will have to keep him informed, though; I still haven't found the right moment to mention the wallet. I'm under specific instructions not to tell you anything that we uncover our end, either. So, you're not to know that Harold Sissons had a private bank account in just his name with £63,000 in.'

Carlos whistled, raising his eyebrows.

'Any recent deposits or withdrawals?'

'We don't know yet. Masters tried to fob Caroline off that the private account was the reason he thought her father had left her mother. I bit my tongue. He only found out about the account yesterday afternoon, but I couldn't say that. I didn't know about it when we met last night or I'd have said. He's put in a request to the bank for access to more information to check for any suspicious activity.

'Meg didn't know anything about the account, or any of their joint accounts, for that matter. She left money matters to her husband. I don't know how she's going to survive without him; she doesn't seem to know how to do anything other than cook and clean.'

'Just as it should be,' he laughed.

Fiona thumped him on the arm. 'Wait till Rachel hears that one. Anyway, I'll let you know if anything crops up on that front. Now, are we going to stand here all day or go into this bedroom?'

Carlos smiled sheepishly. 'In we go, then.'

He flicked the light switch just inside the door to reveal a pendant light that shone brightly through a white lampshade. First impressions were an anticlimax.

'I don't know why, but I was expecting some sort of den of iniquity,' Carlos sighed. The room was similar to downstairs: virtually empty with little sign of it being the personal space of the late Harold Sissons. It was minimalistic, just like the rest of the house, revealing nothing about the man in question.

A huge iron-framed double bed took centre stage, covered in an old-fashioned counterpane. Two pillows lay on top on the right-hand side of the bed. A single lamp stood on the dark mahogany bedside table and a brass windup alarm clock had stopped at 3.30pm.

'You've been watching too many horror films.' Fiona laughed. 'I'll take the wardrobe; you take the drawers.'

Forty-five minutes later and they had found nothing other than confirmation that Harold Sissons lived an ordered obsessive compulsive type of life. Not a thing out of place. His socks were rolled up and stored in orderly rows according to colour – the only colours being black, grey or pale blue. Pants and vests were neatly folded. Other drawers revealed an orderly array of pyjamas, jumpers and cardigans with nothing hidden; even handkerchiefs were ironed and folded. No secret photos, no hidden vices, nothing. Carlos exhaled.

Fiona's search revealed a similar pattern in the wardrobe. Shirts, trousers, jackets and ties all neatly hung according to colour and type.

'I don't think we're going to find any answers in here,' he suggested.

'What a weirdo. How can anyone live like this?'

'As opposed to your lived-in type of place, you mean?' he quipped. Having visited Fiona's flat in London, he understood housework was not her thing. Clutter was her thing.

'Yeah, well. Life's too short to live like this.' She sat on the bed and stared around. 'No photos, no pictures on the wall. This man lived in a vacuum. He doesn't even leave a dirty handkerchief in a jacket pocket. I've been through every one of them. He's got mothballs in there like my grandma used to have. By the way, have you managed to find out what happened between him and Caroline yet?'

'No, nothing, except she won't refer to him as father, dad or anything like that. I'm hoping to quiz her tomorrow. There was definitely a reaction when I suggested I would need to dig into their past.'

'I don't think it's a family crime, this one. It comes from outside. One of the community centre people you mentioned, maybe.' Fiona swept her hand under the mattress, an old-fashioned heavyweight that should have been thrown out years ago. 'You'd think with all that money in the bank, he'd treat himself to a new mattress. I wonder what he was keeping it for.'

Carlos watched her. 'That's what we need to find out. Do you want a hand to lift the mattress?'

'Yep. Might as well. You never know, maybe there's truth in the money under the mattress thing.'

They heaved the mattress up, causing Lady to get up from the floor where she'd been lying in front of an old-fashioned fire grate. Carlos held it up. He could see thick springs attached to a metal frame; he hadn't come across a bed like this in years.

'Nothing,' said Fiona. 'Put it down.'

'This is hopeless; it hasn't helped at all.' Carlos sat on the bed to have one last scan around. 'Right, your turn, Lady. Find, girl.'

Lady jumped to her feet, tail wagging furiously, and put her nose to the floor. She busied herself around the room, taking in every square inch, even sticking her nose up the chimney, which brought giggles from Fiona. Finally, she crawled on her belly to get under the bed. Moments later, she let out a yelp.

Carlos shot down to the floor to find her lying on her side, whimpering.

'What is it, girl?'

Chapter 12

It was dark under the bed. Carlos switched on his phone torch to check what Lady had discovered. He saw the sharp end of a broken spring digging into her neck from the old-fashioned bed above. She was starting to panic, frantically trying to release herself and causing the spring to embed itself even deeper. Blood stained the white fur around her nape.

'Blooming heck. She's going to impale herself in a minute. Stop, Lady. Stay!' The dog stopped struggling, big brown eyes pleading with him to get her out.

'What is it?' asked Fiona.

'One of the springs has collapsed and split. There's a piece in her neck; she's trapped. Damn thing's dug in even more with her trying to wriggle free. We need to move this bed.'

Fiona's hazel eyes widened as she fixed them on the metal-framed monstrosity that dominated the room. 'It's cast iron! It'll weigh a tonne. Let's get the mattress off first.'

They lugged the heavy mattress off the bed and stood it up against a wall. Fiona stood tall at five foot ten, but her lack of fitness was in no doubt as she doubled over to catch her breath.

'Give me a minute.'

Carlos could at least see Lady now through the rusty bed base. Blood oozed from her neck, but she was staying calm.

'Good girl. Nearly there. Stay.' Lady's fearful brown eyes stared up at him, but she didn't move. 'Come on, Fiona.'

His friend stood upright, still breathless but more composed.

'Right, I'm ready. Shall I take this side?' Fiona gripped one side of the foot of the bed while Carlos grasped the other.

'On three. One, two, threeeee.' They heaved, but the bed barely budged. The humungous thing was a dead weight.

'It's a monster. I can't even move it off the floor,' Fiona complained. Carlos had managed to lift his side a couple of inches from the floor, but without the counterbalance from Fiona, it fell back to where it had been in the first place.

'Can you tell Caroline what's happened and nip next door to fetch Gary and Sophie?' He recognised the two of them would not have been able to lift the bed even if Fiona had been fitter. The anniversary date would have to be disturbed.

Carlos reassured Lady and spoke comfortingly to her while waiting for the others to arrive. Caroline came up and tentatively poked her head into the room.

After a quick glance around, she asked, 'Can I help?'

'I'm really sorry about this, but Lady's managed to get a spring embedded in her scruff.'

'Oh, poor thing.' Caroline ventured into the room, although still wary. 'Dreadful thing. I don't know why he kept it after all this time. It belonged to my grandfather.'

Carlos heard footsteps on the stairs and then along the landing, bringing with them a sense of relief. Gary arrived first, followed by Sophie and, finally, a breathless Fiona.

I really need to talk to her about her fitness when this is over, thought Carlos.

Gary assessed the situation and took charge. 'Someone will need to remove the spring once we have the bed up.'

'I'm no good at lifting, but I am a first aider,' said Fiona.

'Right, you're on the dog,' said Gary. He placed each of them, including Caroline, strategically in the best position to distribute the weight of the bed. For once, Carlos was grateful for his geeky brother-in-law.

'Tell us when,' said Sophie.

'On the count of three, we all lift and shift over to the right. Once erm...' Gary glanced at Fiona.

'Fiona,' she said.

'Once Fiona has enough space to release the dog, we can drop it down again rather than try to bring it back to its original position. If you can't remove the spring, we'll put it down and I'll have to come back with a hacksaw and cut it away from the main frame first.' Gary's confidence slipped a little as he saw the blood-soaked white fur around Lady's neck and his face whitened.

'Gary!' Carlos snapped.

Bringing his attention back to the task in hand, Gary counted and they all lifted at the same time. The bed still seemed to weigh a tonne even with four of them lifting it from the foot end, and the head dragged heavily along the carpet.

'Right, hold on. Get the dog free,' panted Gary who was showing remarkable strength.

'Got it!' Fiona shouted triumphantly. 'But I'm stuck under here so you'd better move that thing away before we're both crushed.'

'Okay. Go!' yelled Gary. With the combined strength of four people, they managed to pivot the foot of the bed to one side, freeing Fiona and Lady completely in the process.

'Lady, look at you.' Carlos hugged his dog while Caroline fetched a wet towel. Lady wagged her tail, happy to be free again, but stayed still. He parted her fur to assess the damage. 'She's got a small puncture wound and has managed to tear her collar, but other than that, she'll live.'

Caroline returned with the towel and some disinfectant. Carlos washed his dog's fur and cleaned as much of the rust away from the wound as he could.

'Better take her to the vet's,' suggested Gary, paling again.

'You're right. Sorry about the mess, Caroline. I'll come back tomorrow and clear it up. Are you okay if we don't try to move the bed back?'

'Absolutely!' She stared at it in disgust. 'I'll speak to Mother about getting rid of it.'

'Come on, Lady,' Carlos called. Lady ignored him and returned to the spot where her blood now stained the carpet. She sat stock still and barked. Carlos wiped sweat from his face as his heart dropped to his stomach.

'I need to go. I think I'm going to be sick,' said Gary, rushing out of the room.

'What's the matter with him?' asked Fiona, but said no more as Carlos caught her eye.

'I'll go and check he's all right,' said Sophie.

'What is it?' asked Caroline who stood by the door, trembling.

'I'm not sure. It could be nothing. She's been acting a bit weird lately. Why don't you go downstairs? With permission, I'd like DS Cook and I to remove the carpet and see what's underneath.'

Caroline's eyes widened and her hand flew to her mouth. She turned abruptly and ran from the room.

'I've got a bad feeling about this, Carlos. Do I need to call it in?'

'Not yet. Let's check it out first. For all we know it could be nothing but a dead mouse.'

Carlos pulled and tugged at the carpet by the fireplace, but it wouldn't move. He pulled out an army knife from his pocket and sighed.

'This could cost you your fees,' laughed Fiona.

'Well I'm not going downstairs to ask permission.' Carlos gave Lady a handful of treats. He checked the wound again to make sure she was all right, then dismissed her from her post while he started work on the carpet.

Half an hour later, after fighting with the thickness of the carpet and underlay, he had removed a large square to reveal enough of the floorboards underneath to see six of them had been cut through and replaced. He grimaced.

'Maybe not a dead mouse.'

'You need a crowbar or something.'

Carlos agreed. The boards had been firmly nailed back in place.

At that moment, he heard movement on the stairs. Then Gary

stood in the doorway with a crowbar and a saw.

'Thought you might need these.'

Grateful for his brother-in-law's good sense, Carlos took the tools.

'Thanks, Gary. You don't have to stay if you don't want to.'

Gary half-turned before shrugging. 'What the hell?' He joined Carlos and Fiona, kneeling down beside the floorboards.

The boards moved easily once the first one was prised loose. Gary pulled it up and placed it on the floor. Carlos handed him the next one and observed how he laid it neatly down on top of the other one.

'Really?'

'What?'

'Nothing.'

Carlos went back to the task in hand and removed two more boards.

Fiona shone a phone torch into the space.

'There's something down there. It's a holdall of some kind.'

Carlos went to work on the final two floorboards, and once there was enough space for him to reach down, he donned a glove handed to him by Fiona. Wiping some of the dust from the top, he unzipped the bag, expecting to find a cash hoard.

Gary fell back and retched when it was revealed what was inside. 'Sorry, I need to go.' His loud footsteps could be heard running down the stairs and out the front door.

Fiona stared at Carlos in disbelief. 'Now, that I wasn't expecting.'

'Me neither. When I saw the holdall, I thought it was a stash of jewels or cash. I should have known, though, from Lady's response. We can't smell anything but dust, but she got the scent of death.'

'Who was it, do you think?'

Carlos moved the bag to expose the smallish skeleton, still clothed in a moth-eaten T-shirt and shorts.

'I don't know, but judging by Caroline's reaction, the women downstairs might. Call it in, Fiona, while I go and talk to them. I'll leave the holdall down there for forensics.'

Lady followed Carlos downstairs excitedly, thrilled with her find. Carlos texted Sophie to come and collect her. She arrived seconds later.

'Gary told me. Do you know who it could be?'

'No idea. I'm just going to talk to Meg and Caroline.' He lowered his voice. 'Can you get Lady seen by a vet? I don't want her to get an infection.'

'Of course. At this rate, I'll need a vet and a doctor. One for Lady, one for Gary.'

Carlos rolled his eyes, but stopped himself saying anything other than, 'Gary was really helpful this evening. Tell him that, will you? I've got an idea. See you in a few minutes.'

Carlos found Caroline sitting in a chair, hugging her knees while Meg stared vacantly out of the rear window. Tears flowed down Caroline's cheeks.

'It's Matthew, isn't it?'

'Look, it's going to get a bit chaotic around here for the next few hours. Why don't you and your mum join me next door where we can talk in private?'

Caroline shot up. 'Yes, let's get out of here. Come on, Mother.'

Chapter 13

Gary left with Sophie to go to the vet in the village after calling first, leaving Carlos with Caroline and Meg. After pouring himself and Caroline coffee and Meg a glass of sherry, he joined the two women at the kitchen table, taking out his notepad. Meg hadn't spoken a word since the grim discovery; it was Caroline who'd suggested the sherry. He could have done with a shot of whisky himself, but that would have to wait.

'I'm sorry for the shock of this evening's discovery, ladies, but I do need to ask you both some questions. If you need to leave or move around at any time, please feel free.'

Meg's light grey eyes remained fixed as if frozen in time. The deep lines in her forehead scrunched, the only sign she was confused by the grisly find. Her silence unsettled him.

Turning to Caroline, he asked. 'Who's Matthew?'

'My brother.' Caroline's knee was in overdrive and her confused eyes darted between him and her mother. He suspected that she, like her estranged father, preferred to be in control of her emotions and recognised the struggle.

Carlos swallowed hard. He had guessed something like that, but pressed.

'And?'

'He ran away. At least, we were told he ran away.' The controlled, albeit agitated, woman he had met earlier that day now resembled a pained child. Tears filled the attractive hazel eyes and the knee bashed mercilessly on the underside of the table.

'Please, take your time.' He moved a box of tissues towards her. Taking one, Caroline dabbed her eyes, smudging neatly applied makeup. The tearful eyes and trembling lips fought to regain order. Carlos's heart went out to her. Meg's glacial face remained unchanged.

'It was twenty years ago. I was at university in Edinburgh, but had come home because Mother's sister was ill. Mother and I went away for the weekend to stay with her. It turned out her sister was dying.' Caroline took her mother's hand, but the older woman didn't respond. 'It was the one and only time before my wedding that Mother was allowed to go anywhere without him.' She spat the word "him" out with venom, but still no reaction from Meg. 'He wasn't happy about it, but somehow I persuaded him to let her go. I should have known the manipulative brute would have had some other reason for relenting.

'The atmosphere throughout that week got more and more tense the closer we got to leaving. Matthew was supposed to come with us, but at the last minute, he wasn't allowed.'

'By your father?'

Caroline nodded. 'By the man who was supposed to be my father. I wonder now if this was his spiteful plan all along. When we got back, he told us Matthew had run away. He told me…'

Caroline wiped away the falling tears. Hands shaking, she continued.

'I lived in halls in Edinburgh. Matthew was twelve – he was Mother's miracle, born when she was forty-three. After I was born, the doctors told her she wouldn't be able to have any more children because she almost died giving birth to me. *He* never wanted children in the first place and was livid when Mother got pregnant again. I was only seven years old when she got pregnant. I heard him constantly telling my Mother how useless she was, what a poor mother she was and how she couldn't cope with the one child she already had. I cried myself to sleep most nights, wishing I could do something to protect her from his barrage of abuse.

'He tried to coerce her into having a termination. The pressure triggered some sort of breakdown, and she was admitted to hospital. I was sent to my grandparents for a while. The doctor in the psychiatric hospital kept Mother in until it was too late to terminate the pregnancy – I think she colluded with Mother to help her, but *he* made sure her life was hell throughout the rest of the pregnancy.

'By the time I returned home, things were even worse. He hardly spoke to me and constantly tormented my mother. That man was a beast and a bully; he hated not getting his own way.'

Caroline stole a glance at her mother, who still showed no reaction. Carlos wanted to ask if her father had been violent, but felt it would be better to save some of the conversation for when he could be alone with Caroline.

'I did my best for my brother growing up, but I couldn't stay any longer. I was a selfish teenager and went as far away as possible.' Caroline stopped speaking for a moment and appealed to her mother. 'You know why I left, Mum. He was impossible.'

With no response from Meg, Caroline turned back to Carlos.

'I left home when Matthew was ten, first, to stay with my grandparents again – my mother's parents – then I went to uni.' Her shoulders slumped. The knee stopped knocking on the underneath of the table. Caroline sprung up.

'I need to call Aiden.'

'Would you like some privacy?'

Caroline nodded.

'You can phone from the lounge.'

Carlos poured two more coffees. Noticing Meg hadn't moved a muscle, he left them on the table and followed Caroline through to the lounge-diner. Before she could dial her husband's number, he took her arm.

'I'm going to call a doctor for your mother. She's in shock.'

Caroline's watery eyes were wide. She nodded. 'As you wish. I really need to speak to my husband.' She pulled her arm away.

'You might be more comfortable in the snug. It's back there.' Carlos nodded to a door off the side of the lounge. Caroline went in and closed the door.

The front door opened and Lady bounded in, leaping at him joyfully. He bent down to stroke her, taking a look at the shaved part of her neck surrounding a dressing. She reeked of antiseptic.

'She's had an antibiotic injection and there's a course of antibiotics and anti-inflammatories. Mr Mahud suggested no more rusty springs and a few days' rest. He also presented you with a nice bill.'

'As if rest's going to happen.' Carlos ruffled his beloved dog's fur. 'Good girl. Best girl.' His jaw dropped open when he checked the bill Sophie handed him. 'I'm in the wrong job.'

Gary took over. 'He couldn't stitch the wound. He said puncture wounds are best left unstitched because there's a risk of abscess developing beneath. He's packed it with a hydrogel. We need to pack it each day and take her back if there's any sign of infection.'

'Thanks, guys.'

'How's things?' Gary asked. 'There's a host of police cars in the road. Thank Heavens we live at the end of the village, but it won't be long before news gets around.'

Carlos tilted his head towards the kitchen and lowered his voice.

'Meg's in a bad way. She's shut down. Shock, I think. Can you call a doctor?'

Gary grimaced. 'I could do with seeing one myself. I'll give them a ring.'

'Caroline's in your snug, calling her husband. Meg and Harold had a son.'

Sophie gasped. 'And is that who you believe the skeleton belongs to?'

Carlos nodded grimly.

'Size and clothes fit the picture. He was twelve.'

Sophie's hand went to her mouth. Eyes wide, shaking her head, she rushed to the kitchen.

'I'll check on Meg.'

Gary called 111 and, after a lengthy time waiting to be put through and a call-back, he turned to Carlos who was mulling over what Caroline had revealed.

'It won't be our local doctor, I'm afraid. They have an out-of-hours system so we could get anyone. I've explained the urgency. A doctor will visit. No idea when.'

'I'll check whether Caroline's finished on the phone. Can I leave you and Sophie to see to Meg?' Not waiting for an answer, Carlos continued, 'There's no point me trying to question her. If a DCI Masters turns up, come and get me. I don't want him anywhere near Meg in her state.'

Gary stared down at his hands. 'I'll stay in here and wait for the doctor. No use me going in there. I wouldn't know what to say.'

'Good idea. I take it you'll be all right? I'll leave Lady with you, if that helps.'

Gary looked down at the dog lying on his rug.

'Thanks. I'd like that. I'll study the sheet the vet gave us.'

Carlos felt that would be the best thing for his brother-in-law to do, as he'd met with more unpredictability than he could handle. Gary would be safer with something practical and scientific to distract his mind. Moving to the kitchen to retrieve the second round of coffees he'd poured earlier, Carlos carried them through to the snug. He gently knocked and poked his head around the door before entering.

Caroline was sitting in an armchair. She jolted upright and composed herself. The rigidity he'd noticed when they met returned.

'Can I come in?'

'Of course. It's your house. I just needed some time alone.'

Carlos didn't correct her on the house thing and handed her a coffee.

'Would you like something stronger?'

'I would, if you don't mind. Do you have brandy?'

'I'll ask.' Carlos went back to Gary, who happened to be pouring himself one.

'Could you pour two more of those?'

With brandies in hand, Carlos returned to the snug. He handed Caroline the larger one and sat down in one of the armchairs nearby.

'Is your husband coming down?'

'No. We have children. I don't want them knowing anything about this. It's traumatic enough.'

'How old are your children?'

'Nine and seven. The in-laws are staying. I think I might have told you that before. Aiden will tell the children Mother's not well. When I return, meeting their grandmother for the first time will detract attention away from my having been away. They often speak on the phone when he's not around – when he wasn't around – but now they can meet her face-to-face.'

Carlos wasn't certain Meg would be in any fit state to travel anytime soon, but Caroline had cheered up considerably at the prospect. Now wasn't the time to burst any bubbles.

'I believed my brother had gone missing after running away to find me all those years ago. I've lived with that guilt for twenty years, thinking something horrible happened to him because I didn't fight to take him away with us. I was convinced he'd been abducted and it was all my fault. On good days, I imagined he'd turn up one day out of the blue and grin that mischievous...' Caroline's eyes welled up.

'Did your father tell you your brother had gone after you?'

Caroline pursed her lips, trying to control the trembling. 'He told us Matthew cried all weekend. He said Matthew yelled at him and stormed out, saying he was going to Edinburgh. That was something that nagged me for years. Matthew was terrified of the man. We all were. I should have known he wouldn't have shouted at him.'

'Caroline, was your father violent?'

'Not with his fists, no. But he undermined everything we ever did. He dominated my Mother so much that I don't think I ever knew the *real* her. The closest I got to seeing her happy was when she told him about being pregnant with my brother. He coldly told her she couldn't have another child and went off to one of his meetings. I sat with her as she stared into space, much like she's doing now. It frightened me. Afterwards, I never saw her happy again.

'I found some photos once, pictures of when she was first married. She was smiling, but even then there was no real happiness. My grandparents told me, before they died, they didn't approve of the marriage, but they were of the belief that you made your bed and all that... Well, we certainly had to lie in it. *He* was hard on Matthew from the minute he was born. Matthew was always a sensitive, shy boy, more like my mother.'

'Did your mother also believe Matthew came after you?'

'I assumed she did. We never talked about it. Mother went into meltdown, shut down like she has now. That man put the blame on me for everything and I believed it. I'm ashamed to say, I left the next day and returned to Edinburgh. Partly because I couldn't stand to be in that house for a moment longer, partly because I was holding down a full-time job and partly because...'

'You were hoping your brother would come home?'

Tears fell to the floor as Caroline lifted a tissue to her face. Her shoulders shook, years of torment coming to the surface.

Chapter 14

Carlos squeezed Caroline's shoulder and left her to cry.

Gary was heading for the snug. 'You said to let you know if a DCI Masters arrived. He's here,' he whispered.

'Jacobi, I need to have words with Mrs Sissons and Mrs Winslow,' bellowed an all too familiar voice from the hall.

Gary was letting another person, a grey-haired man wearing an ill-fitting suit carrying a medical bag, in the front door when Carlos appeared in the hall. He led the new arrival through to the kitchen before returning to stare down the DCI.

'Mrs Sissons isn't in a fit state to be interviewed. As you can see, the doctor's just arrived to examine her.' Gary raised himself up to his full lanky height.

'How convenient,' Masters snarled, not taking his eyes off Carlos.

'Mrs Winslow's also out of bounds, I'm afraid,' said Carlos.

Caroline heard the last part of the conversation as she emerged from the snug. 'I've told Carlos all I'm prepared to say for now, Chief Inspector. Perhaps you can ask him anything you need to know. Now I need to be with my mother.'

Caroline marched through to the kitchen, leaving Masters, Carlos and Gary in a standoff. Gary returned his focus to Lady, who was delivering a low growl Masters's way.

Carlos compromised first. 'Why don't you join me through here and I'll tell you what I know.'

Masters glared towards the kitchen just as Fiona arrived, dispelling the tension a little.

'All sorted next door, sir. Have you found anything out, Mr Jacobi?'

'I was just about to fill the chief inspector in on what I've discovered. Perhaps you'd like to join us?'

'Don't mind if I do. Is that okay, sir? I can take notes. It sounds a bit busy in there.' She nodded towards the kitchen, where muffled voices could be heard. 'Is there somewhere else we can talk?'

Carlos gestured towards the snug. Masters nodded curtly.

'Right. Lead the way. Tell us what you've got, Jacobi.'

Once seated in the snug, Masters relaxed a little. Lady followed them, not willing to leave her master with this man without her being present. Fiona stroked the dog's head, causing her to go into a happy whining frenzy.

'How are you, girl? She's the heroine of the hour, sir. Found the spot where the body was hidden and got herself injured in the process, didn't you, girl?' Fiona ruffled Lady's fur again. Even Masters smiled at his ebullient sergeant crouching down on the floor, cuddling the dog.

Carlos inhaled and exhaled, relieved the tension was dissipating. He related everything Caroline had told him so far. Masters, for all his stroppy attitude, listened carefully, only interrupting occasionally.

'So,' he summarised, 'we have the body of a man found in the woods two nights ago. Now we have the skeleton of a minor who may turn out to be the late man's son. And from what Mrs Winslow has told you, it appears her brother went missing twenty years ago while she and her mother were away for a few days, which leaves us to conclude that, in all likelihood, Harold Sissons killed the boy.'

'That's about the sum of it,' answered Carlos wryly. 'What we don't know yet is whether the two deaths are connected.'

'Of course they're connected. Someone found out the man murdered his son—'

'If it is his son, sir,' Fiona interrupted.

'I agree, Sergeant, but I think for now, we assume it is.' Masters grinned; he clearly liked Fiona. Who wouldn't? 'Which narrows it down somewhat. It's a shame the body was buried or we could have hoped the monster's conscience had caught up with him and he'd killed himself. Hopefully we'll be able to make an arrest tomorrow.'

Carlos's jaw dropped open. 'How so?'

Masters snorted. 'The wife may have had a lover. Jealous and controlling man finds out, takes it out on the boy. The rest of this is police business, Jacobi, so I suggest you back off now. Mrs Sissons's ex-lover, if there is one, goes to the top of the suspect list, otherwise it's the daughter. It could seriously harm your reputation if you continue working for this family.'

'Meg Sissons did not have a lover, and Mrs Winslow was in Edinburgh. No-one else could have known about the boy's murder, otherwise it would have come out long before now.' Carlos regretted it as soon as the anger and astonishment spilled out of his mouth, but it appeared Masters was too triumphant to notice he'd disagreed with his verdict.

'Thank you for your time, Jacobi. Cook? Time to leave. We need to talk.'

Fiona shot Carlos a worried glance, but followed her boss. An astounded Carlos sat in the armchair for some minutes, polishing off his brandy.

***

Before leaving, Masters told Caroline he would need to question her and her mother the next morning. Carlos accompanied the DCI and Fiona to the door, but Masters didn't wait. He slammed it on the way out.

Annoyed at having the door slammed in his face, albeit shutting him inside rather than out, Carlos peered through the blinds to check whether Masters and Fiona were leaving altogether or returning next door. Masters gesticulated under the streetlight outside Meg's house, then he jumped into his car. Tyres screeched again as the insensitive DCI left the scene.

Fiona returned to the house next door. All the other police cars had left, along with the pathologist's white BMW. He hoped Fiona would come back before she went home, but for now, he refocused himself on events taking place in the kitchen.

The doctor suggested Meg have an injection of sedative. She still hadn't spoken a word since the horrific find in the house next door.

'Would you and Meg like to stay here tonight?' Sophie asked Caroline.

'That's kind of you. I'd appreciate it if Mother could stay. I don't think it would be good for her to go home just yet. I'd better go back next door to sleep, as well as clear up any mess left by that buffoon and his gang. I also promised I'd phone my husband again once the police had gone. He'll be beside himself. Nothing like this has ever happened to us. I couldn't believe someone had killed that horrible man, but now this.' The knee began its jerking under the dining room table again as Caroline fought to maintain control.

'Try not to worry. We'll look after your mum. I'm so sorry...' Carlos offered.

'Er hum...' The doctor coughed. 'Shall we get the patient upstairs now?' The man had bags under his eyes. His phone had gone off at least three times in the past fifteen minutes. Carlos sympathised. Medics had a tough life, but he felt more sympathy for the pathologist who would have been called next door, trying to piece together the last hours and cause of death of a child.

Caroline led Meg by the hand, following Sophie upstairs to a spare bedroom. The doctor followed. Five minutes later, the medic returned. Carlos and Gary saw him out.

'I've given her a strong sedative. She should sleep all night. I suggest you call her own doctor in the morning if there's no improvement. If she's still like this tomorrow, she's going to need admission. She's in a severe state of shock, poor woman.'

'The police want to interview her tomorrow,' said Carlos.

'Then they will have to want. Unless she makes a miraculous recovery overnight, she's in no fit state and will be of no use to them like this. The woman's completely shut down. Your sister told me what had happened. First her husband, and now this.'

'Thanks for your help, Doctor. Is there anything we should do if she does wake in the night?' asked Gary.

'I've left some pills with your wife. You can give her two of those, but I doubt you'll need them.' The doctor returned to his marked car, where a driver waited. Carlos heard him direct the driver to the next visit. Clearly his night was not over yet, either.

'More brandy?' asked Gary.

Carlos nodded. Gary poured two large shots while they waited for Sophie and Caroline to come downstairs. Carlos checked his phone for messages, but no word from Fiona. Her car had left by the time they saw the doctor out. She'd have all the paperwork to complete; he couldn't imagine Masters doing it.

He and Gary finished their brandies and Lady settled herself at Carlos's feet. Twenty minutes later, they heard the front door open and close.

Sophie joined them.

'Meg's asleep. Caroline's just gone back next door. Can you pour me one of those?'

Sophie looked exhausted and dishevelled after the evening's events. Gary did as she asked and poured her a brandy.

I need to get them another bottle of this stuff if tonight's anything to go by, Carlos thought.

Gary joined Sophie where she had slumped down on the settee and put his arm around her. Although he was still wan himself, he had recovered enough to be of use to his wife.

'Thanks for all you did tonight, you two.'

'I'm only sorry now you're involved in this, Carlo,' Sophie used her pet name for him. 'What if that detective's right and someone we know killed Harold? He mentioned Caroline. Meg couldn't have done it, although who would blame them after tonight's disturbing discovery?'

'How did you know that's what Masters thinks?' asked Carlos.

'I'm surprised the whole street doesn't know what he thinks. He's hardly discreet. I heard him bragging from the kitchen how he'll make an arrest within days.'

'Did anyone else hear?' Carlos was surprised Caroline had opted to go back to the house she insisted she hates, although she appeared to be a woman who liked to be in control.

'No. Caroline was using the bathroom upstairs because Gary was in the downstairs loo, soaking a flannel to clean Lady's fur, and the doctor had his stethoscope in his ears, listening to Meg's chest.'

'But Caroline was down here. I saw Masters talking to her.'

'She'd just come down. Carlos, she didn't hear. I checked who was around when the loudmouth said it. Honest.'

'What about Meg?'

'Well, she was around, obviously, but if she did hear, she didn't respond. Not a flicker of change crossed her face. I don't think she was actually listening or hearing anything. She just stared into space. Funnily enough, I noticed the same vacant look yesterday when I went to stay with her before the police came. The lights were on but no-one was home, you know what I mean?'

Gary raised his eyebrows quizzically. Sophie nudged him, giggling.

'She means Meg looked vacant. It's an expression my aunt used to use when people weren't with it, and Sophie uses it whenever she gets the chance.' Carlos laughed. 'I'm surprised you haven't heard it.'

Gary smiled at his mischievous wife. 'I'm pleased you can laugh at a time like this.'

'Anyway, back to Meg. If she heard anything, she wouldn't have processed it. As I said, the lights were on...'

'We get it, Sofia,' Carlos scolded her, using her real name, but nodded thoughtfully. His sister pretend-scowled, but Carlos's thoughts were elsewhere. He didn't have either Meg or Caroline down as the murderer of Harold Sissons. Meg was weak and frail, and Caroline lived in Edinburgh and hadn't seen her father for twenty years. Not only that, she would have to be a good actress to have fooled him. But he couldn't rule either out altogether. Both had motive, especially if they'd found out what had happened to Matthew Sissons, but he couldn't see how they could have known. And there were still the goings-on at the community centre and Harold's disagreement with Colonel Webb.

'You're quiet, Carlos,' Gary interrupted his thoughts.

'Just trying to process the two crimes. A long time's passed for either of them to want to take revenge, and by all accounts, Meg and Caroline believed the boy, Matthew, had run away while they were staying with Meg's sister some twenty years ago. Their shock was genuine; they didn't know Matthew was under the floorboards upstairs. I'm certain of that.'

'You obviously know more than we do; you'd better fill us in. Shall I make hot chocolate?' Sophie asked.

After Carlos had taken Lady for a quick walk up the lane and they were settled with hot milky drinks, he told them everything he had learned from Caroline.

'She never spoke to her father again,' he said when he had come to the end of the sorry tale, 'only having telephone contact with her mother, except for her wedding fifteen years ago.'

'I'm surprised he allowed her to the wedding,' said Gary.

'It was the one and only time Meg's parents intervened on her behalf. Harold went away on a manufactured business trip according to Caroline, but she didn't want him there anyway.'

'So what about the police? Didn't they try to find Matthew?' asked Sophie, tutting.

'I suppose they must have been informed. I expect they'll pull the files from the missing persons case in the morning or on Monday if they haven't done so already. Everyone assumed he'd either come to harm on the journey or run off elsewhere. That's what Caroline told me. Her horror at the find seemed genuine.'

'And was she in Edinburgh last week?' asked Gary.

'I guess so, and sincerely hope she was, for her sake,' answered Carlos, knocking back the final dregs of the hot chocolate. 'All alibis will be checked by Fiona, whatever Masters may do.'

'There has to be some other reason for Harold's murder,' said Gary. 'Some local feud or a tragic accident. Perhaps he fell over in the woods and hit his head on a stone or something.'

'And buried himself?' Carlos chuckled.

'Oh yes. I forgot about that. I've been trying to put it out of my mind, to be honest.'

'And so you should,' said Carlos kindly. 'He wasn't a popular man with some, though, according to the locals, and he did have an argument on the day he went missing. That's something I'll be chasing up. We need to go to the carol service tomorrow evening so I can talk to people again about Harold Sissons. Preferably before they find out he was possibly a child killer.'

'Why do you say that?' asked Gary.

'Because, my dear brother-in-law, when people find out things like that, they tend to imagine all sorts of things and embellish the truth. Before you know it, we'll have witnesses swearing he's a serial killer. I need them to give unbiased accounts.'

'Carlos, why don't you drop the case? You are on holiday, after all, and it turns out Harold wasn't the man we thought he was. He...' Sophie tailed off, lifting her large brown eyes pleadingly.

'I know, Sophie. I find the whole thing as distasteful as you do, but the man was still murdered. We don't know what the motive was yet, but whether you and I think he deserved to die or not, there's a killer out there, probably in your village. Don't you want to know who it is?'

Sophie shook her head, tears falling. 'I'm not sure I care. Is that terrible?'

Gary took his wife's hand. 'Me neither. I'd rather the police find whoever is responsible.'

'And what if the deaths are related?' asked Carlos.

'Then good luck to them, I say.' Gary pulled Sophie close.

Feelings were running high. Carlos believed that when morning came, his sister and brother-in-law would think differently. It had been a long day.

'On a happier note, how did the anniversary meal go?'

Sophie's eyes brightened. 'At least we finished it before your Sergeant Cook came round. Look what he bought me.'

She held out her left hand to show an eternity ring studded with five black diamonds cushioned between her wedding and engagement ring.

'If you're not careful, you won't be able to use that hand with all the weight.'

As they managed to laugh again and relax a little, Carlos decided to stay off the subject of bodies and murder. Lady fidgeted at his feet; he stroked her head. Poor girl, she had certainly earned her bread over the past few days, he mused.

Gary and Sophie went to bed and Carlos sat for some time, mulling again over the events of the day. He checked his phone in case he'd missed a text from Fiona. Then he texted her and waited, but no reply. Frustrated, he decided it was time to get to bed himself. Just as his head hit the pillow, his phone vibrated.

'On the night train to Edinburgh. Signal intermittent. Speak tomorrow. F x'.

Chapter 15

The Edinburgh train pulled in at 6am. Fiona grabbed her rucksack from the luggage rack and joined the queue lining up to try to be off first, leaving behind crisp and biscuit crumbs on the seat. She'd barely slept despite having a sleeper compartment; instead, she had spent the night wondering how she was going to deal with DCI Masters and his loathing of Carlos. Their animosity was a threat to the investigation, of that she had no doubt.

She had only worked with Masters a few times and, despite his surliness, they got on. He liked her humour. If she was honest, she found him attractive, but over the past couple of days she had seen a different side to him.

He hadn't shown any interest in her as a woman, but even if he had, she wouldn't have given in. He had a reputation around the station with regards to his flings, none of which were known to his wife. He also went for the younger, slimmer model. Fiona had recently turned thirty-seven and her figure left a lot to be desired.

Edinburgh station was illuminated with Christmas decorations and festive songs played over the loudspeakers in between regular, if not continuous, announcements of what train was arriving or departing from what platform. The station was busy; it was the last Sunday before Christmas, so many people were arriving or departing for the holidays.

Masters had insisted she speak to Aiden Winslow in person and also check Caroline's alibi with her boss. Fiona had argued the toss, suggesting the checks could be carried out by the local force and over the phone, but with Masters's mood worsening by the minute, she had given in.

Poor Caroline Winslow had no idea she was under suspicion, and Fiona wasn't at all convinced that she was anything other than a victim, born into a dysfunctional family. There was a deep sadness about this family, and now Meg Sissons had closed down. Fiona had been a DS for almost a year now, and was a PC for many years before that, but she never got used to speaking to people ripped apart by tragedy. Not only had this woman lost her husband, it looked like she had also lost her son at the man's hands. Now Terry Masters was determined to put the old woman's daughter behind bars, mostly because she'd hurt his pride by hiring Carlos.

There was no reason for a police sergeant to travel all the way from Derbyshire for this mission; perhaps she should have dug her heels in. Had Masters found out about her friendship with Carlos? That's what had really bothered her all night, but no-one else at the station knew, so she couldn't see how he could have worked it out.

She walked along the concourse. Gurgling sounds in her gut reminded her of how hungry she was. The smell of bacon and sausages reached her nostrils. She spotted an open café.

'Food is just what I need,' she said out loud, marching towards the smell.

Twenty minutes later, the empty plate that had once held a full fry up with potato scones and black pudding – the only differences between a Scottish and an English breakfast – sat on the table in front of her. Downing a second mug of strong tea, she dialled.

'Fiona! I hoped you'd call this morning,' Carlos sounded out of breath.

'Good morning to you, too,' she laughed.

'Sorry, I'm out for a run with Lady. That wasn't the politest greeting. How was the journey, and need I ask what you are doing in Edinburgh?'

'The journey was long, too long, but not really long enough for an overnighter. Couldn't sleep.'

An announcement in the background drew her attention away from the call.

'Could Fiona Cook please make her way to the customer services desk.'

Fiona groaned. 'That'll be Steve.'

'Did I hear that right?' Carlos sounded concerned. 'Your brother lives in Edinburgh?'

'Just outside. It's going to be hell, but I wasn't going to try to find an empty hotel or B&B. It's almost

Christmas. Not to mention the fact the DCI might not sign the expenses sheet, the mood he's in.'

She heard Carlos chuckling. Ignoring the reference to Masters, he replied, 'Blimey, I've just remembered your brother. Isn't he a criminal?'

Fiona sighed heavily. 'Yep, that's the one. He's got a flat and a floor I can sleep on, so let's drop that conversation,' she snapped.

Her little brother was a sore subject at the best of times. In the old days, he would have been referred to as a scoundrel, but he was a constant source of embarrassment to Fiona and her dad. Nevertheless, they loved him.

'He's a trouble magnet, that's all. Look, I'd better find him. I'll call you later and fill you in, but suffice it to say, I'm here to speak to Aiden Winslow and Caroline's boss.'

'Good luck with the latter. There aren't many civil service departments open over Christmas week.'

'Just a quickie, how's Meg?'

'Fast asleep when I left. The doctor gave her a heavy dose of sedation, and as far as I'm aware, it worked. I haven't seen Caroline yet. Speak later, ciao.'

'Bye, Carlos.' Fiona slipped the phone back into her mac pocket and headed across the concourse towards customer services. A pleasant surprise greeted her when she caught sight of Steve. He'd smartened up, a good sign that he wasn't drinking or doing drugs. The glow in his dark green eyes melted her heart.

'Hey, Fiona.' He pulled her into a hug.

'Hello, you.' Not comfortable with the sudden demonstrative hug from her brother, Fiona pulled away and automatically checked his pupils. No signs of opiate or cannabis use, just the happy eyes she remembered from their youth before they went their separate ways.

'What?' He stepped back as she continued staring.

'Nothing.' She shrugged. 'Good to see you, sorry it's been so long.'

'And now you're using me for a place to stay,' he joked.

'That's about it. Where's your car?'

'I don't have a car. I came on my bike.'

Irritated, Fiona gawped. 'How the hell…'

He burst out laughing just like he used to and grabbed her bag before putting his arm around her shoulders.

'Gotcha!'

Fiona melted again and joined in his laughter. Perhaps this wasn't such a bad idea after all.

'You haven't changed at all,' but the truth was, he had changed dramatically since the last time she'd seen him. She'd collected him from prison when he finished a sentence for dealing. He'd promised her and her dad he'd change, but was back to his old tricks soon afterwards. Now they only kept in touch through the odd phone call.

She realised as she followed this confident, well-dressed man out of the station that they hadn't spoken in a while. The designer clothes concerned her, if she was honest. Where had he got the money for them? Then she got a glimpse of the Rolex on his wrist and her heart sank.

'What ya doing up here, then, sis?' he asked. She was struggling to get used to this new brother who wouldn't normally show any interest in her, or anyone else for that matter.

'Work,' she answered, hoping that would be the end of the conversation.

The Volvo parked in the station car park, although old, was in immaculate condition. The interior was polished and clean. Steve continued the chat as they drove out of the city to the suburbs of leafy tree-lined avenues. If she'd been surprised at her brother's confident air and happy demeanour, she was more surprised by his sudden interest in her and her world.

Fiona found herself checking around the car for any sign of drugs and felt guilty doing so, but this area was posh. Even though she was almost falling asleep by the time they pulled on to a large driveway, her stomach knotted. Was he dealing again?

'Where are we?' she asked.

'Home,' he answered, studying her reaction. 'Come on, Fi.' He leapt out of the car with an agility she'd never witnessed before. The more she looked at him, the more she didn't recognise her own brother. Guilt pangs at not keeping in touch settled over her stomach.

She moved cautiously, stepping on to the pristine block-paved driveway. The large house was Victorian with huge bay windows and painted blue frames. A blue composite front door swung open.

A shapely young woman emerged and hurried towards Fiona, enveloping her in a hug before she had time to react.

'Fiona, I've heard so much about you.' The woman smiled warmly. Fiona disentangled herself from the stranger's embrace, her jaw dropping open.

'Hi,' she replied. *That's good, because I've heard nothing about you*, remained unsaid.

The two women stood for a moment, appraising each other.

'Fi, this is Jen.' Steve kissed the woman, who gazed adoringly into his eyes.

Okay, now I feel sick. Was it the fry up or the twee suburban couple in front of her making her realise her brother was a stranger?

Jen broke the silence. 'You must be tired. I heard you got the overnight. Come on in, I've put the kettle on.'

The woman sounded nervous and Fiona would have to get used to the posh Edinburgh accent. Suddenly, she felt scruffy. Her precious plastic mac had seen better days and was fraying at the wrists; her brown ankle boots with flat heels were akin to walkers' boots. She must have looked like she had hiked to Edinburgh rather than taking the train.

She followed Steve and Jen up four stone steps and through the front door into a wide high-ceilinged hallway with polished real-wood floors. They turned left into an expansive lounge.

Steve and Jen removed their shoes on entry and stepped into fur-lined slippers, but Fiona kept her shoes on. She didn't do *fancy pants show* at the best of times, and she was preparing for a swift exit if required. If it had been possible to have a double, she could well believe that this was her brother's double, or that someone else had inhabited his body – the transformation was frightening and maybe a bit forced.

Now you're just being unkind, she chastised herself.

The polite conversation dried up an hour later and Fiona noticed Jen's mask slip once or twice as she exchanged glances with her brother and stared wide-eyed at Fiona's boots. Or was it the trail of leaves that had accompanied them, parking themselves on the highly polished floor? A large white fur rug took centre stage; at least she hadn't stepped on that.

Eventually, Steve cleared his throat.

'Erm, I wonder, Fi...?'

Fiona sensed his discomfort but was saved by the ringtone of *Fight Song* coming from the hallway where she'd hung her mac. *Apt*, she thought.

'I need to take this,' she said.

Once in the hall, she rolled her eyes when she saw who was calling.

'Hello, sir.'

'What have you got?'

'The train was late, I've only just arrived,' she lied.

A pause at the other end. 'We need to wrap this up, Cook. There's pressure coming down from on high. We need to teach these civil servants they can't throw their weight around, understand?'

'Yes, sir, but—'

'But what?' he snapped.

'What if she's innocent, sir? There's no proof Caroline Winslow's done anything wrong.' She swallowed hard, waiting for a barrage of abuse, but Masters seemed to be thinking about what she'd said.

'Just find out what you can. If she's innocent, we'll go after the old girl, find out if she had an affair.'

Another lead weight settled in Fiona's stomach. *I wish I hadn't had the big breakfast now*, she thought, but replied, 'I'll do my best, sir. I'll contact you as soon as I have anything.'

'Not today. I'm, erm... busy. We'll talk tomorrow.'

Fiona heard a woman's voice in the background. *Playing away again, sir?* she thought.

'Righto, I'll call you in the morning after I've contacted Mrs Winslow's boss.'

Masters rang off, leaving Fiona standing in the huge hallway, angry. Muffled voices came from the lounge. She made a few 'Mm' sounds as if she was still on the phone and crept closer to the slightly ajar doorway.

'You didn't tell me she was a slob,' hissed Jen.

'She's not a slob, she's just... she's just Fi.'

Fiona smiled, grateful for her brother's attempted defence, then remembered how unkempt he'd looked the last time they met. At least she washed!

'Well she's not going up my stairs in those clodhoppers. Look at all that mud! I'm going to have to get the cleaner in again, and it's Christmas week.'

'It's just a few leaves, Jen. You could...' Fiona's brother decided not to finish the sentence. 'Look, she'll be gone in the morning. She's been good to me, I told you that.'

'A thousand times,' Jen huffed.

Fiona exhaled heavily, sat on the stairs and untied her laces. She pulled off her boots and lay them on a shoe rack in the hall.

'Behave yourselves,' she muttered to them before rejoining Steve and

Jen in the lounge. 'My boss,' she explained, 'never a moment's peace. By the way, Jen, I'm sorry I forgot my manners. I've left my boots in the hall. If you have a vacuum, I can clean up my mess.'

Jen's face reddened as Steve shot her an "I told you so" look.

'Oh, no. No problem. I have a cleaner. I am a little house-proud. Steve likes it that way.' Jen giggled nervously.

Now it was Steve's turn to blush.

'Yeah, I remember,' Fiona answered sarcastically.

Chapter 16

Meg awoke in a strange but comfortable bed. Winter sun found its way through a crack in the curtains. Grogginess threatened to send her back to sleep. Her eyelids too heavy to keep open, she felt herself drifting.

She overlooked flourishing green trees, not a care in the world. The sky appeared a deeper blue than usual. Her eyes imagined she could see through to heaven. She belted out her own rendition of *I Believe*, felt so alive. Happiness. Immeasurable joy filled her heart, the letter in her hand the reason for the elation. Here was the fulfilment of all her hopes and dreams.

She paused her singing for a moment and sat down on a rock on top of High Tor, overlooking Matlock Bath. How had she managed to reach the top without pausing for breath? She read the letter again.

'Dear Miss Russell,

We have pleasure in offering you a scholarship at the Arts Educational School...'

Her heart missed a beat as she clutched the letter to her chest. She couldn't wait to tell Harold.

Suddenly, the sky above her turned grey and a storm threatened. Her parents often reminded her how quickly the weather could change in the Peak District. It was time to descend back into town.

Meg tucked the letter into her dress pocket and, in her mind, heard her mother scolding her for climbing the tor inappropriately dressed. At least she had thought to put on sturdy shoes before leaving home. Her parents were at work when the letter came and her sister was at a birthday party. She would have run straight round to Harold's, but they weren't due to meet until four and he didn't like interruptions. He was working with his dad for the summer before going to college. He would be so excited when she told him the news; he loved her singing.

As she clambered down the hill, she wondered why she hadn't told him about her application. Was it really because she didn't want to share the disappointment if she wasn't accepted or was there something more?

The rain lashed down as she reached the main road into Matlock Bath. Her sky-blue cotton summer dress was drenched, as was her hair. Even the change in the weather couldn't dampen her mood today.

This was her day.

Wednesday 4 August 1954.

Nothing could go wrong.

***

Harold read the letter as she waited in excited anticipation for him to congratulate her and share in her happiness. His face clouded over as he stared up from the page.

'Is this some kind of joke?' He spoke at last, throwing her precious letter to the floor.

Nervousness replaced the joy that had filled her heart all day. She retrieved the letter and folded it neatly in the lap of the dress she'd changed into before coming to tell Harold her news.

'I thought you'd be pleased for me.' She couldn't yet look up from the letter.

'Why would I be pleased? You dump this on me when I've been working hard all day, and you didn't even ask me about this before applying.'

Harold was older than Meg at sixteen and sometimes treated her like a child. She was thirteen.

Although she would be starting her new school as a second year, the teachers had been impressed with her audition.

'Sorry,' she muttered as tears threatened to fall. This wasn't going how she'd expected it to, but deep down she realised it was going exactly how she'd expected, otherwise she would have told Harold before now.

'I should think so. Look, Meg, I know you have this crazy dream about being a singer, but you have to face reality. You're just not good enough.'

His words stung like never before. 'What do you mean? You've always told me you like my singing – that I'm good – that I should be on the stage.'

'Well the truth is, you're not. You're just making a fool of yourself, Meggie.'

She hated it when he called her Meggie. She had tried asking him not to, but that made him angry.

'When you sing to me, of course I like it, because it's for me. Don't you see? This will ruin everything.'

He couldn't have hurt her more if he'd put a knife through her heart and twisted it. Her shoulders shook as sobs broke through. The dreams she'd held on to fell to the floor with every tear she shed.

'There's no use crying, Meg. Crying doesn't help anything.' Harold's voice was cold as he admonished her.

She ran from his house, down the street and into the countryside once again. This time there was no joy in her heart. No hope. No ambition. Everything had been snatched away in an instant.

So this was it. She wasn't good enough. She would never perform on stage, never become like Julie Andrews. It was all an impossible dream.

Meg stopped running, drying her eyes as she pulled the letter from her pocket. The rain had stopped, but the wind was howling through the trees as she tore the letter into tiny pieces and threw it in the air. She watched the wind carry her dreams away and felt a stranglehold gather around her heart.

She vowed she would never sing again.

***

Meg opened her bleary eyes and felt the damp patch on the strange pillow. The sun was stronger now, bringing shafts of light into the room.

A familiar fear gripped her heart as she heard Caroline's voice coming from somewhere in the distance. Shattered memories like shards of glass pierced through her brain.

A room where they tried to get her to talk. Pills that gave her nightmares and the darkness that followed injections. A hospital, they had called it, but it was more like a prison. Helplessness threatened to overwhelm her. Was that where she was now heading? Harold had told her again and again she would end up in a psychiatric ward without him to look after her. His nagging voice filled her head, all the poisonous things he'd told her about herself screamed, closing in, threatening to suffocate her.

'Stop it!' she yelled, putting her hands to her ears.

Harold's not here. A small voice from within sparked a glimmer of hope like the shaft of the sunbeam forcing its way through the crack in the curtains.

***

Sophie tapped on the door of the bedroom where Meg had been sleeping since last night. No reply. She gently opened the door and peered inside. Light coming through a gap in the curtains revealed Meg sitting up in bed, humming a song Sophie didn't recognise.

'Good morning, Meg.'

The older woman continued to hum.

'Caroline's arrived downstairs. Can I get you a cup of tea?'

Meg stopped humming and for a brief moment the confused eyes displayed panic.

'Meg?' Sophie tried again.

'Where am I?'

'You're in our house. You stayed the night after, erm…'

Meg moved suddenly, removing the bedcovers and sitting on the edge of the bed.

'I must get home. Harold will want his breakfast.'

'Mother, he's not here. Remember? He was found in the woods.'

Sophie was relieved when Caroline appeared behind her, marching into the room like a woman on a mission.

'How are you feeling?' Caroline asked Meg, her tone softening.

'A bit groggy. Have I been unwell?'

'You had a shock, Mum. The doctor sedated you last night. Are you ready to get up?'

Meg tried to stand, but slumped back into a sitting position.

'My legs don't seem to be working. Perhaps I'll stay here.' The older woman climbed back beneath the covers and lay down. As Caroline and Sophie turned to leave, they both heard humming.

'What is that song?' asked Sophie.

'Sounds like *This is My Life.* Shirley Bassey sang it, I think.' Caroline frowned, a concerned furrow in her brows. She was very much in control this morning, dressed in a smart woollen dress that hugged her curves. If Sophie hadn't known, she wouldn't have guessed what had been unearthed the previous night.

'She can certainly hold a tune,' she said.

'I've never heard her sing before, or maybe – a long time ago – when I was a child – I once found her singing to Matthew.' A cloud appeared over Caroline's face.

'Can I get you some tea? Carlos should be back any minute. He went out for a run about an hour ago.'

'If it wouldn't be an imposition. I couldn't face tea leaves again. It was something he always insisted upon. Mother never got a choice in the matter. I'm sorry for the trouble we seem to be bringing to your home. Are you okay about Mother staying here until the drugs wear off?'

'Please don't apologise. We're glad to help. Your mum was friendly when we moved in. Brought us sandwiches round on the day we moved, and cake. It's horrible what you're both going through.'

Sophie meant what she said, although she wasn't keen to have a rather unpredictable Meg staying upstairs. The responsibility bore down on her chest. She'd hardly slept, worrying about her neighbour. Thank Goodness Carlos was here.

'Hopefully your mum will feel better later,' she added.

Caroline's look said it all. They both doubted Meg would be feeling better for some time.

Sophie led the way through to the kitchen and invited Caroline to join her. Caroline sat at the breakfast bar, mobile phone in hand, tapping into the screen, her face racked in concentration. Sophie placed a mug of tea down on the bar in front of her guest.

'Can I get you some breakfast?'

'No thanks. I don't eat breakfast.'

No wonder you're so thin, thought Sophie.

Caroline didn't look up from the screen except to lift the mug to her mouth. The right knee was bouncing up and down from the barstool. She tutted a few times and tapped frantically again, clearly not going to engage in small talk.

'I think I'll take your mum a cup of tea upstairs just in case,' Sophie said.

'Yes, good idea,' replied Caroline.

'Do you think she would prefer tea leaves?'

'Probably,' Caroline made no effort to move, frowning at the phone in her hand as she blew out a huff.

'I don't have any. Would you mind?'

'What? Oh, yes. I'll pop next door and get some. Aiden's parents are spoiling the kids already. I knew they would. I can't leave them like this for long, I need to get back to Edinburgh.'

Sophie understood. It must be hard being so far away just before Christmas, and now Caroline had her mother to deal with. A sudden dread settled on her stomach. Surely Caroline wouldn't leave her mother in Peaks Hollow, or worse, in her and Gary's home?

Sophie boiled the kettle again and was just about to remind Caroline about the tea leaves when the other woman plonked the phone back in her handbag, finished her tea and marched out at pace, presumably to go next door. Whilst Sophie had every sympathy for the agitated woman, she could feel her own nerves fraying. Gary had hardly slept either, so she'd left him in bed this morning. Carlos had been dashing out with Lady when she arrived downstairs in her dressing gown. Now she was left babysitting her neighbour and Meg's anorexic daughter, and all she could feel was her stomach rumbling, complaining it hadn't been fed since dinner last night.

She heard the door open and sighed, waiting for Caroline to appear with the tea leaves, but was delighted when Lady came bounding into the kitchen and threw herself at

Sophie's legs, dancing around with pure joy.

'Am I pleased to see you.' Sophie stroked the dog's head and filled her water bowl. 'Where have you been? Caroline will be back any minute.'

Carlos's sweaty frame enveloped her in a hug as she burst into tears.

Chapter 17

Carlos took a quick shower, then insisted Sophie sit while he made breakfast. His sister had been a rock over the past couple of days, but he wasn't surprised she was feeling the pressure. What was supposed to be a happy first Christmas in her new home was turning into something out of a horror movie. Dead bodies, strange neighbours and a neurotic, albeit bereft, stranger landing all at once.

'Here, drink this,' he placed a mug of strong coffee in front of her. 'Are you up to a fry up? I'm starving.'

Sophie's huge eyes lit up. 'I would have had one cooking, but Caroline doesn't eat breakfast.'

Carlos chuckled at his sister's mimicking. She had Caroline Winslow almost to perfection.

'I thought she'd gone to get tea leaves?' he said.

'She has, supposedly. Should I go and check?'

'No, Sis. You need to eat. Meg's probably gone back to sleep anyway. And she's going to need it before she goes back home.'

Carlos handed Sophie the Sunday paper he'd picked up on his way home. The deaths were unlikely to make national headlines, but he wanted to be sure. He found bacon, eggs, sausages and mushrooms in the American-style larder fridge and started cooking. Fifteen minutes later, he and Sophie were tucking into a substantial breakfast.

'You're not going to be able to eat like this if you marry Rachel,' teased Sophie.

He grinned. 'I'd give up anything to marry Rachel, although she does have the odd unhealthy meal. Speaking of unhealthy, I spoke to Fiona this morning. She's in Edinburgh.'

Sophie lifted her eyes from cutting up a sausage.

'Why?'

'Following up on Caroline's alibi.' He lowered his voice in case the other woman appeared.

Sophie's jaw dropped. 'They can't think...'

'Trust me, Terry Masters can think anything he likes. None of it will make sense to ordinary people like you and me, but he'll go his own way, do his own thing. Besides, Caroline's challenged his machismo, he hates that. He'd love it to be her.'

'But she was in Edinburgh when Harold went missing and away with her mother the weekend her brother disappeared.'

Carlos finished his breakfast and cleared the table before getting up. 'I don't think she's in the frame for her brother's death – at least, I hope not. Look, I'm going next door to see where Caroline is. Do you have any plans for today?'

'We had mooted going up to Yorkshire early to see Gary's parents until all this happened. He's in no fit state now, and I can't leave Meg while she's staying here. We can put off the Yorkshire visit, but we can't have Meg for much longer. I don't want to be rude, Carlos, but Caroline will need to take responsibility for her mother.' Sophie pleaded with her eyes. 'But judging by the fact she can't be relied upon to fetch tea leaves, I'm not hopeful.'

'Understood. I'll have a word with Caroline, see if I can get her to make plans.' He looked at his watch. 'She's been gone over an hour; we've given her long enough.' He hesitated. 'Are you sure you're happy for me to stay on with my appendage?' He looked down at Lady fast asleep on the make-do bed on the kitchen floor.

'Yes, of course! Sorry, I didn't mean to make it sound like you're intruding. Look, I could just about cope with all this, but Gary's not made of stern stuff. He works hard and is bogged down with his secret project without coming home to murder and mayhem. He could do with taking a day off to visit his parents, but he says he doesn't have time. That's why we were going to try today.'

'Perhaps he'll feel better when he gets up. What if I can get Caroline to take Meg home? Will that help? You could still go.'

'Enormously.' Sophie's eyes threatened tears again.

'You get Gary up. I'll see to Caroline.'

Sophie's ebullience was under strain. Carlos could see that and he'd do anything to protect his little sister.

She smiled weakly. 'I feel better after eating. Thanks. You're right, I'll see if Gary's up to the trip today, as long as you make good on your promise.'

'Consider it done. Stay, Lady.'

Carlos arrived next door and knocked. No reply. He walked through the side gate and went around the back of the house. The garden was as pristine as the inside. The night frost was clearing and the sun's rays were reasonably strong, but it was much colder than it had been in London before he left.

The sturdy wooden door at the back of the house was closed. He knocked again and called out.

'Caroline? It's Carlos, are you in there?' Still no reply. He didn't like this at all and wondered whether Sophie had a key.

I'll just check the garage before I go.

The old garage had two wooden doors. He pulled the handle and the door opened, letting light into the otherwise dark detached building. There was no car. He took a few steps inside, drawn to an old bicycle that must have belonged to one of the children. It had a boy's crossbar.

'Must have been Matthew's,' he said out loud.

A rustling sound near the garage entrance caused him to turn just in time to see a man's figure running down the lane, away from the village. He went to give chase, but was almost run over by a car whizzing into the cobbled driveway.

Caroline leapt out of the driver's side. 'I almost ran you over. Are you all right?' she yelled rather than asked.

Carlos checked his ankle; he'd twisted it jumping out of the way.

'No great damage. I'll be fine.'

'What were you doing sneaking around in the garage?' Her eyes narrowed.

'Looking for you. Sophie was expecting you back with tea leaves.'

Caroline straightened up. 'I should have said. Mum's run out, so I had to go to the out-of-town supermarket. The local doesn't open on Sundays.'

'Is that your brother's bike in the garage?'

'Where?'

Carlos pointed through the door. Caroline's face softened, although her colour remained wan.

'Yes, it is. My grandparents bought it for his twelfth birthday. He went everywhere on that thing. I wonder why they kept it.'

'Perhaps they didn't get around to doing anything with it. Did you say it was nearly new?'

'A few months old, but yes. I suppose it's rusted through now.' Caroline didn't move to inspect it.

Carlos debated whether to bring her attention to its mangled state. He wouldn't be able to keep it from her for long, but how much more could she or her mother take right now?

'Why don't we get that tea to your mother? Sophie and Gary need to go up to Yorkshire soon, so it's probably best if your mum comes home, if you feel she's up to it.'

'If not, we can stay at a pub in Eyam. I've booked a room just in case. Did the doctor say he was coming back today? I can't remember.'

'No. We were to call if she doesn't improve. He wondered if she might need to go to hospital.'

Caroline stiffened. Flintlike eyes bored into Carlos's.

'My mother is not going into a psychiatric hospital again. I won't allow it.'

Carlos didn't think she'd have much choice if Meg didn't improve, but he was willing to go along with Caroline for now.

'Let's see how she is.'

Caroline left the car on the driveway, smirking. 'Harold Sissons would have hated that.'

They returned to Sophie and Gary's in silence, Carlos trying to work out what had happened to the bike and who he'd disturbed hiding in the garage. A vagrant? He doubted it, or Caroline would have seen something when she took the car out. The car, though ten years old, had been in perfect condition, from what he'd managed to make out. A blue Vauxhall Astra that had probably not seen much use since it had been bought.

'Does your mum drive?'

'Not unless she took lessons after I left home. She never mentioned it if she did.'

'Was the garage locked when you took the car out?'

'I think so. I can't remember. Why?'

'No reason. Are you expecting to speak to the police today? I thought I heard the chief inspector arranging to see you.'

'The sergeant called first thing, said they would be in touch tomorrow. The chief inspector's busy today, she said.'

Carlos was pleased.

Once back at Sophie's, he made tea while Caroline tapped into her mobile phone. Sophie had left a teapot out. He could hear voices coming from upstairs, and singing.

Weird.

Caroline lifted her head from the phone. 'It's that song again,' she said, staring in disbelief at the door.

'What song?'

'Mum was singing it this morning. I need to go.' Caroline marched from the room, leaving Carlos putting a cup and saucer on a tray. Sophie had picked up on the fact Meg used a cup and saucer from Friday's visit and was doing her best to make Meg feel calm. He lifted the tray, noticing Caroline had left her mobile on the breakfast bar. He reached out to pick it up and saw a new message had come through.

'Don't tell them. Whatever you do.' The sender's name was Aiden.

Now what's that all about? Don't tell who what? Secrets seemed to abound in this family. He just hoped Caroline's alibi would hold firm.

The singing continued as he reached the top of the stairs, becoming louder as he approached the room where Meg had slept. The door was wide open and Meg was sitting up in bed, belting out a ballad in exquisite fashion while Caroline gawped. Sophie and Gary nodded approval, holding hands.

'She won't stop until she's finished,' whispered Caroline.

When the song ended, Meg came out of a trance and noticed people in the room. She appeared unsure of herself again.

'What happened?'

Sophie and Gary, who had been clapping, stopped.

'Nothing, Mum. Look, here's some tea.'

Caroline took the tray from Carlos and he left them to it. His sister and brother-in-law also made a discreet exit.

'She's got a gorgeous voice,' said Sophie.

'What happened?'

'Gary had just dressed when we heard singing coming from Meg's room. We went to see if you and Caroline were in there, but instead, found Meg performing as if she were on stage. She didn't seem to see us at all. Caroline arrived and tried to say something, but Meg carried on as if she wasn't there. We suggested we let her finish, then you came in. Do you think we should call the doctor again?'

Sophie stared up at Gary. Carlos intervened.

'No. You two do what you have to do. Caroline has agreed to take her mother home or to a pub B&B. If she needs a doctor, Caroline and I will deal with it.' He didn't mention the bike or the near-miss next door, but Gary noticed.

'Carlos, you're limping.'

'I tripped next door, round the back. I was trying to find Caroline, but she'd taken Harold's car and gone to buy tea leaves.'

'That's why she was so long.'

'Yes. Now go on. You should get up and down today if you leave soon.'

'Erm... we've decided to stay the night,' said Gary. 'We'll drive back down in the morning. I'll drop Sophie and go straight to work. Do you mind?'

'Not at all. It will do you good, and I'm sure your parents will be pleased to see you for longer. Don't worry, the house will be back to normal by the time you get home. Lady and I will manage.'

'I've left mince in the fridge, or there's a frozen lasagne in the freezer. Help yourself to anything while we're gone.'

Carlos thought it would be better for them to be out of the way, particularly as he wanted to call Fiona about the mangled bike and try to interview Meg and Caroline at some point. He intended to find out what the person in the garage had been up to as well, so there was plenty to keep him busy.

'Thanks, I'll do a ragu with the mince. Lady and I will take a leisurely stroll this afternoon.'

'As if you're going to have time for that,' quipped Sophie.

'You know me. Forever the optimist.'

Caroline joined them downstairs. 'Mother's getting dressed, she'll wash at home.'

'Will you both be staying there tonight?' asked Sophie.

'We'll have to see how she is later. I expect you'll want to ask some more questions.' She held Carlos's gaze.

'If your mum's up to it.

'Right. I need to go.' She walked briskly into the kitchen, retrieved the mobile and left without saying another word.

Chapter 18

With the house empty, Carlos called Fiona. She answered almost immediately, sounding breathless.

'How's it going up there?'

'Interesting. Steve's hooked up with some wealthy woman with OCD.'

'I never knew there was so much OCD in the world. We ex-army bods are bad enough, but ours pales into insignificance compared to the

Sissons's house. You sound breathless, are you okay?'

'Just come out to get some fresh air. Conversation dried up about an hour ago. We ended up waiting for whoever had anything to say to speak next.'

'That's not like you,' Carlos laughed. 'You can always keep a conversation going.'

'Yeah, but this one I'm more likely to turn into an interrogation. I want to know where the money's coming from and if it's legit, but Jen – that's the girlfriend – needs to be out of the way before I can quiz my brother, and she's sticking to him like glue.'

'Maybe he's just landed on his feet.'

'And maybe cows have joined the pigs flying. I don't mean to sound cynical, and Steve seems happy, but this is real money, Carlos. I just hope he's not dealing again.'

'Does he look like he's using?'

'No, not at all. He's well-dressed, healthy, putting on the pounds – he looks great.'

Carlos paused, not knowing what to say. He remembered the state Steve had been in when Fiona bailed him out of trouble the last time, and it wasn't pretty. He hoped rather than believed that her brother had turned his life around.

'I'm sure you'll get the chance to ask.'

'I just wish he'd warned me. We arrived at this suburban mansion of sorts when I was expecting a poky flat. Anyway, how's things down there? I spoke to Caroline briefly this morning to let her know we wouldn't be interviewing them today. She didn't give anything away other than she was busy buying tea leaves – I'm surrounded by odd people at the minute. Is Meg talking yet?'

'Not really. She's singing and going in and out of reality from what I can tell. I'm no psychiatrist, but I'd say she's manic.'

'Did you say she's singing? I lost you for a minute.'

'Yep. That's what I said. Caroline's taken her back next door to see if being in familiar surroundings helps. If not, she'll call the doctor again. It could be side effects from the sedation.'

'Or she's still in shock.'

'That too. I wanted to talk to you about something else.'

'Go ahead. I've just arrived at a park of some sort; I'll find a bench.'

Carlos relayed the morning's events, including finding the bike in the garage, along with someone hiding inside and running away, followed by him almost being knocked over by Harold's car.

'Wow! All before breakfast, Carlos. You are having a time of it.'

He laughed, 'Yours hardly sounds harmonious either.'

'Touché.'

'I wonder if forensics should check the garage,' he said finally.

'What are you thinking?' asked Fiona.

'Well, Caroline told me Matthew had the bike for his birthday and went everywhere on it – a present from his grandparents – and from the looks of it, the bike was involved in an accident.'

'You think Harold ran the boy over?'

'Maybe. I'm not jumping to conclusions, but that could have been what happened. There's a blind spot when you come into that drive. That's why I almost got run over by Caroline.'

'So, it could have been an accident. If so, why did Harold cover it up?'

'I'm not getting ahead of myself. First, we need to know if there was a road traffic accident around that time, then we need to investigate whether it was actually an accident or not. It might have nothing to do with the case. Caroline wasn't home often, so the boy could have been in an accident she didn't know about some time before that fateful weekend.'

'I can run a check for reported RTAs in the months prior to his disappearance. I'll do that in the morning. I'll call the boss and ask if he's willing to send forensics out on a Sunday, otherwise it'll be tomorrow. You'd better warn Caroline.'

Carlos's heart sank. 'I know. I didn't want to add to their pain. If I can get any sense out of Meg, I'll ask her if Matthew was involved in any accidents around that time. It's something a mother would remember.'

'Good idea. Do that before I ring Masters. There's no need to rattle his cage until we have more information. I'll still check on RTA reports in the morning. I've phoned

Aiden Winslow and arranged to meet him privately tomorrow morning. The grandparents are taking the kids into town to get some last-minute Christmas presents.'

Carlos remembered the text message. 'This might be nothing, but I happened to see a message from Aiden on Caroline's phone. It said not to tell them anything. I don't know who the "them" is he was referring to.'

'Mm. I'll keep that in mind. It could be something to do with not telling the kids or his parents about what's been happening.'

'Good thinking. Makes sense. What a Christmas they're having.'

'Not to mention your poor sister and her husband.'

'Sophie's taking it hard. She likes Meg, but Gary's in a state and stressed out with work, so it's not the easiest time for them. By nature, she'd want to help as much as she could, but Gary's sensitive. They've gone up to Yorkshire for an overnight to see his parents.'

'Poor Carlos. All alone in a strange village with bodies everywhere and two crazy women next door. Definitely no holiday for you.'

Carlos laughed. 'Not to mention the mysterious stranger in the garage and the colonel from the community centre.'

'It could be the vicar. It's always the vicar...'

They bantered for a while before Carlos brought the conversation to a close.

'I'd better go next door and see if Meg's up to talking.'

'And I'd better go back to my brother's – or rather, his girlfriend's – to try to find out what he's got himself mixed up in. Let me know later if I need to break up the boss's illicit liaison. I might just call him at home,' she cackled.

'Not if you want to keep your job! I'll text or call you later.'

Carlos put the phone in his jeans pocket, grabbed a quick coffee and left Lady sleeping on Sophie's rug in the lounge: a fluffy cream faux-fur effort that was looking decidedly muddy.

'Looks like you're going to cost me a new rug,' he said, stroking her head. She wagged her tail in her sleep and opened one eye. 'You stay there, girl. I'll be back soon.' Lady watched him leave, but didn't move, seemingly pleased to get some rest after the excitement of the past few days.

Caroline let him in and explained that Meg had slept most of the time since returning home, but was now awake and able to speak.

'Try not to mention last night,' Caroline suggested.

Meg lifted her head as Carlos came in, a weak smile greeting him.

'Hello Mrs... erm... Meg. Good to see you looking a little better.'

'We were just going to have tea. Would you like some?' asked Caroline.

'Tea would be lovely,' he replied.

'Do sit down,' suggested Meg. Carlos remembered Sophie telling him about Harold's chair, so he sat in the one Meg had used yesterday afternoon. Meg was on the settee with her feet on a footstool.

Once Caroline and her mother had performed the tea ritual, Carlos felt he could begin.

'Do you remember I said yesterday that I would need to ask you both some questions if I was to find out who might have killed Harold?'

Meg's eyes shot nervously around as if expecting her husband to turn up and find her doing some forbidden activity.

'It's all right, Mother. He's dead, remember.'

Meg relaxed, taking a sip of tea.

'Would you be able to tell me about the day your husband went missing, Meg?'

Meg seemed uncertain, but with a little nod of encouragement from Caroline, she began.

'They didn't believe me. I told them he was missing and they laughed.'

Caroline bristled, opening her mouth to speak, but Carlos shook his head.

'Was that the police?'

'I called them an hour after Harold didn't come home for his dinner. I knew something had happened. He's never late.'

'What happened before he went missing? Do you know where he was that day?' Carlos didn't want to get into a conversation about police incompetency until he heard Meg's recollections.

'It was a Thursday. Harold goes to the community centre on a Thursday. The historical society meet and there's always a talk. I enjoy history. I read his notes while he has his evening bath. He has a bath on Thursday evenings.'

Carlos noted she still spoke as if Harold was alive. 'Why didn't you go with him to the meeting? Was it men only?' He knew it wasn't from his visit to the community centre, but wanted to dig into the unusual relationship without seeming threatening.

Meg lowered her head. 'Harold doesn't like me going out, except when we go shopping together. We shop on a Monday. I sometimes go into the village on other days when we run out of things. That's when I phone Caroline.'

'Was there anything different about Harold on that day? Did he change his routine at all?'

'He usually comes straight home from the centre and I get dinner ready for five o'clock. That's when we eat.'

'And did he come home that afternoon before he went missing?'

Meg seemed unsure. She scratched her head, trying to remember.

'I don't think so.' She glanced at Caroline for support.

'I wasn't here, Mum, so I don't know. You told the police he didn't come home that day.'

'There you are, then. He didn't come home that day. As I told the police, he disappeared.'

Carlos suppressed his irritation at Caroline's intervention and moved on.

'Can you remember anything happening on the Thursday morning before your husband went to the community centre?'

'He went to the library at ten, the school at eleven and came home for lunch at twelve-thirty.'

'Is that what he usually did or what he actually did that day?' asked Carlos.

'He always does those things on a Thursday morning.'

Carlos couldn't be certain Meg's recollection aligned with the reality of the day in question or whether she was assuming Harold had kept to his usual routine.

'Why did he go to the school?'

'He's a school governor. I think he meets the head on Thursday mornings, but I'm not certain.'

'Did Harold have any close friends?'

Confusion crossed Meg's face and Carlos, aware that the window of opportunity might close soon, pressed.

'Meg?'

'I don't know his friends. We know a few people in the village, we've lived here for decades, but Harold keeps himself to himself. I don't go out much. The vicar's wife visits on a Wednesday afternoon while Harold plays bridge.'

'This is really helpful, Meg. Just one more question. Does your husband own a spade?'

Meg's head shot up, eyes pleading with Caroline to help.

'Is that what killed him?' Caroline asked.

'They believe he was hit with a spade, yes.' Carlos didn't take his eyes off Meg, and she in turn didn't take hers off Caroline.

'He would have had a spade. He's a keen gardener, as you probably noticed when you were round the back this morning. Mother, where does he keep the spade?'

Meg's bottom lip trembled. 'In the shed at the bottom of the garden. Why would someone hit him with his own spade?'

'My thoughts exactly, Mother. I think she's had enough, Carlos. Mother, why don't you go for a lie down and I'll try to answer any further questions?'

Meg dutifully got up and made her way upstairs.

'Will she be all right up there?'

'I don't think she remembers anything from last night. It's as if she's blanked it out. She asked about the police tape when I took her up to shower after we got home and I just told her that the police wanted to keep his bedroom sealed off. What's this about his spade?'

'The police wonder if he took his spade to the woods that afternoon. Apparently people go metal detecting, collect mushrooms and plant winter flowering plants. As your dad was a keen gardener, he may have had the spade with him.'

'And someone attacked him with it?'

'That's one theory.'

'Well it's easy to check. You can look in the shed. I expect the key will be on the rack in the kitchen. Everything's labelled.'

There are some pluses to being OCD, thought Carlos. 'Thanks. I'll take a look.'

'If the police think that, why haven't they asked my mother about this before now?'

'I expect they were going to before we found Matthew's remains.'

Tears threatened to spill from Caroline's eyes. She blinked rapidly. Carlos gave her space and headed up the garden path after retrieving a key marked "shed".

The lock was well-used and opened easily. Inside tools hung or were stored in labelled containers. Each tool was polished and oiled. A spade hung next to a garden fork, a hoe and a rake. The tools were spotless, well-maintained. There were no gaps on the labelled hooks.

It was not Harold's spade that had killed him.

Chapter 19

Carlos didn't get any further by questioning Caroline, who insisted she didn't know any more than he did. Once he informed her all was well in the shed, she became agitated and irritable. Deciding the stress was getting to her again, he returned next door.

He took Lady for a long walk in the woods and couldn't resist having another quick recce of the crime scene, but there was nothing else to be found. When he arrived back at Sophie's, he started cooking, changing Lady's dressing while the ragu simmered. The wound looked clean and he repacked it, as instructed by Gary, before feeding her.

'Good girl.'

The aroma of ragu permeated the kitchen as he sat down to eat at the table. The kitchen clock on the wall in front of him caught his attention as he cleared his plate. He leapt off the chair, ramming the remnants of the spaghetti in his mouth.

'I almost forgot, Lady. I have to go to church.'

Lady sat up, her saucer eyes pleading with him not to take her out again.

'You and Sophie have identical eyes, you know that? Speaking of which, notice how she neglected to say she wouldn't be around for the carol service when I mentioned it on Friday. It's all right, girl, you don't have to come for this one. No bodies in the church.'

He laughed out loud and was still chuckling when he turned the corner to the village church. He stopped laughing when he spotted the graveyard enveloping the ancient building. The bells rang out a clarion call, letting villagers know it was time to attend the evening service, and it seemed they all obeyed.

Well, it is a carol service. Perhaps attendance is better than usual.

The gloomy darkness of the surrounding graveyard was dispelled by lights shining through ornate stained glass windows. Carlos followed a crowd of people along the meandering path and entered the church through towering oak doors. It had traditional high ceilings, stone walls and rows of pews. The warmth of people smiling and chattering enthusiastically pricked his heart.

Rachel would love this.

He missed her. He'd only called her once to let her know he'd arrived safely – he was avoiding disturbing her sleep during the day, as she was on night shift. They'd texted the morning after he found the body and she'd sent him a sarcastic message about her not being the only one to investigate murder when on holiday – Rachel had become quite the cruise ship sleuth, seeming to get involved in an investigation every time she cruised, often egged on by their mutual friend, the irrepressible octogenarian Lady Marjorie Snellthorpe.

A deep voice from behind pulled Carlos away from his reverie.

'Didn't we meet on Friday at the community centre?' Carlos turned, recognising the neatly trimmed moustache and the curt tone, although the greeting was warm. Colonel Martin Webb shook his hand vigorously.

'We did. How are you?' *Stupid question*, thought Carlos.

'Can't complain. I hear you're investigating the death of Harold Sissons. Got what he deserved, if you ask me. Nasty fellow if ever I met one.'

'Now, now, Martin. We're in church.' The flirtatious woman named Clara was clinging to the colonel's arm. Carlos remembered her from his visit to the community centre and her comments about Harold being controlling. He couldn't avoid noticing the scarlet miniskirt that barely reached her thighs and a low-cut silk blouse leaving little to the imagination. She had a good figure for her age, the voluptuous breasts hitting Martin on the side almost deliberately. She giggled.

'Looking at you, I thought we were in a brothel,' Martin replied scornfully, disentangling her hand from his arm. Carlos didn't get to hear her response as Doreen Milnthorpe, the vicar's wife, tapped his elbow.

'Pleased to see you made it. We're packed tonight. Most people in the village come to the carol service. I don't see Gary or Sophie. Are they here?'

'They've driven up to Yorkshire to visit Gary's parents. They'll be back tomorrow. Sophie sends her apologies.'

'It's important to see family at Christmas time.' The vicar's wife sounded resentful. 'Ours can't make it this year, but they'll all be here for New Year. I think they had enough of their father's preaching growing up, if I'm honest.'

Carlos chuckled politely. 'How many children do you have?'

'Just the three. Barney Junior's our oldest. He and his wife are spending Christmas with the in-laws. They're expecting their first child. Priscilla's our youngest, she's recently got engaged, and Lorna's a journalist. Works in London. She's covering a story – so she says – but I think the nightlife is preferable to that of

Derbyshire. I miss them at this time of year, but we can rarely holiday over the Christmas season.'

'I understand. My girlfriend's father's a vicar.'

Doreen raised an eyebrow, but their conversation was interrupted by murmuring running through the assembled congregation. Carlos turned to see what had caused the stir and was surprised to spot Meg and Caroline making their way through an astonished crowd. Doreen left Carlos's side immediately, but Martin beat her in the race to greet them.

'Meg, how are you, my dear? What a pleasure to see you without that…'

A nudge from Doreen prevented him saying anything else. Meg smiled shyly as her eyes met his. They held each other's gaze for longer than the usual customary greeting.

Caroline took her mother's arm and barged past the gawping colonel while Doreen followed immediately behind, determined to add her welcome once Caroline stopped marching. The only person not happy to see Meg was Clara, who shot daggers at her back and pulled the colonel away from staring after her.

'You're making a fool of yourself,' she snarled.

Regaining control, Martin shrugged and found a seat on the end of a pew. Clara tried to force herself in, but in the end gave up and sat on the opposite row, glaring first at Martin, then at Meg's back. Carlos noticed the colonel whisper something to the woman next to him. The woman said something back, then stood and stormed out of the pew to another one on the opposite side of the church. It was the nurse, Josie, whom Carlos had also met on Friday.

Definitely some animosity between the two of them. He wasn't surprised. The colonel was the sort of man who would think nothing of offending people, from what he'd witnessed so far.

He wondered if, on other occasions, the brusque colonel was more attentive to the effusive Clara. If not, the woman needed to take the hint. He reflected on the greeting between Martin Webb and Meg.

Now that was interesting. He determined to chat with the colonel some more at the earliest opportunity.

Carlos tucked himself into a pew next to a young family. The man nodded to him, but said nothing as the organist stopped playing and the congregation hushed while the Reverend Barney Milnthorpe took to the lectern.

Carlos enjoyed himself. The service engaged the villagers, while a nativity play drew oohs and ahs from the assembled crowds and parents scrambled to take photos of their children. Carlos watched Meg and Caroline throughout the service, but they didn't budge. When he glanced over to Martin, he realised that the colonel's eyes were boring holes into the back of the head of one woman in particular – Meg Sissons.

Carlos's thoughts returned to Rachel and how much she would have enjoyed this. He shot his own little prayer silently into the air that she would be kept safe from danger.

Barney concluded the service with a short sermon and then rattled off some local announcements. After the service was over, parishioners were invited to stay for mulled wine and mince pies. A scrum headed towards a side door, where Carlos assumed they could get their refreshments.

Barney had been dressed in traditional church regalia, but when he reappeared a few minutes later, just the black shirt and white collar remained. He greeted many of the parishioners as he made his way towards Carlos, who was waiting for the scramble to die down.

'You'd better join the queue if you want to sample my best mulled wine. It goes down a treat at this time of year, and I'm afraid not all my congregation understand the word "moderation".' The friendly vicar's shoulders shook as he laughed. 'Look, that's Billy Slade. Only comes in once a year and always joins the queue three times, pretending he's not had a drink. Afterwards, he'll be off to the local.'

'Don't you mind?' asked Carlos.

'Not at all. One day he might even take the message into his heart. The angels in heaven rejoice over one sinner who repents, you know.'

Carlos looked from Billy Slade to the optimistic vicar and couldn't help but like this enthusiastic man.

'Perhaps I'd better join the queue then,' he replied.

'Looks like you have no need.' Barney grinned widely, showing off polished white teeth. Doreen appeared with a tray carrying two glasses of mulled wine and two mince pies.

'I thought I'd better get these to you before we run out. I guessed my husband would want to speak to you. He's got something to say.'

'Oh?' Carlos said as he helped himself to the heated wine. It was topped with cinnamon and cloves, and when he took a sip, he felt the warm liquid go straight down to his stomach and its effects straight to his head. 'That packs a punch,' he said to the vicar, who was waiting for his verdict.

'Winemaking's my hobby. I save my best for this service each year, and my wife does the rest.'

'Including making these fine mince pies?' Carlos tasted the succulent mincemeat and short crust pastry that melted in his mouth. 'It's delicious.'

'Thank you,' said Doreen. 'Barney, I'd better get back to help the others. Clara's being shirty with them. I don't know what's got into her.'

'Mm,' replied the vicar, casting his eyes towards Meg who was in conversation with Martin. 'I do. Clara Fisher's got a rival for the colonel's affections.'

Doreen followed his gaze. 'You can't think there's anything to those rumours? It's just village gossip. I'm sure Martin is offering his condolences. Now, I really must go.'

Carlos watched the exchange between Martin Webb and Meg

Sissons. Caroline was out of sight, so he assumed she was collecting mulled wine for her mother.

'What rumours?' he asked.

'Do you think it will have any bearing on your investigation? I don't like to gossip.'

'It might. Everything matters at this stage in proceedings.'

'In that case, I'll tell you what I know. It's rumoured that Martin had a thing for Meg when they were teenagers, but she was besotted with Harold, despite many feeling it was not a good match.'

'Do you know why?'

'Sorry, no. After so many years, it's difficult to differentiate between fact and fiction. Anyway, soon after Meg married – I'm told – the colonel also married – a local girl – and soon afterwards he joined the army.

Martin and Valerie travelled all over the world with his job. He retired when he was sixty, and he and Valerie returned to the village. I only got to know them then. They seemed happy to me, but you never know, do you?' Barney sighed. 'But Harold's reaction to the colonel's return caused a lot of friction. Valerie Webb died seven years later – cancer – that's when the rumours started.'

'And do you believe them?'

'You've heard the saying – there's no smoke without fire – but I would have said no until tonight.' Barney's eyes fixed on the couple again.

'It could be as your wife said, he's offering his condolences, particularly if they do go back a long way.'

'You're right. I almost hope there is something between them. Perhaps

Meg can find happiness in her old age. I feel so guilty. I have to ask, are the rumours true about young Matthew being found buried in the house?'

'I'm afraid so. Did you know the boy?'

'A little. He came to Sunday school a couple of times. He was the same age as my Lorna. They were in the same class at school, and she swore he wouldn't have run away, but there was nothing to suggest otherwise. I can't help feeling I should have done something. How could we not have known this stuff was going on under our noses?'

'You shouldn't feel guilty. People are brilliant at putting on a show of being the perfect couple or family. We all have something to hide – but for most of us, it doesn't involve murder or domestic abuse.'

'Is that what was going on?'

'Not physical abuse, from what I've gleaned, but yes – I would say that Meg was the victim of domestic abuse in every other way. Harold Sissons has caused that woman more harm than we may ever know. Like you, I hope for some form of recovery now the shackles are off.'

Carlos and Barney drank their wine, each lost in their own thoughts. The vicar blew out a huge breath.

'As for not feeling guilty, I'm afraid this one will be hard to get through. Doreen visited Meg every week, but Meg never said a word about abuse. They were an odd couple, for sure, but we didn't see it. I do regular training to spot signs of child abuse, but if Matthew was killed by his own father, it was well hidden.'

Carlos put his hand on the other man's shoulder.

'Don't punish yourself. No-one knew.'

'Except perhaps my Lorna.' The vicar's hand went to his head. 'I hope this doesn't hit the national headlines. She won't let it go if she finds out. The story is personal to her. I hope you find out who killed Harold Sissons soon.'

Barney stood up and headed towards the mêlée to chat to his parishioners.

'Me too,' muttered Carlos.

Chapter 20

Following the conversation with Carlos, Fiona mulled over what he'd told her. The mangled bike suggested an accident, but why hadn't anyone mentioned it when interviewed? Admittedly, she'd not managed to interview Caroline yet thanks to her boss sending her on this unnecessary trip.

She'd been grateful at first. The opportunity to catch up with her wayward brother was a bonus, but now she wished she'd never come. Her suspicion antenna was on high alert having seen the luxury Steve and his new girlfriend were living in. Why hadn't he mentioned it when she'd phoned him to arrange her stay? Because he knew she would quiz him on where the money was coming from.

Well he's going to be quizzed, like it or not, once I get that woman out of the way.

Fiona wished she'd disturbed Aiden Winslow today rather than putting it off until tomorrow. Making polite conversation with Jen after dinner was wearing thin. The Chateau Musar at over £30 a bottle hadn't escaped her notice either and worried her all the more. Jen was sticking to Steve like they were attached at the navel, not giving

Fiona any opportunity to talk to him in private.

So be it.

Fiona drew in a deep breath, causing the couple to exchange "here we go" glances.

'How did you two meet?' The innocent question was loaded and they knew it.

'Through my father's work,' answered Jen, a little too hastily. 'Steve was doing odd jobs for him.' Now Jen's tone became condescending. Steve shot her a warning look. The wine was affecting Jen, who had been slurping it back much more quickly than Fiona or her brother. Fiona leaned forward and picked up the second bottle from the table.

'Great wine. Here, let me pour you another.'

Jen held out her glass greedily. Steve covered his with his hand, glaring at Jen, trying to warn her, but she was too far gone.

The phone rang, but Jen made no effort to move.

'Are you going to get that?' Steve asked through gritted teeth.

Jen reached for the phone. 'Hi, Dad. Yeah. He's here. It's Dad,' she stated the obvious, handing the phone to Steve.

'Hey. Oh, right. Hang on. My sister's staying the night, can we talk about this in the morning?'

An angry response caused Steve to stiffen. He glanced at Fiona and Jen.

'Don't mind me,' Fiona said, smirking. 'You go ahead.'

Steve shrugged and headed into the hall, closing the door behind him. She couldn't hear what he was saying so turned her attention back to Jen.

'You said Steve was doing odd jobs for your father. What sort of jobs?'

'Contacts, you know?' The conspiratorial whisper caused Fiona's ears to prick up.

'You mean his criminal contacts?'

'You know about them then?'

Fiona's heart rate increased. 'He might have mentioned doing some work with people he met inside. Which friends in particular?'

'I don't know, but he's been useful to Dad, and now we're together, he works in the firm.'

'What is it your dad does?'

'He has a law firm.'

That certainly wasn't what Fiona had expected to hear. Perhaps her brother had gone legit after all. Steve's raised voice coming from the hallway suggested things might not be going as well as intended.

'What sort of law does your dad practise?'

'Criminal law. He's a defence attorney and famous in these parts.'

Fiona stared down at her hands. What work could Steve possibly do to help a defence attorney other than research? A knot in her stomach tightened as she remembered some of the contacts Steve had had in London. These people were dangerous.

'Are you a lawyer too?' *Bimbo more like,* Fiona thought.

Jen stared at her acrylic nails and cackled. 'No. I can't think of anything more boring. I do hospitality for him, though. Put on corporate dos for some of the big shots he represents.'

'You must meet some highflyers in your work, then?'

'No celebrities, I'm afraid. Most of Dad's clients are CEOs of major companies in Scotland. A few from England, but they're boring people most of the time. Dad's wary of some of them. He likes to keep them happy, you know?'

The sinking feeling at what her brother might be involved in wasn't going away. Steve reappeared, preventing her asking the next question.

'Why don't you go to bed, love?' he suggested to Jen as she closed her eyes.

'Your brother's so domineering,' Jen slurred before prising herself unsteadily from the settee. 'I like my men... dangerous.' She winked at

Steve before staggering from the room.

'I think I'll go up, too. We've got an early start in the morning. I've got to go over to Jen's father's. Looks like I'm going to be working over Christmas now.'

Fiona's mouth dropped open. 'You're meant to be going to Dad's,' she gasped.

'Not anymore. Something's come up.'

'You can't do that to him, Steve. He's been looking forward to this for months. I bet he doesn't even know about your new, erm… setup.'

'I'll make it up to him. Can you call him for me?'

'Oh no! You do your own dirty work. There's no way…' but she knew Steve wouldn't face up to the responsibility and she would have to do it.

'I have to work, Fiona. You of all people should understand that.'

'And just what sort of work are you involved in, Steve?'

Her brother's shoulders slumped before he shot her a steely gaze. 'Well-paid work, as it happens. Look around you, Fi. I'm living in a way I've always dreamed of. No more poverty for me.'

'And what does it cost to live like this?' she muttered. 'At what cost?' she repeated, returning her brother's glare.

'I knew you wouldn't understand. You can be so self-righteous sometimes, you know that? I'm earning a good living; why do you have to knock it? I've got a decent woman and a good job. You're the one who told me to find those two things when I last saw you.'

'That's just it, though, isn't it? You've got neither here. Jen told me what sort of work you're involved in.'

'She can't have. She doesn't know,' he yelled before realising what he'd said. His hand flew to his mouth. 'You always do that to me.' He slumped back down in a chair.

'I just don't want you to end up in prison again, Steve. Don't you see? It won't be Jen's father who takes the rap, it'll be you.'

'I'm not doing anything wrong, Fi.' He stood up, heading towards the door. 'Tell Dad I'm sorry. I'll make it up to him.'

Fiona's head spun as she heard her brother go upstairs. What had he got himself into this time? She poured herself a glass of the red.

'Someone might as well finish the bottle. Too expensive to waste.' She gave a wry smile and called Carlos.

'Hi, Fiona, how's it going up there?'

'Could be better,' she muttered.

'Steve?'

'Yeah. I don't know what he's into, Carlos, but it involves some big shot defence lawyer, his new bimbo girlfriend's daddy. I'm worried about him.'

'He's an adult, Fiona. He makes his own choices.'

'I know, but I'm torn apart when he makes the wrong ones. I've got this huge guilt feeling that I didn't do enough for him growing up. Mum died when he was nine. Dad's been in a wheelchair for donkey's years after an accident at work. I should have been there for him.'

She could hear Carlos's deep intake of breath. She never usually talked about her background for this reason. People didn't know how to react.

He spoke, breaking the silence. 'Fiona, I know you. You would have done everything you could for your headstrong brother. He has to take responsibility for his own actions. Are you worried he's breaking the law?'

'In my gut, I'm positive he is. But the question is, what do I do about it? A part of me wants to dig deeper, but another part wants to steer clear. I don't want to put myself in a position of having to rat on my own brother. Dad would never forgive me.'

'You'll make the right decision.' Carlos sighed again. 'He's family, and you can't be certain he's up to no good. Perhaps you should put the matter on hold and wait for him to reach out to you when he needs to.'

'I just hope he doesn't leave it too late.' She took a large gulp of wine. 'Anyway, that's not why I rang. How's our case? Any news on what caused the bike to be in tatters?'

'I didn't get round to asking Caroline or Meg about it. Things went a bit crazy, to be honest. Meg's acting strange – singing and humming one minute, quiet and fearful the next. She still believes Harold is alive at times, and as for her son – she's not said a word about Matthew. I suspect she's lived in a nightmare, barely allowed out of the house from the sounds of it.

'I went to church this evening to see if I could find out anything else from the locals about who might have wanted Sissons dead. I haven't found anyone who liked him yet. Even the friendly vicar is at a loss to say anything good about the man.'

'Did you speak to that colonel you mentioned? Sounds like he could be a person of interest.'

'Only briefly, but I did discover he held a torch for Meg in his younger days, and from what I witnessed tonight, he still does.'

'Tell me more.'

'Meg and Caroline made a surprise appearance at the carol service. Martin Webb was the first to greet them and spent ages after the service talking to Meg. The vicar tells me there was village gossip about him and Harold being at odds with each other for years. To be honest, Colonel Webb makes no secret of his dislike for Harold Sissons, so there could be no more to it than an old love rivalry. I can't help hoping something good happens to Meg soon. She deserves it.'

'You're going soft, Jacobi.' Fiona thought for a moment, then added, 'Anyone else of interest?'

'No-one obvious. There's a nurse who doesn't get on with the colonel, she might be worth talking to. We need to find out if there's more to the animosity between the two men. Enough to cause Webb to kill Sissons. I'd really like to wrap this case up before Christmas.'

'Me too. I'm gonna have to fit in a visit to Dad. Steve's let him down big time.'

'And I'd like to catch up with Rachel at some point. One other thing that could be something or nothing: Meg's recollection of events on the day Harold went missing is muddled. I don't know whether she's got things mixed up in her mind. She went to bed after I asked a few questions, couldn't cope. I did find his spade, though. Neatly polished and hanging in the shed alongside his other garden tools, so that's not the murder weapon.'

'Get me away from all these OCD freaks. Give me a messy room any day.'

Carlos laughed along with Fiona. 'You'll get that when you're home.'

'What do you want me to do about the bike?'

'Leave it for now. I'll ask Caroline tomorrow. When do you think you'll be back?'

'Tomorrow, I hope. Once I've finished this pointless exercise, I'll be on the first train. This could have been done over the phone. One thing's certain, if I do have to stay any longer, I'll find a B&B.'

'Are you sure? It's Christmas week.'

'Yes, I know, and now, thanks to my brother, I have to call my father and tell him his beloved son won't be home for Christmas like he promised. Goodnight, Carlos.'

Chapter 21

The insistent ringing of his phone woke Carlos out of an unsettled sleep. He checked the time, five-thirty.

'Hi, Sophie. Are you on your way back?'

'Yes. We're stuck in traffic on the M1, there's been an accident. Just to let you know we're running late, so Gary's going to drop me off in town to do some last-minute Christmas shopping.'

Carlos could hear vehicles and background noise, but the line kept breaking up.

'Gary's mum slipped on the ice last night, so we spent most of the evening in casualty, but all's well. Gary's stressed about finishing his project.'

'I bet he is, poor guy. And he's had all the trauma of the past few days.'

'I know. How's things down there? Is Meg okay?'

'She's up and down, not always with it. Hopefully I can get to the bottom of this case and she can move on. I went to the carol service last night, had an interesting chat with the vicar about Colonel Webb.'

'Sorry, Carlos, I missed most of that, the line is terrible.'

'Don't worry, we'll speak later.'

'I'll see you later, then. Bye.'
Sophie ended the call.

Carlos lay back on the bed, staring at the ceiling. What a break this was turning out to be. He went downstairs to make coffee and let Lady out before dialling Rachel.

'You must have read my mind. I thought about calling you, but it was too early.' Her cheerful but tired tone was wonderful to hear.

'I just wanted to hear your voice. I miss you.'

'Same here,' she answered.

'How's the night stint?'

'Full of drunks and brawls so far. There's been a spate of violent robberies around the town centre, but we caught the perps last night. Led to a dawn raid this morning on an Eastern European gang moving in on the city.'

'Dawn must arrive early in Leeds, it's still dark here.'

She yawned. 'You know what I mean. How's your investigation going?'

Carlos filled her in on where he'd got to so far. Talking to Rachel helped him organise his thoughts.

'I believe we're looking at two separate incidents. One where Harold Sissons killed his son, either through malice or by accident, and one where someone killed Harold.'

Rachel asked the question on his mind. 'You don't think they're connected?'

'Not unless someone else knew about the boy's death, and the only person I've found – but not met – is one of the vicar's daughters, who didn't believe Matthew Sissons

– that's the son – ran away from home. Meg and Caroline had no idea about the grisly secret, as far as I can tell.'

'What about the mysterious person in the garage you mentioned?'

'Could have been an opportunist thief looking to nick something, but the bike thing bothers me.'

'Do you think Harold could have run his own son over?'

'It's a possibility.'

'If it was an accident, he would have called an ambulance, surely?'

'Most normal people would, but Harold Sissons is turning out to be a complex and devious individual. Caroline – their daughter – says he never wanted the boy in the first place. He was misogynistic enough to believe Meg should have complied with his wishes – he wanted her to have an abortion, so in his twisted head, he may well have believed Matthew had no right to live...'

'Go on...' Rachel encouraged.

'Say it was an accident. He could have convinced himself it was for the best. Now it seems Harold Sissons got what he deserved – karma.'

'Who do you suspect might have killed him if you exclude immediate family? Colonel Webb must be high on your list.'

'Yep. He is, but I hope it's not him. He's a curt but likeable chap, and I'm hoping he can bring Meg some happiness out of all this.'

'You're going soft.'

'That's what Fiona says.'

'Who's Fiona? Should I be jealous?'

'Blimey, Rachel, I forgot to mention it. Fiona Cook's down here working for CID. Her DCI is an old nemesis from my army days. I never thought I'd see him again.' A cloud weighed heavily on Carlos's head at the mention of Masters. 'Look, you need to get some sleep. I'll fill you in when we meet. I'll try to get up there on Christmas Eve or between Christmas and New Year and take you out for dinner before shift.'

'You're on.' She yawned again. 'Give Fiona my love and give Lady a big hug and plenty of treats from me. Take care, darling.'

Speaking to Rachel brightened his morning. Now he could focus on clearing up this investigation. He was going to have to ask Meg and Caroline some tough questions if the old lady could take it. But first, it was time to take Lady for a run.

***

Running always cleared Carlos's head, but the morning was flying by. He'd been delayed on his way back by every villager seeming to want to say hello, many remembering him from church the previous evening. He asked a few questions about Harold and Meg, but other than reiterating how unpopular Harold had been, none of the people he spoke with knew him well.

He spotted the nurse, Josie, about to get into her car and hailed her. 'Good morning. I wonder if I could ask a few questions about Harold and Meg Sissons, if you have the time.'

Her green eyes narrowed as she assessed him. 'What's your interest? I don't speak to the press.'

'I'm a private investigator. Carlos, Carlos Jacobi,' he handed her his card. 'I'm staying with my sister and brother-in-law next door to Meg. They've hired me to find out who might be responsible for Harold's death.'

Carlos could have sworn the nurse was there when he'd been at the community centre on Friday. Why was she pretending not to know him?

'Josie Reynolds.' She held out her hand. Carlos shook it. 'I heard about the tragic finding of young Matthew; so sad. We all believed he'd gone missing.'

'You knew him then?'

'Everybody knows who everyone is in this village, but that doesn't mean we know each other. I remember him going missing. He's... was the same age as my youngest.'

'Did you know Harold?'

'Other than passing the time of day, I barely knew either of the Sissons'. They keep... kept themselves to themselves.'

'I was wondering if you could tell me a little about Colonel Martin Webb?'

Josie flicked back her long ponytail of black hair. A glimmer of annoyance crossed her face.

'I'm in a rush. I need to get to work.'

'Thank you for your time.' The car door slammed and Josie Reynolds was gone.

As soon as he and Lady got home, Carlos showered, dressed and prepared breakfast. He changed

Lady's dressing, pleased the wound was healing nicely.

'Good girl,' he said as he applied a new dressing to stop her licking it. 'I need to go next door. You stay here, okay?'

Lady flopped down on the old blanket Sophie had provided by way of a make-do bed. Her eyes didn't leave him until he closed the door to the lounge. His phone rang while he was wrestling with a jumper.

'Hi, Fiona. Are you on your way home?'

'I'm on my way to the train station, but Carlos, I'm calling to warn you. Caroline Winslow has played us.'

'What do you mean?'

'She was in Derbyshire on the day Harold Sissons went missing. She met with colleagues at The Derby

Conference Centre. It was an all-day meeting, but she left early, telling a friend she was going to see her mother in Peaks Hollow!'

'What time did she leave the conference?' Carlos drew in a deep breath, annoyed with Caroline for lying to him.

'Two-thirty. Plenty of time to get up there and kill Harold.'

'Have you spoken to her husband?'

'Yeah, he's covering for her. Says she left early to drive home because she hates night driving. He's lying, I can tell, but he's sticking to the story.'

'That explains the text message,' Carlos sighed. 'Unless he's telling the truth.'

'I'll request traffic cam footage, which I'm sure will place her on one of the motorways after the death of

Harold Sissons. I've got to call Masters now and tell him, but wanted to give you the heads up first.'

'Thanks, Fiona. Do me a favour, can you delay calling him for fifteen minutes? I'm heading next door to speak to Caroline.'

'Okay. You've got fifteen minutes.'

Two minutes later, Caroline answered the door. She was dressed in a lime-green suit, but with wet hair dripping on to a towel around her neck.

'Can you come back? I'm just out the shower.'

'No. It can't wait. We need to talk, Caroline. You lied to me.'

Her eyes widened and she stood aside to allow him entry.

'Mother's gone into the village for some shopping.'

'Why didn't you tell me you were in Derbyshire on the day your father went missing?'

'Why do you think?' she snapped.

'Did you kill him, Caroline?'

'You'd better come through to the kitchen,' she said, gathering herself. Once there, she poured them both tea. 'In answer to your question – no, I did not kill Harold Sissons. The first I heard of him going missing was when your sister told Aiden. How do you think I felt when I found out he went missing about the time I was in the area?' Tears filled her eyes, then bitterness. 'Trust that man to die and leave me in the firing line. The irony of it all. He's probably down there, laughing right now.' Caroline pointed to the ground.

'Your husband told DS Cook you left the conference early and arrived home sooner than expected.'

'I told him not to do that if you found out. I hoped you'd have found the killer by now and it would be immaterial.' She sat down, knee jerking frantically. 'Mother doesn't know, but yes, I was just a few miles away on that day.'

'We haven't got much time, Caroline. DCI Masters will be here soon to take you in for questioning, so you need to tell me everything that happened a week last Thursday.'

Caroline's knee continued to jerk up and down as she clasped the mug of tea with both hands.

'As you now know, I was at a conference. Over lunch, I got it into my head I was going to come home and demand to see my mother. I'd invited her to come for Christmas; I was worried about her. Each time we spoke, she sounded more distant and fearful. He was suffocating the little bit of life she had left in her.'

Caroline blinked tears away before continuing.

'I drove like a woman possessed all the way up here and stopped at a small café in Bakewell to gather my thoughts and plan how to tackle him.'

'So what happened?'

'Years of coercive control happened,' she stared down at her trembling hands. 'I chickened out. I knew I wouldn't win, and recognised it would only make things worse for Mum. He'd make her life hell, but she couldn't see through it, or didn't want to – I don't know which. The thought of her being too afraid to ring me again once he found out about the phone calls brought me to my senses. I resigned myself to the reality that any contact was better than no contact.

'I sat in a car park for almost an hour, crying, if you must know. Bawling my eyes out for my kids, who've never met their grandmother, then for myself for losing my mother, and for... Matthew's disappearance all those years ago.'

Carlos took her trembling hands in his and held them. She didn't pull away.

'You should have told me.'

Her eyes met his. 'I wanted to. I know how it looks, but I wanted to. What I didn't want to do was to admit how that man still had a hold over me after all these years.'

Carlos swallowed back a lump in his throat. 'You were trying to protect your mum. Caroline, you were a child. Men like your... like Harold Sissons thrive on creating a cycle of fear.'

'Thank you.'

'For what?'

'For understanding. But you see, it's more important than ever you find out who killed him now I have no alibi.'

'What time were you in that coffee shop?'

'I left around five. As I said, I sat in the car. I remember the six o'clock news was on the radio when I started the journey home. I did go back into the coffee shop to wash my face before the drive, but I doubt anyone would remember me. The place was empty.'

The sound of car doors outside told Carlos he'd run out of time. Moments later, Masters was in the living room, pompously reading Caroline her rights. With the towel still wrapped around her wet hair, he placed her in handcuffs.

'Is that necessary?' snapped Carlos, fists clenched at his sides. Masters's smug face closed in, facing-off. Carlos could smell the aftershave on the odious man's chin and coffee on his breath.

'As I said before, Jacobi, leave it to the professionals; we know what we're doing. Amateur hour is over.'

Carlos thrust his fists in his trouser pockets to stop himself lashing out and wiping the grin off the prat's face.

'You're making a mistake, Masters.'

Ignoring Carlos, Masters turned to the officers with him.

'Take her away, lads.'

Caroline's fear-filled eyes implored Carlos. 'Please find out who did it and look after my mother.'

He nodded, following the entourage to the door. Three police cars were parked outside. Masters had clearly wanted to make a statement, but thankfully it went largely unnoticed, as the lane appeared quiet.

Carlos punched the wall in frustration as he watched the convoy drive away.

Chapter 22

Carlos walked into the village, crossing the green. A large stone-bricked building stood a few minutes from the church. The sign displayed from a post at the head of a stone wall read simply: 'Vicarage'.

Carlos headed up a tree-lined pathway to the front of the impressive house. His attention was drawn to the right by sounds of an axe being wielded. He followed the path around one side of the house

384

where he found the affable vicar chopping wood.

'Good morning, Vicar. I'm impressed.'

Barney looked up from what he was doing, his bulging cheeks reddened by the cold and exertion.

'Good morning, Carlos, although I think it's afternoon,' he corrected. 'Do call me Barney, as you're staying around for a while. Everybody else does, except for those who call me all sorts of things, but not usually to my face.' He laughed before throwing a few pieces of wood on to a woodpile. 'We have a wood burner, and the exercise is good for me, so the local quack tells me. I have to keep my blood pressure down, she says. Now, what can I do for you?' Barney placed his axe in a small storage space to the side of the woodpile.

'I'm sorry to disturb you. It was Doreen I was looking for. Is she around?'

Barney glanced at his watch. 'She'll be preparing lunch. Why don't you join us? Follow me.'

Carlos didn't get the opportunity to reply, so followed the vicar around to the back of the vicarage where a stable door, top half-opened, led to the kitchen. They paused at the entrance. The smell of homemade soup reminded him he was hungry and the baking aroma made him doubly aware.

'Doreen!' Barney called, but he didn't open the bottom half of the door. Doreen turned from stirring soup and spied Carlos. She lowered the heat on the gas hob, and then beamed.

'Hello again, Carlos. Is your sister back from Yorkshire?'

'Not yet. They were stuck in traffic this morning when I spoke to Sophie. She's gone into Derby for some last-minute bits and pieces.'

'Did they have a good time?'

'Not particularly; they spent the evening in casualty. Gary's mother had a fall, but no fractures. She's back home safe and sound.'

Doreen's eyes widened. 'Heavens! It has been rather icy over the past few weeks. All the rain freezing up. I heard it was bad in their part of the world. That reminds me, Barney, snow's forecast for Christmas Day. I hope you've chopped enough wood.'

'Don't you worry, I've massacred the stumps Mason sent over.'

'Well that's something. Mason's a local farmer – I bake for him and he gives us wood from an overgrown patch he's clearing.' Doreen addressed this at Carlos. 'I hope Barney's invited you to stay for lunch. I assume you're here as part of your investigation.'

'Your husband has been kind enough to invite me for lunch, and yes, partly that's what I'm here about. I was wondering if you could keep an eye on Meg. I'm sorry to say that Caroline's been taken to Chesterfield police station for questioning. I'm not sure when she'll be released. I'd rather people didn't know about this, but Meg will need someone.'

Barney's jaw dropped open, mirroring that of his wife.

'When? Why? Surely they can't think she had anything to do with her father's death. She hasn't been here in years.' Barney's hand went to his head. His bulging sea-blue eyes threatened to burst through his face. 'Oh no! Don't tell me she murdered her brother?'

'Barney, you're running away with yourself again. Please go and get washed up and Carlos can tell us what's happened over lunch. It's ready now anyway.'

'Good idea,' Barney declared. 'I do get carried away sometimes.'

Looking at Carlos, Doreen added, 'Whatever's going on, no-one will hear anything from us.'

'Come with me, Carlos. Servants' entrance for me until I'm cleaned up. I'll point you to the dining room.' Barney started off towards the opposite side of the house to the wood pile.

Lunch comprised a tasty winter vegetable soup seasoned with cinnamon and mint.

'This is superb. You're a wonderful cook, Doreen,' Carlos said.

Doreen kept the conversation to trivia, discussing people they had spoken to the night before, allowing Carlos to enjoy his lunch. And – he suspected – her husband's blood pressure to settle. Only when he put his soup spoon down did the couple stop talking and turn towards him expectantly.

'All I can tell you is that Caroline swears she had nothing to do with Harold's death. It's that the police are questioning her about. They don't doubt Harold killed his son, as far as I'm aware. Caroline was away with her mother when the boy disappeared.'

'I remember that now. Lorna reminded me when we spoke on the phone this morning,' said Barney. 'You were at the shops, Doreen.'

'You didn't tell her about Matthew, did you?' she asked.

'I didn't need to. That's what she was asking about. The local press have reported the story and are running with a piece in tonight's paper. Lorna gets alerts about stories to do with Peaks Hollow; she says it could make national headlines, but I doubt it. Harold's death only made the inside of local pages, not the nationals. I was keeping the sad news until after Christmas, but now she's coming up after work tonight.'

Doreen sighed. 'Ordinarily, I'd be pleased to see our daughter, but she'll be more determined than ever to unveil the truth concerning Matthew's disappearance. She took it very hard at the time.'

'From the sounds of it, it's clear what happened. That should keep her out of mischief. Unless she decides to go after the Harold Sissons story. She can be dogged when she wants to.'

'In that case, it might be better if I ask someone else to watch over Meg,' said Carlos.

'I feel it would,' said Doreen. 'Although, I'll pop in this afternoon and see how she is. So why have they taken Caroline? I don't understand.'

Carlos trusted Doreen and Barney, but he didn't want to compromise them with their daughter, knowing what journalists could be like.

'I'm not really sure. It seems she attended a conference in Derby on the day her father disappeared and they want to clarify the time between when she left the event and when she arrived home. Her husband told the sergeant that she came home early as she doesn't like driving at night. I'm sure it will all be cleared up, but just in case of red tape, someone needs to keep an eye on Meg. I would have asked Sophie, but I don't know when she'll be home, and Gary's found the whole experience distressing.'

'I wonder if Isabel Daniels from the village shop would look in on her if it drags out?' said Doreen. 'We don't need to tell her why. She's the only one who sees Meg regularly, apart from me.'

'Doesn't she have family visiting for Christmas?' enquired Barney.

'No. They've gone on a cruise, but her Frank won't sail. Not since he was parachuted into the sea on an RAF exercise.'

Barney chuckled. 'He tells everyone that story. It was in the 1960s. They were out on manoeuvres when his co-pilot accidentally pressed the eject button and Frank Daniels ended up in the North Sea.'

Carlos joined their laughter. The thought of an RAF pilot being accidentally ejected from his plane appealed to an ex-army soldier like himself. The RAF were renowned for having it easy while soldiers traipsed through mud and much worse. He remembered when he and two men lived on a tin of spam for a week while RAF colleagues stayed in first-class hotels.

'Did the plane crash?' he asked.

'No. The co-pilot realised his mistake and landed it, reporting the whereabouts of Frank so the air-sea rescue could bring him in. Frank has hated the sea ever since.'

'Anyway, I'll ask Isabel to look in on Meg until Caroline returns,' suggested Doreen.

'What does Meg know about Caroline?' asked Barney.

'Nothing yet. She was shopping when Caroline was taken in. I'm going to see her now; I'll just tell her Caroline's gone to the station to answer some questions.'

'Which is the truth,' said Barney. He handed Carlos a card with the address and telephone number of the vicarage. 'In case you need it.'

'Thank you,' Carlos said, handing one of his own PI cards to the vicar. 'In case you need it.' Smiling wryly, Carlos went to shake hands with the couple, but was pulled into a warm embrace by both.

'I'll pop round and see Isabel this afternoon, and then go to see Meg myself,' said Doreen. 'Whether this will keep our tenacious daughter away from you, Carlos, is another matter.'

Carlos hoped he didn't meet Lorna Milnthorpe if she was an interfering journalist.

'I do hope we're not going to be inundated with press.' Doreen added.

That's all I need, on both counts, thought Carlos.

***

Carlos went straight to the Sissons's house from the vicarage. A flushed Meg opened the door a couple of inches.

'Is it okay for me to come in?' he asked.

'I've got a visitor and have just made tea. We don't like to be disturbed when we're having tea. Would you come back later?'

Back to the OCD Meg, he mused. Despite being curious to know who the visitor was, he decided against asking.

'Right. I'll call later if I need to. It's just, erm... I need to let you know that Caroline is—'

'At the police station. Yes, Aiden called. He's driving down later today.'

Why didn't I think of that? Carlos berated himself.

'That will be nice for you. I'll call round later if I need to speak to you again. You know where I am if you need me.'

Meg closed the door, leaving him staring at the dark blue wood. He pulled the vicar's card out of his pocket and punched in the number on his way back next door. Barney answered.

'Hello, Reverend Milnthorpe here.'

'Barney, it's Carlos. Emergency over, Meg's son-in-law's driving down from Edinburgh,' he explained. 'Mrs Daniels won't be needed. I'm not sure Doreen needs to visit either. Meg has a visitor just now and wouldn't let me disturb her.'

'Well I must say, my prayers aren't usually answered this quickly. I must be doing something right,' laughed the vicar. 'Thanks for letting us know, Carlos.'

Carlos ended the call. Lady hurled herself at his legs as soon as he entered the cottage, almost sending him flying out again.

'Lady! We've talked about this. You have to control yourself.' Sometimes the doggie issues that made her unsuitable as a police dog resurfaced when he least expected. He bent down to stroke her. She placed her front paws on his shoulders. 'That's not allowed either. What is it with you? You find a body or two and think you can do what you like.'

He tickled her tummy as she withdrew her paws and rolled on to her back. Disentangling himself from his overexcited dog, he closed the front door, spying a note in the letterbox. He withdrew a folded piece of expensive stationery addressed to Carlos Jacobi. It had no other name on.

Opening it out, he read:

'IF YOU WANT TO KNOW WHAT HAPPENED TO THE BOY, ASK THE COLONEL.'

Carlos stared at the piece of paper and made his way into the kitchen. He prepared coffee in the machine.

'Mm. What does this mean, Lady?'

Lady barked and waited at the back door.

'Sorry, girl,' he said, opening the door to let her out. He poured coffee and checked the note front to back.

Nothing else to be seen. Manila paper, thicker than the usual 80gsm most people used in printers these days. It could have been typed in an office and he was certain the top part, which would have revealed a company or personal address, had been cut off.

Carlos smoothed his hair from his forehead as Lady came back inside, leaving a trail of muddy pawprints after her. The frost from the morning had well and truly melted. He shut the back door, towelling her paws before opening cupboards beneath the sink to find floor wipes. After cleaning up his dog's mess, he picked up the mug of hot coffee.

'And there I was thinking at least the Matthew part of the puzzle was solved. Who could have sent such a note and why?'

His phone vibrated on the kitchen bar where he'd put it when he came in.

'Hello, Fiona. When do you get in?'

'Not until six-thirty. Why don't you meet me at my place? There's a pub down the road where we can eat, or an Indian not too far away. Apologies to your sister and brother-in-law, but I don't want to be seen at yours. Masters believes he's got his killer.'

'She didn't do it.' Carlos recounted what Caroline had told him this morning.

'And you believe her?'

'It would be hard to make up, although she's had time to work on a story if I'm being cynical. We need to track down the café she stopped at and see if anyone remembers seeing her. You'll be able to ask her if she remembers anything about it tomorrow. That's if you're still holding her.'

'Oh, Masters will hold her all right, even if he believes her story – however unlikely that might be – if only for hiring you. I can't really talk right now. I'm in the loo, balancing this damn phone while trying to take a pee. The carriage is packed with Christmas travellers. Blast...'

He heard her scrambling around and the familiar loud chugging of a train in motion.

'Fiona? Are you okay?'

'Yeah, dropped the phone. I'd better go before I lose the damn thing down the hole. I'll text you my address when I get back to my seat. That's if I still have a seat and the bloke with his three kids from hell haven't ensconced themselves in it by now.'

Carlos laughed at both visions Fiona had conjured up in his head. Busy train toilets were not where you wanted to be when trying to have a serious conversation.

'I don't suppose the man will stay there for too long if he has.'

'Seven-thirty okay with you?'

'I'll be there. See you later.'

A minute or so after he rang off, his phone pinged with the address, causing him to put his head in his hands again.

'Drat, Lady. I forgot she lived on a boat!'

Chapter 23

The suspension of Carlos's Capri struggled with the contours and bumps along the dark country roads. He'd virtually rebuilt the car from the inside out, installing original parts which were not always easy to find. The outer body remained in good condition following a respray and he garaged it overnight whenever he could. It wasn't unusual for him to travel hundreds of miles to collect a part for his precious vehicle.

Now he was bouncing up and down on the leather seats, thankful he'd had new seatbelts fitted. His satnav had given up the ghost, but he remembered there should be a turnoff to the left before a junction.

Arriving at the staggered junction, he realised he'd come too far. There was no room to turn, so he crossed the junction, turning on the opposite side of the road and pointing his car back the way he'd just come. He drove more slowly this time and spotted the turnoff after about a mile.

Turning right, he entered an even bumpier unmaintained track and drove cautiously along with lights on full beam. Finally, he arrived at a pothole filled car park, found a space and switched off the engine, letting out a sigh of relief.

Lady leapt from the car as soon as he opened the door and released her seatbelt.

'Not the best journey, was it, girl? Good job I strapped you in.'

The car park was dark and heavy rain pelted down, soaking his waxed jacket on the outside. He jumped back inside the car, leaving Lady to explore while he texted Fiona.

'We're here.'

'Be right out,' came the reply.

Five minutes later, Fiona tapped on the window of the passenger door and climbed in. Carlos called Lady, who jumped in the back seat where a dry blanket awaited her.

'You look wet,' Fiona chuckled.

'Great place you chose to live. I'm lucky my shock absorbers haven't snapped.' He kissed her on the cheek. 'Your mac comes in handy round here, I bet.'

'Do you like the hat? It's a new addition and almost matches.' Fiona removed the darker blue bucket hat dripping water over her mac.

'You're starting to look like a country bumpkin,' he laughed.

'That's my type of gal. Come on, I'm starving. I guess it's pub grub as you've brought Lady.'

'Yep. That will do nicely, if we ever make it out of here.'

'I would have shown you the boat, but it's muddy down there along the towpath, and I knew you'd be wearing your designer shoes!'

He laughed again, staring down at his soaked tan Barbour boots.

'These babies can take a bit of rain. I've got my jeans on, if that helps?'

'Also designer, no doubt.'

Carlos conceded. 'You win. Where to?'

'Back out to the main road, down to the next junction, across the staggered junction. There's a pub two miles along on the right.'

'I met the staggered junction and realised I'd gone too far. This place really is off the beaten track. Couldn't you find a mooring in a better place?'

'Not on my wages. I spent everything buying the boat and paid the first year's mooring in advance. That way, I have somewhere to live, no matter what happens. Most of my salary goes on care fees for my dad, so I hope you realise you're paying tonight.' She laughed heartily.

'It will be my pleasure.' He pushed the gearstick into first and began the tentative drive back to normal roads. 'I didn't realise you supported your dad, Fiona. Isn't there any income support?'

'He gets the maximum, but he's in debt up to his ears after bailing Steve out over the years. Steve would be dead in some backstreet alley if he hadn't. I want to keep Dad at home for as long as possible so pay top-up fees for a live-in carer.'

'I'm sorry.'

'Don't be. Dad's happy, and the best news is, I don't have to try to race down to Surrey in between working over Christmas. I was surprised; he almost sounded relieved when I told him Steve was working over Christmas and couldn't make it. Seems he's joined some disabled club where the old codgers go on outings and play chess competitions. He's always been good at chess – he sounded happier than I've heard him in years. Seems the men in the family have both had personality transplants!' She laughed. 'Anyway, the community centre that formed the club is providing them with a slap-up Christmas dinner, courtesy of the local church. It's a great weight off my mind, and don't worry, I exaggerate slightly – my wages do leave me with some spending money.'

They arrived at the pub car park and Carlos found the last space.

'Busy,' he remarked.

'A lot of people from the marina come here, and there's a village up the road within walking distance.'

Fiona nodded to a few people on the way in and they hustled their way towards the bar.

'Keep your eye out for a table,' she yelled to be heard above the din. 'Lager, is it?'

He gave her a thumbs-up sign and did as instructed while Fiona ordered drinks. He turned to pay, but she pushed his hand away.

'You can get dinner and put it on expenses,' she laughed.

'You're on. Look, there's a small table coming up in that corner.' Carlos grabbed his pint and headed in the direction of the table, managing to sit down before anyone else noticed it was vacant. Fiona joined him.

'Nice one,' she smirked. 'I've asked Ted to bring us his specials, unless you want to wait all night to eat.'

'No. The specials will be fine. I hope.'

'You can go get Lady now we're settled.'

Carlos took a swig of lager and headed outside to the car. Fiona had told him well-behaved dogs were allowed in, but he was pleased she'd suggested they find a seat first. It had been challenging enough to find space in the packed bar without an excited dog in tow.

He opened the car door and Lady sat up expectantly. Her drenched fur and look of sheer delight pulled at his heart.

'Come on, girl. Best behaviour, though. None of your quirky issues tonight. All right?'

Lady barked as if she understood and allowed him to put her on the lead before they headed back inside the pub. A few minutes later, they were at the table. Lady licked Fiona's hand and lay down partly under the table with her head on Carlos's foot.

'She'll dry off now. I can feel the heat from that fire over there.' Carlos was delighted to see an open fire roaring a few feet away. Fiona laughed.

'Why do you think it's so popular with boat people? Free heating.'

A heavyweight barman came over to their table bringing two large plates stacked with chilli con carné and rice.

'Here you go, Ms Cook. Enjoy your meal.' The man winked.

'I take it that's Ted?'

'Yeah. We get on. I helped him out after a burglary and he's been good to me ever since. You'll get a ten per cent discount, by the way.'

'Thanks. I approve of the special. Right up my street.'

'I knew it would be when I saw what it was.' Fiona glanced around as she forked chilli con carne into her mouth. 'Right. What have you got?'

'I'll tell you what I've gathered so far. Caroline was in the vicinity, but a few miles away in Bakewell. She says she stopped at a café to pluck up the courage to challenge her father, but once the adrenaline surge had dropped from her initial bravado, she couldn't face it. She was worried she'd make things worse for Meg.'

'A well-founded worry, I should imagine,' said Fiona, polishing off some more chilli.

'I agree. She said she cried her eyes out in the car park for a long time before returning to the café to wash, and then drove back to Edinburgh.'

'So why did her husband lie?'

'He was trying to protect her. He knew how it would look. She'd told him not to, but it seems he did anyway. He's on his way down to Peaks Hollow, probably at Meg's by now.'

'He mentioned he might when I spoke to him this morning. I'm still annoyed at being sent up there. It could have all been done by telephone, and by working with the local police. Now, Masters has got their backs up.'

'Something else I need to share.' Carlos removed the secretive note from his inside jacket pocket and placed it on the table.

'What does it mean?'

'I have no clue. No idea who sent it or anything. I haven't had time to follow it up. I need to find out where the colonel lives, but don't want to involve Barney and Doreen Milnthorpe any further. Their daughter, who's a journalist with an interest in Matthew's case, is also on her way up here.'

'Goodness! That picturesque village is going to be marauded by overenthusiastic busybodies by the sounds of it. What's her interest? Apart from being a nosy journalist, that is.'

'She went to school with Matthew and never believed he'd run away.

No-one would listen to her and she's had a thing about it ever since, according to her father. They believe his death is an open-and-shut case, so I feel it's better they don't know anything about this note.'

'Quite right. Hopefully she's a fashion reporter or something.'

'Rather a sexist remark, Fiona.'

'You won't get me being part of the PC brigade. But no, I'm all for women doing great things. I just don't want her to get in our way, that's all.'

'I'm going to have to disappoint you. I did an internet search and it turns out she's an investigative journalist.'

'Why doesn't that surprise me? I think I blame it on the mirror I smashed last week!' Fiona finished her meal and moved her plate to a nearby table which had been vacated. The pub was quieter; it was getting late. 'Isn't it wonderful! We have two dead bodies; a government highflyer from Scotland in custody; a mysterious note; a private eye; a short-sighted DCI; and now, a flaming investigative journalist.' Fiona blew air through her lips.

'You forgot to mention the savvy sergeant and the dog!' Carlos laughed.

She grinned. 'There is that. I need another pint.'

'Lager?'

'Yeah, this pub's draught lager's the best there is.'

Carlos returned with two more drinks and watched as Fiona attended to messages on her phone.

'So what about you? What have you got?'

'Not a lot other than what you know. I ran a check on RTAs about the time of the boy's disappearance. It came back negative. If he was involved in an accident, it was either minor or not reported. Mind you, recordkeeping wasn't the best back then, so the report could have been misfiled or something like that.'

'What about Caroline?'

'The boss's keeping her in overnight. He's convinced she's Harold Sissons's killer. I'm joining him at the nick to question her tomorrow.'

'So there's no-one else under suspicion regarding Harold's murder?'

'Nope. And to be honest, Carlos, she could be spinning you a web of lies. She's already lied about her whereabouts on the day her father disappeared. Her husband then gives a false statement to cover for her. I don't need to remind you she also has motive. Motive and opportunity without a concrete alibi.'

'I know all that,' Carlos snapped. 'But why kill him now, after all these years? I could understand it if we'd found out about her brother beforehand, but we hadn't.'

Fiona's head shot up from her glass. 'We hadn't, but what if she had?'

'Go on...'

'What if the person who sent you the note does know something about Matthew's disappearance and they also contacted Caroline Winslow? You've seen her, Carlos. She's a bomb waiting to explode. All that knee jerking and snapping. Say she knew Harold had killed her brother. As you pointed out, that would have caused something to snap.'

Carlos leaned back in his chair, putting his pint glass down.

'Okay, so let's work on that theory. We also know the colonel was previously in love with Meg, and from what I witnessed in church last night, he still is. What if he's in on it? Colluded with Caroline to put an end to Harold? He may have even done the deed for her.'

'It's plausible, but I can't see a reputable citizen getting involved just for the sake of it. Okay, so he might be in love with Meg, but why now? Do you really think that's what happened?'

'No. But we need to explore the possibility. The only thing is, I'd rather Masters not know about the note for now.'

'Is this about losing face, Carlos? Because if it is, I'm having nothing to do with it. If we have our killer, I'd rather wrap this case up and enjoy my Christmas than protect your machismo.'

Carlos laughed loudly. 'Protect my what? You know me better than that. No, it's not that. When I was with Caroline this morning, she seemed lost. Her whole life has been overshadowed by this control freak who happened to be her father. Three lives have been ruined by that man. I can't see Meg recovering if her daughter's sent to prison on top of everything else.'

'I told you you're going soft. Caroline's trauma also provides more reason for her to kill him.

Break free and start a new life. You're forgetting she has a loving husband and three children of her own, so she's not that lost.'

'But these scars run deep. What I saw this morning was a child. A young girl who had tried and failed to protect her mother from a monster. I think if she'd killed him, she would almost be proud to say she had done it, but instead, she had to confess to failing yet again. That sort of failure isn't easy to acknowledge, either. She's tormented by grief over her brother and loss of her own childhood and forced alienation from her mother.

'Please, Fiona, let me talk to the colonel before you mention the note. I'll happily say I kept it from you. You go ahead and push Caroline with your theory and see if she cracks. We have to be certain. I don't want Caroline Winslow locked up for a crime she didn't commit just because Masters holds a grudge against me.'

'So what did happen between you and Masters?'

'That's a conversation for another day.'

Fiona finished the dregs of her drink. 'You've got until tomorrow evening. I want my Christmas to be peaceful. And you're also forgetting something, Carlos.'

'What?'

'She's a mother. A mother would not want to leave her children and go to prison without a fight, so she's not going to confess easily. It's admirable to be in touch with your feminine side, mate, but don't let it cloud your judgement. Now, I'm going to the ladies for a wash before returning to the boat.'

Carlos sat waiting, deep in thought.

Chapter 24

The next morning Carlos noticed the BMW that had been parked on Meg's driveway when he left for his run was no longer there.

'Good. Let's take another peek in the garage, Lady.' He paused at the front door, but assumed if Aiden had left already, Meg must be up. He rapped the brass knocker.

Moments later, he heard the chain being removed from its place and bolts moving. Meg stood, small and frail in the doorway. Her faraway eyes stared, seeing but not comprehending, he thought.

'Sorry it's early, Meg. Can I come in?'

'I was about to make tea. Would you like some?'

'That's very kind of you. Yes, please. Is it all right if my dog comes in too?'

A moment's hesitation. 'Harold didn't like dogs, but he's no longer here, so yes, do bring him in.'

'She's a girl. Lady's her name.'

'As in *Lady and the Tramp*?'

'I think so. I inherited her from a friend who emigrated to Australia.'

'I would love to visit Australia.' Meg headed straight to the kitchen, where she made tea using mugs and tea bags. Understanding there had been much fuss over compulsory tea leaves previously, Carlos was surprised, but didn't comment.

'I'm told it's a beautiful country. I haven't been there myself yet, but hope to get out to visit him once he and his family are settled.'

'Visit who?' Meg's face blanked.

'A friend in Australia... never mind. How are you, Meg? Did your son-in-law stay over?'

'Yes, I'm quite well. My son-in-law's out at the moment. I can tell him you were looking for him.'

Carlos took the mug Meg handed to him and followed her through to the lounge. Cautious not to upset her, he sipped the heavily sugared tea and stopped himself gagging.

Lady went to examine one of a number of empty cartons that were spread about the room.

'Lady's fascinated by your boxes. Are you having a clear out?'

'Aiden's helping me to get rid of Harold's things. No point hanging on to them, is there? He won't be coming back.' Meg hummed a tune under her breath.

'It makes sense, but are you sure now's the time?'

'Time for what?'

Carlos was losing the battle for her attention, and her clear out was none of his business anyway, so he got to the point.

'I wonder if you would you mind if I took a look in your garage, Meg?'

'That's Harold's garage. No-one's allowed in there,' she said gravely.

'I don't think he can object now, Meg,' he spoke softly.

'No, I suppose not. Martin was in there yesterday. He's been so kind.

He might not like anyone else being in there.'

'Martin Webb? The colonel? Is that who was here when I popped round yesterday?'

'I suppose it must have been. I didn't see you yesterday.'

He didn't see any point in reminding her of his visit yesterday. What the heck was Martin Webb doing in Harold's garage? 'I'm sure people won't mind, Meg. It's your garage now. It might help me with the investigation into Harold's death. Is it locked?' Carlos drained the mug of tea, fighting nausea. He was in a hurry to get into the garage now he knew someone else had been in there.

'The keys are labelled on the hook in the kitchen.'

'Oh yes. Caroline showed me. Can I help myself?'

'Yes, I don't need anything from out there.'

Carlos unlocked the garage and pulled open the wooden door. Harold's car was parked where Caroline had left it. He marched around the car to find an empty space where the bike had been.

'Damn!'

He returned the key, said goodbye to Meg and went next door. Sophie was just up.

'Hello, big brother. Did you manage down here all alone?'

Carlos had left a note for Sophie the night before, explaining he was out with Fiona. By the time he got back, she and Gary were in bed.

'Just about. How was your time up north?'

'Freda's okay, but we had a fright. Gary was in a right state. He's gone into work.'

'We're ships in the night!'

'I popped in on Meg when I got back yesterday. She told me her son-in-law was coming down. I thought he couldn't make it because of the children? She was very muddled.'

'I've just been in there myself. She's got that vacant look again – in between humming tunes, that is.'

'I've noticed that too. I think Caroline should call a doctor.'

'Meg didn't tell you?'

'Tell me what?'

'Caroline's been taken in for questioning. It turns out she was in Derbyshire on the day Harold went missing.'

Sophie's mouth opened wide. Her hand went to her face. 'She didn't...?'

'I'm pretty sure she didn't, but it doesn't look good. She has motive, opportunity and no alibi. As you can imagine, DCI Masters made a right show of taking her into custody yesterday.'

Sophie recovered enough to pour them coffees. 'Poor Meg. Can things get any worse for her?'

'In a way, it's a relief she isn't taking it all in, but that presents its own problems. I can't get any real sense out of her. Did you know Colonel Webb had a thing for her?'

'Really? I haven't been here long enough to hear village gossip. I suppose you heard it at the carol service.'

'Saw him with my own eyes. There was real affection between the two of them.'

Sophie seemed puzzled. 'Did you take Meg to the carol service?'

'No. She turned up with Caroline, and the colonel made a beeline for her. Look, I want to go and speak to him. Do you know where he lives.'

'He's not involved, is he?'

'I don't know. I hope not, for Meg's sake.'

'If you go past Meg's heading out of the village, he lives in a short row of cottages on the same side of the road. His is the first one, big red door.'

'Thanks, sis. What are you doing today?'

'I've got to go to a farm to collect the turkey and a few other bits. In fact, I'd better get a move on. I'll pop in and see Meg when I get back. I'm afraid we're out again tonight. It's Gary's work's do.'

'I thought he might accompany me to find another body.'

'Not funny, Carlos. Not funny at all.'

He leaned down to kiss his sister while she put on her coat.

'Speak later.'

'Ciao.'

Funny how the colonel lives in the direction the other morning's intruder ran in. This is starting to make sense.

He took a quick shower, fed and watered Lady, and went to leave.

'You can sit this one out.'

Lady whined and rushed to the door, blocking his path.

'No, Lady. Stay. No tantrums.'

Lady continued blocking the entrance. She had previously shown some of the behavioural issues his friend had told him about, but this was a first. Perhaps finding the two bodies had brought out some deep-seated insecurities in her.

He knelt down. 'Look, girl, I don't know if this man likes dogs, okay? If he does, I'll come back for you. Now stay!'

She moved over and sat, but she was agitated. He could hear whining, followed by howling as he walked along Sophie's drive.

What's got into her? Good job the cottage is detached. He wondered whether to go back for her, but if he gave in to poor behaviour he might regret it later. He fastened his coat to shut out the ice-cold headwind forcing its way round him and thrust his hands in his pockets.

Carlos arrived at the cottage Sophie had described. It was in keeping with the vicarage, possibly built from the same local stone. A white Mondeo was parked in the drive. A sign was pinned to the front door.

'VISITORS ROUND THE BACK.'

He obeyed, walking around a narrow path to a stable door painted in the same red as the one at the front. Unlike the one at the vicarage, top and bottom were bolted together.

He knocked. The door inched open, but there was no reply. He knocked again, causing the door to open a little further. He peered around the door and shouted.

'Hello?'

He was debating whether to go inside when he heard rustling coming from behind. Before he got a chance to see who it was, he felt a sharp pain in the back of his head. His knees buckled and he fell to the ground, reaching out, trying to grab the door handle. A second blow rained down, this time to the side of his head. Through blurred vision, he saw a lanky figure bearing down on him, holding what looked like a spade.

'Sorry, Lady, I should have listened,' he murmured as everything went black.

Chapter 25

Fiona tossed and turned all night,
disturbing thoughts invading her
subconscious. Her sleep wasn't
helped by rain hammering down on
the fragile roof of the boat. The leak
in the corner of the sitting room – if
she could call it that – was worse
than ever. Drips seeped through,
falling into the pan she had placed
on the floor before she went to bed.
Too tired to inspect the damage

properly, she got up and placed a larger saucepan on the floor.

The rain now sounded heavier than ever. One of the things she liked about living on the boat was the pattering of rain on the roof, but not right now. Worried about what might be happening, she dragged herself up and left the bedroom. She knew her way around in the dark, but flicked the light switch before going over to the corner and checking. Rainwater had spilled over the sides of the pan and soaked the floor beneath it.

'Blimey! I knew I should have fixed that leak.' She found a large bath towel amongst a pile of washing and mopped up the mess, placing the sodden towel in a plastic bag that served as a laundry basket. 'I suppose that means a trip to the launderette,' she groaned.

Replacing the emptied pan, she was grateful she could no longer hear the rain. It was almost morning anyway.

'*Things always seem better in the morning.*' She heard her mum's voice whisper in her head, just like when she used to reassure her after Fiona arrived home from school, crying from being teased about her scruffy clothes. But then her mum went and died, and things weren't better in the morning. Not for many years.

Just as they were getting back on their feet as a family, her dad had an accident at work that left him in a wheelchair. Fiona ended up being a teenage carer while her dad's compensation money was eaten away by her younger brother who couldn't keep away from trouble. Fiona's bubbly personality was inherited from her mother, because life hadn't given it to her.

Boiling the kettle, she made a mug of tea and flopped down on the only piece of the sofa visible. She knew her life was spiralling out of control again. Money was tighter than she'd let on to Carlos, and her happy-go-lucky attitude was under constant threat as the realities of her situation closed in. She was a messy person both by nature and through stubbornness, but the chaos she lived in now was worse than it had ever been.

Sipping her tea, Fiona contemplated her situation. It wasn't so bad. At least she had a place of her own. She loved her boat and all it needed was a little bit of a clean. She'd sort it on her next day off. Soon, if she could solve this case.

Why was Carlos so convinced Caroline was innocent? Caroline Winslow was just the type to have snapped in a moment of madness. She could have belted the man she obviously hated over the head with a spade. The bad blood between Fiona's boss and Carlos was spilling over just like that damn rainwater, clouding both their judgements.

'Male testosterone. Thank goodness I'm a woman, I don't know how they get through the week. The pair of them need their heads banging together. Why do men have to take things so personally and why are they so damn competitive?' She raised her voice to the empty room. 'And what the heck have you got yourself into, little brother?' She and Carlos hadn't mentioned Steve last night, but he was on her mind constantly. At least her dad was happy. That phone call could have been a lot worse.

After showering, Fiona called her boss.

'Hello, Cook. You're back, then?'

'Yes, sir. I understand you'd like me with you to interview Mrs Winslow this morning?'

'We've been granted an extension for questioning, so no rush. Let's leave it till this afternoon, let her stew a bit. I'll meet you back at the nick. Perhaps you could question the mother again. See if she knew her daughter was in the area the day her husband went missing. They could be in it together.'

Fiona punched the air, imagining it was her boss's nose. Another pointless exercise. Meg Sissons was not on this planet. How could she get any sense out of the old lady? She'd be lucky if Meg remembered what she'd had for breakfast.

'Yes, sir. Anything specific you'd like me to ask?'

'Find out if she knew about her daughter being in the area. Didn't you hear me, Cook?' he snapped.

'Bad line. I must have missed it.'

'And Fiona?'

'Yeah?'

'Keep Jacobi out of it. Understand?'

'I'll do my best, sir. Where will you be if I need you?'

'I've got to drop the family off at the in-laws in Matlock. We're staying there for Christmas. I hate this time of year. Nonstop rounds of people I'd rather not see. What are you doing over Christmas, Cook?'

'Erm... having dinner with friends,' she lied.

'Good, so let's get this case wrapped up neatly. See you later, then.'

Well, that's a first. Terry Masters has never asked anything about me before. Too busy flirting with the next woman on his list. Everyone knew about his extramarital affairs apart from his wife and kids.

'Poor woman.'

Fiona eventually stepped on to the towpath as sunlight appeared through the clouds. The only sign of the previous night's rain was the raised water level in the canal and deep puddles in the potholes along the path. Carlos was right. There were plenty of better mooring spots. This marina barely survived the last recession, but the boat owners were loyal and she liked being out of the way. At least she was unlikely to come across anyone from the day job here.

Her faithful black Mini, also in need of replacing, was where she'd parked it the night before. Squeezing in, she turned the key in the ignition, holding her breath. Relief flooded through her as the engine burst into life at the first attempt.

Forty minutes later, she pulled up outside Carlos's sister's. Ignoring Masters's request to leave him out of it, she wanted to see if Carlos would like to accompany her, knowing her boss wouldn't be heading this way this morning.

Carlos's pride and joy was parked in the driveway. The Volkswagen Golf she assumed belonged to his sister wasn't there. Distraught barking was coming from inside and the door banged as Lady threw herself at the wood from the other side.

Fiona's pulse quickened. Worried something might have happened to Carlos, she rang the bell and peered through the letterbox. The barking got louder. One of those draught excluders that must be a postman or postwoman's nightmare blocked her vision. She pressed the bristles down and felt hot dog breath panting in her face.

The dog stopped barking temporarily as Fiona tried to reassure her through the letterbox. *Perhaps he's gone out and left her desperate for the toilet*, she reasoned. No sound came from inside. Fiona dialled Carlos's number and tried to listen through the letterbox. Still no sound. The phone went to voicemail.

'Hi, Carlos Jacobi here. Sorry I'm not available at present. Leave a message and I'll get back to you as soon as I'm free.'

'Carlos, it's Fiona. Your dog's going demented in your sister's house. I'm going next door to speak to Meg. Join me if you're free.'

As Fiona turned back down the drive, Lady's barking got louder and more desperate. Carlos had told her Lady had issues. Perhaps she suffered from separation anxiety?

Fiona shook her head and headed next door.

Chapter 26

Fiona knocked on Meg's door. Aiden Winslow answered.

'We meet again, Sergeant,' he said with a wry smile that didn't reach his eyes. 'Where's my wife? Why are you holding her?' he growled.

'She's assisting us with our enquiries. She lied to us, Mr Winslow. And so did you. You're lucky I'm not arresting you for obstruction.' The lack of sleep was catching up on her. She was in no mood for games. 'Is your mother-in-law home? I need to speak to her.'

'She's gone to the shops in the village. You can wait if you like. Look, I'm sorry about just now. I'm worried about Caroline. I believe her when she says she didn't see Harold on that day, and my wife's not capable of killing anyone.'

'We are all capable, Mr Winslow, given the right circumstances. If you want to help your wife, you need to be honest with yourself. Maybe she snapped. Her dad sounds like he'd cause anyone to snap.'

'I repeat, Caroline would not kill anyone. She's highly strung, but she's rational. She wouldn't risk being away from the children. They are her life. My wife has issues from her past, Sergeant, but we are working through them. She's a good mother and a wonderful wife.'

'So why lie in the first place? If she's innocent as you say she is, why didn't she tell us about being in the area?'

'Once she realised Harold Sissons had disappeared on the same day she was in Derbyshire, she was going to tell the police if you asked. But when Meg told her about how incompetent you lot had been when she reported Harold missing, Caroline knew what would happen. And now she's being held against her will to assist with your enquiries. It's just as she feared.'

'My wife tells me everything, Sergeant. We share things; she would have told me if she'd done this. Personally, I wouldn't blame her, but she didn't do it. She came home on the Thursday night upset, feeling she'd failed her mother again and hating herself for it. I'm telling you, Caroline did not do this.'

'That's what Carlos believes. Have you spoken to him?'

'Is he the private detective?'

Fiona nodded.

'No, I haven't met him yet. Meg told me he came round earlier – wanted to look in the garage, then left in a hurry, she said.'

'Do you know what he was looking at in the garage?'

'I'm sorry, I don't know, Meg didn't go with him. Harold didn't allow her in the garage,' he mocked. 'I only met that man once, but now I know what he did to Matthew, I wish I'd come down here years ago and rescued Caroline's mother myself.'

Something nagged in the back of Fiona's mind. 'I went next door before I came here. Carlos's dog's there, but he's not. I think she might be desperate for the loo. Does Meg have a key?'

'I'm not sure. There's a key rack by the front door and one in the kitchen, but that one's for outside stuff.' Aiden stepped back into the hallway and examined the keys. 'What's the surname?'

'Cole...'

'Here you are.' He handed her a front door key labelled, "Coles".

'Thanks. I'll bring it back later.' She took the key and headed next door. Lady's barking sounded hoarse, but she was just as determined, throwing herself at the door. Fiona inserted the key and opened it.

'It's all right, Lady...'

Lady was past her in an instant, running down the drive. The crazed dog paused for a moment outside, putting her nose to the ground, and then raced off out of the village.

'Now what have I done? The stupid dog's going to get run over.' Fiona pulled the door to and managed to arrive at the road in time to see Lady disappearing in the distance. Wishing she was fitter, she gave chase.

'This is ridiculous, Fiona Cook,' she complained to herself.

Lady turned a bend and was out of sight. Fiona was bent over double, gasping for breath, when she heard barking in the distance. Breaking into a slow trot, she followed the sound. She arrived at a row of cottages and heard the barking coming from the back of the first one.

'What's she got now? A cat?'

Fiona paused again and walked slowly, sucking in breaths as she went. The ice-cold air caused her to go into a coughing fit. She could hear Lady hurling herself at a door.

'What is it with this dog?'

She turned into the back garden just in time to see a man leaning over the top half of a stable-type door, pointing a rifle at Lady. Fiona stopped coughing and found her voice.

'Sir, stop! It's all right. I'm police.' She took the ID out of her pocket and showed it to the tall, wiry elderly gentleman.

'That dog's mad. Needs putting down. Is it yours?'

'No. She belongs to a friend. Lady, sit!' Lady stopped barking and sat next to Fiona, letting out a low, persistent growl. Something wasn't right, but Fiona wasn't about to tackle a man wielding a rifle.

'I hope you have a licence for that, sir?'

'Of course I have a flaming licence,' he snarled. 'People should have licences for dangerous dogs, if you ask me.' He was still pointing the rifle at Lady's head.

'Perhaps you could put the weapon down, sir.'

'What? Oh yes. Of course, Sergeant... Cook, was it?'

'Yes. And you are?'

'Webb. Colonel Martin Webb.'

Fiona's warning siren blared inside her head. 'Has a private detective been to see you this morning, Colonel? This is his dog.'

Fiona leaned down to stroke Lady's head. She calmed as if understanding.

'Carlos Jacobi, you mean? I've met him a couple of times. He was at the church service on Sunday evening. Nice fellow. He's investigating the death of Harold Sissons, isn't he? No, he's not been here. Why would he?'

'He was speaking to everyone who was at the community centre on the day Mr Sissons disappeared. He told me you were on his list, that's all.' Fiona watched for a reaction, but the colonel didn't blink.

'No. He hasn't been here. Now I'd thank you to take that wretched dog off my property before it gets hurt.'

'I don't suppose you have a piece of rope?' Fiona gave her best smile.

The colonel hesitated, before saying, 'Hang on a minute.' He returned with a piece of rope. Fiona tied it around Lady's collar. The dog was growling and reluctant to leave, but Fiona pulled her away.

'Thank you for your time, Colonel Webb. And your understanding. Come on, Lady.'

We'll be back later with a warrant, but she kept that thought to herself.

Fiona started the walk back up the path to the road and felt the rope slip from her hand as Lady pulled away. She gave chase again and caught sight of the rear end of the dog as Lady leapt over the lower half of the stable door into the house. Fiona leaned over undoing the bolt and followed cautiously.

There was no sign of Webb. Fiona walked across the kitchen, treading quietly. Lady was no longer barking, but she could hear her snuffling.

Fiona found Lady sniffing the bottom of a door that looked like it led to a cellar. She held her fingers to her lips.

'Shush.'

She looked around, but Webb was nowhere to be seen. *Perhaps he's gone to lock the gun away*. Fiona opened the cellar door and Lady hurtled down the steps. She felt the wall and found a light switch. Seconds later, she felt the rifle pressing between her shoulder blades.

'Down you go, Sergeant Cook,' Webb commanded.

***

Carlos grimaced in pain as he tried to open his eyes. Every move of his head brought a thumping into his temples. It reminded him of his one and only experience of captivity in Greece when he'd been rescued by a friend. He felt a cold stone floor beneath him and shifted uncomfortably.

When he finally opened his eyes, he couldn't see a thing. The room was pitch-black. From the musty smell, he gathered he was in an outbuilding or cellar. His hands were tied behind his back. He tried to sit up, but discovered his feet were also tied. The pounding in his head caused him to moan out loud. What had happened?

Webb! It's been Webb all along.

He called out, 'Hello! Is anyone there? Hey?' At least he wasn't gagged, which meant either he was out of the way somewhere no-one could hear or the room was soundproof. Neither scenario boded well.

Why the heck didn't I listen to Lady? She tried to warn me. That dog has a sixth sense, Barry had told him. He'd laughed at the time, but he should have brought her with him.

No. Webb would have killed her.

'Think,' he told himself. His eyes became accustomed to the dark and he could make out shapes. Nothing else.

He felt the phone buzzing in his cargo pants pocket. Struggling to move, he forced himself on to his back, lifting his legs in the air. The phone dropped out, but landed face down. Shuffling into a sitting position, he flipped the phone over between his feet. Fiona's name was on the screen. He couldn't hit the answer button and sat helplessly as he watched it go to voicemail; he'd been meaning to set voice activation on the phone for ages, but hadn't got around to it.

If I get out of this mess, that's the first thing I'm going to do.

He fought the urge to pass out as he lay in the darkness, the minutes ticking by. Carlos eventually heard movement coming from somewhere above him. A door opened and light burst through, revealing a set of stone steps. Lady came bounding down and hurled herself towards him, licking him all over.

'Good girl. You found me. Is Fiona with you?'

A light came on. 'Oh yes, she's here,' came the curt reply.

Carlos's heart sank as he saw Fiona heading down the steps with a rifle pointed at her back. Lady growled.

'Tell that dog to stay put or I'll put a bullet through it right now. These rifles can create an awful mess.'

'Lady, sit!' Carlos commanded. She obeyed, but continued to give a low growl. Fiona looked at Carlos apologetically before speaking.

'Colonel, you won't get away with this. My DCI knows exactly where I am. If I don't call in, you'll find yourself surrounded.'

'You don't fool me, Sergeant. I saw the state you were in, chasing the mutt. No-one knows where you are.

Why didn't you leave when you had the chance?'

Carlos wondered the same thing. She should have called for reinforcements. Now they were all going to be killed.

'What happened?' he asked.

'Lady wouldn't leave, slipped the rope. Before I knew it, she'd hurdled the door and was in the house.'

'So what happens now, Martin? You kill us. Then what? Where does it end?'

'You're trespassers. I'm an old man living alone. I have to defend myself.'

Carlos spotted Fiona giving him a three-two-one signal with her fingers. He waited. As soon as she got down to one, she back kicked the colonel in the shins and Carlos gave the command.

'Disarm, Lady.'

The dog leapt at the colonel who'd stumbled following the kick and grabbed his rifle arm, causing him to cry out in pain. The rifle went off and a bullet skimmed past Carlos's arm, but Fiona had the colonel in an arm grip and swiftly applied handcuffs. Lady's growl warned the colonel not to move again. Fiona kicked the rifle away and headed towards Carlos.

'Nice one,' he said.

'You too,' she replied as she untied the rope from his hands and feet. 'By the way, you look a mess.' She grinned. He felt the side of his face where congealed blood had formed a lump over a large gash.

'I've got a thumping headache. The colonel's spade hit me with some force.'

***

Forty minutes later, Carlos was sitting on a wall in the bright winter sunshine, asking for sunglasses and thankful to be alive. The paramedics who'd responded to Fiona's call for assistance had insisted he go to hospital for a concussion test. After arguing for a while, he'd finally agreed to go in.

Just as he was getting into the ambulance, Masters arrived. Ignoring Carlos, he joined Fiona who was briefing the uniformed officers before they took Martin Webb away. Carlos's thoughts turned to Meg. If there was any love left between the two of them, she had been failed by the male species again.

Poor woman.

Chapter 27

Carlos was examined by a consultant in the accident and emergency department. The doctor wanted to keep him in overnight, but he refused. They'd compromised at a CT scan. Now he sat waiting for the results.

Dr Singh reappeared just as Carlos was running out of patience. The smile on the doctor's face made him feel better.

'You can go home, Mr Jacobi. Please call immediately if you start to feel drowsy, and I insist you are not alone for the next twenty-four hours.'

'Don't worry about him, Doc; I'll stick to him like glue.' Fiona had not long turned up after Carlos had called her to give him a lift home. 'Either he stays with me or I stay with him. I won't let him out of my sight.'

The doctor nodded. 'Any problems, he's to come straight back by ambulance.' He shook Carlos's hand and moved on to the next patient.

'You don't have to...'

'Oh yes I do. I've spoken to Sophie, who was going to cancel her night out, but I said you were fine, just a slight bump, so unless you want me to call her and tell her otherwise...?'

'Okay. You win.'

'Besides, I wouldn't want to be the one to tell Rachel you died of a brain haemorrhage because you were too stubborn to stay in hospital.'

He laughed. 'I've got the message, Fiona. Anyway, I'm too tired to argue. Wouldn't it be better going to yours in case Masters turns up in the village?'

'I was looking forward to a warm bed. We've got work to do, anyway, so that should keep you awake for a while.'

'What work?'

'Colonel Webb is not co-operating. He says we trespassed on his property and he thought we were burglars and hit out, not knowing who we were.'

'That's ridiculous. He must know his story won't stand the test.'

'I'm sure he does. In the meantime, he's determined to make a fool of us and give us the runaround for as long as he can. I've given my statement. I need to take one from you.'

'Shouldn't someone else be taking it from me?'

'Masters says he'll sign it. He doesn't want to talk to you, and I'm happy to go along with him on this occasion, because I know exactly what happened. We were almost shot. Come on, I've got Lady in my car.'

Lady ran in circles around Carlos's legs when Fiona opened the car door. He bent down and hugged her close.

'Thanks, girl. You saved my life.'

'Both our lives,' said Fiona, causing Lady's helicopter tail to bash against the side of the car.

'In you go,' he commanded and the dog jumped in the back, while Carlos managed to squeeze his tall frame into Fiona's Mini after pushing the seat back as far as it would go. He put his hand to the dressing on his forehead and ripped it off.

Fiona's jaw dropped open. 'What the...'

'It was irritating me. They've stitched the wound, it'll be fine. If I'd been in Afghanistan, I'd have stitched it myself.'

'You're going to be a difficult patient, aren't you?'

'What makes you think that?' He grinned. 'I need to go home and pack a bag, and ring Sophie. Are you sure this is necessary?'

'Do you want me to take you back in there?' She nodded towards the hospital.

'No. Let's go.' He shook his head in disbelief at Martin Webb's arrogance. He'd liked the man, but not anymore.

After phoning Sophie and reassuring her he'd sustained a minor injury and the hospital had made a fuss over nothing, he told her to go ahead and enjoy her evening. Fiona drove in silence for most of the journey, lost in her own thoughts.

'So it looks like Caroline's innocent after all,' said Carlos eventually.

'Don't gloat, Jacobi. It's not becoming.'

'Has Masters let her go?'

'Nope, not yet. He'd already been granted an extension to hold her for questioning for 96 hours, so he's in no rush. He'll have to soon enough, though. The spade's gone for DNA sampling; hopefully they'll find traces of Harold Sissons's skull as well as yours.' She laughed.

'That's not even funny. What put you on to Webb in the first place? Weren't you supposed to be interviewing Caroline?'

'I was, but the boss wanted to leave her to stew. He told me to interview Meg Sissons again. Ironic, isn't it? You owe your life to Terry Masters.'

'Don't push it, Fiona.'

'When I got to Meg's, she was out. Aiden Winslow told me you'd rushed off after going into Harold's garage. I had a bad feeling about it all, especially with Lady howling like a pack of wolves. Was it to do with the bike?'

Carlos rubbed his head. 'I'd forgotten about that. Yep, the bike was missing from the garage, and once I found out where Webb lived, I put the pieces together and figured he'd been the one in the garage the other day. He knows about the bike, so there must be a connection between him and the death of Matthew. It must be what the note alluded to. I bet we'll find the bike at his house.'

'Sorry to disappoint, but I searched the place right through with Masters after you left. Forensics did their bit, too. No bike anywhere.'

'He's dumped it somewhere, then. He would know this countryside well enough to do that.'

'So what's your theory?'

'He must have been involved in Matthew's death. Maybe a hit and run that neither he nor Sissons reported.'

'But why? He and Sissons hated each other by all accounts, so why would they collude? Perhaps Webb buried the boy and Sissons was innocent all along.'

Carlos's head ached. 'I can't see how. The stench of a rotting body would have permeated that room for weeks, if not months. Matthew's body must have been kept elsewhere, and later moved. Where? For some reason, if the colonel was involved, they kept this secret between them. Harold kept that bike for a reason.'

'Blackmail, you mean?'

'Maybe. We might never know if you can't get a confession out of

Martin Webb. He's not going to capitulate easily if his story so far is anything to go by.'

'So I guess he had enough of being blackmailed and killed Harold Sissons, hoping to move in on Meg as soon as he could.'

'That's about the sum of it, as far as I can see,' said Carlos. 'All we need now is proof.'

It was dark by the time Fiona pulled into Sophie's driveway. Meg's lights were on, but the curtains were closed. As soon as Carlos slammed the car door, Aiden Winslow appeared behind him. Fiona got out, as did Lady, keen to stretch her legs.

'I hear you've arrested someone on suspicion of Harold's murder. Why hasn't my wife been released?'

Fiona replied, 'We have taken someone else in for questioning. I can't say any more at the moment. Be patient, Mr Winslow. If your wife is innocent, she'll be released.'

'You're our employee. You tell us what's going on,' Winslow snapped at Carlos.

'I'm employed by your mother-in-law and your wife. I will give one or both of them a full report as soon as I have anything to say, but for now, I've got a splitting headache,' Carlos snapped before softening. 'Rest easy. I don't think it will be long before your wife's home.' He gripped the other man's shoulder.

'Was it really Colonel Webb? Meg says he's been so kind since Harold died.'

'We can't say anything more now, Mr Winslow,' intervened Fiona. 'Mr Jacobi needs to rest.'

'Of course. Sorry. It's just I don't know what to do. It's nearly Christmas. They won't let me see Caroline. Your smug DCI tells me she'll need a good lawyer.'

Both Carlos and Fiona straightened at this news. Carlos glanced at his friend.

'We'll be in touch as soon as we can,' she said. 'Give it until tomorrow. We won't hold her any longer than that, I'm sure.'

Carlos wasn't so certain. What was Masters up to now? Surely he couldn't still believe Caroline was involved.

'Aiden?' he called after the man as he left.

'Yes.'

'I wouldn't tell Meg about this for now.'

'I haven't and I won't. It was the colonel's neighbour who told me. I went to get some fresh air as the police were driving him away.'

'Goodnight.'

Carlos opened up Sophie's house and invited Fiona in. 'Look, Masters isn't going to turn up tonight. Why don't we stay here? You said you need a warm place for the night. You can borrow one of Sophie's nightdresses – you're about the same size. I'll text her, then she'll be able to enjoy her night out for Gary's sake.'

Fiona grinned. 'You'll get no argument from me. What's for dinner?'

***

Carlos's dreams were filled with flashbacks of Martin Webb standing over him with a spade interspersed with being under fire in Afghanistan. Masters laughed as he fell down next to his best friend, who was lying dead on a dusty road. Next, Webb fired a shot at Lady.

He woke in a pool of sweat, relieved it was just a dream. Memories of Afghanistan had haunted him continually since he'd crossed paths with Masters. He had gone two years without flashbacks; now he felt like he was back to square one. At least Lady was very much alive, sleeping at the foot of his bed.

'It was just a dream, man. Get it together,' he told himself. What was real was the splitting headache he woke with. He reached for paracetamol and swallowed two whole.

He could hear Fiona downstairs, so he got up gingerly and went for a shower, hoping the paracetamol would kick in soon. He felt the lump on the back of his head when he tried to wash his hair. *No wonder I've got a headache*. The front of his forehead was swollen and bruised around the stitches from the hospital.

He walked cautiously downstairs, stimulated by the smell of fresh coffee and followed by an excited dog.

'Hey. You're up, then. I managed to work out how to use this thing. This coffee's good.' Fiona beamed. 'You look dreadful.'

Carlos helped himself to coffee and opened the door to let Lady out into the garden.

'Thanks,' he said, joining her at the kitchen table. 'Any news?'

'Masters just phoned. He wants me to join him to question Caroline again, because we didn't get around to it yesterday. We're expecting results back on the spade this morning. As far as I know, Webb is still in denial. He'll cough today, I'm sure.'

'Yeah, I expect you're right. What I don't understand is why he covered for Harold if it was an accident. They weren't friends, so why would he do that?'

'Beats me. I can't get my head around these criminal types, especially why anyone would cover up an accident. I still think it was deliberate.'

'You mean by Harold or by Colonel Webb?'

'I don't know where Webb fits into it. Maybe he blackmailed Harold if he found out about it.'

'So he could have taken the bike to cover up the cause of death.'

Fiona slurped back some coffee before answering. 'Could have. Or someone else might have removed the bike. Caroline, for instance.'

Carlos huffed. 'Why have you got it in for her?'

'And why are you trying to protect her?'

'Touché. I don't believe Caroline had anything to do with the death of her brother. She was genuinely surprised when I showed her the bike. I concede she could have got rid of it to protect her mum from seeing it. For that matter, so could Martin or Aiden.'

'Now you're talking sense. Yep, I suspect one of them moved it to protect Meg from the trauma – as you say, she's been through enough. So, the theory is Harold killed his son, either deliberately or by accident, and hid the body. It would help if the pathologist pulled his finger out; he's not been in a hurry to sort out the bones, but we should hear today on best guess cause of death. I suspect Caroline was the one who got rid of the bike to protect her mother. Harold was killed by Martin Webb for reasons as yet unknown, and Caroline is either in partnership with him or completely innocent.'

'That all makes sense and fits neatly along the lines I was thinking. Webb and Sissons argued on the day Harold disappeared. It could have been about Meg,' suggested Carlos.

'Or money. The bank's being cagey about Harold's finances, but the DCI's going over there at lunchtime to meet the manager. Once we have that information, one of the team will rake through the transactions and see if there are any coming from or going to Martin Webb. Anyway, I'd better get going. Are you all right to be left alone now? Your sister didn't get home until 3am; her husband left for work an hour ago.'

He grinned. 'Thanks for babysitting me. I'll be fine. Do you want me to follow up with Meg? You said you wanted to quiz her yesterday, but didn't get around to it.'

'Oh, I forgot. Yes, I wanted to find out if she could remember anything else about the day her husband was murdered, and to ask if she met with Caroline. All pretty pointless now, but it would be good to tie up any loose ends. They could all be in cahoots.'

'The trio?'

'Yeah. Unlikely, but it's worth checking.'

'Okay, I'll speak to her later. Do you think Masters will let Caroline go today?'

'Hard to say. He's convinced she's involved and she still has no alibi. He's got grounds to charge her, particularly if he can link her to Webb.'

'His prejudice against a woman who stood up to him has nothing to do with it, of course!' Carlos spat the words out.

Fiona shrugged. 'Look, I'll be there the whole time she's interviewed. If we can't get a confession, perhaps I can veer his focus towards the colonel. Don't worry. If she's innocent, she'll be out in time to get home for Christmas Day. Try to get some rest, Carlos. And look on the positive side. You found Harold's murderer, Webb. You've got a nice payday coming just in time for Christmas.'

She laughed loudly, and Carlos was grinning long after she left. She brought the fresh air he needed right now; her sense of humour was therapeutic.

Lady came in from the garden and sat by his side, excitedly wagging her tail.

'Sorry, girl. It'll be a short walk this morning. I'm bushed.'

Chapter 28

The interview with Caroline Winslow wasn't going well. Masters and the suspect were at loggerheads, with neither prepared to compromise. Fiona's frustration with the pair was at boiling point; she'd had to get her boss to stop badgering and yelling more than once. The so-called defence lawyer from a local firm was worse than useless. Barely out of school, he spent more time looking at his watch than he did listening and didn't even attempt to defend his client.

'Just admit it, Mrs Winslow, and we – those who are innocent, that is – can all go home for Christmas,' Masters growled and leaned in, invading Caroline's personal space. The brief checked his watch again.

'Do you have somewhere else to be?' Fiona snapped, fixing her gaze on him. All eyes turned to her. Masters, annoyed at the interruption, stared at her, and then at the brief, who blushed.

'Erm... I do have another appointment. Perhaps we can resume later?'

Masters shook his head. 'Unbelievable. Well, don't let us keep you – seems we're not getting anywhere here anyway.' He got up and stormed out of the interview room.

'Interview suspended 11.34 am at the request of defence. DCI Masters leaves the room.' Fiona spoke into the tape and switched it off.

The embarrassed, flustered young man gathered his papers together and hurriedly pushed them into a brand-new leather briefcase.

'Excuse me,' he said to Fiona, not acknowledging his client.

Caroline put her head in her hands. Fiona noticed the trembling and heard the telltale sound of the knee knocking on the underside of the table.

'Can I get you some coffee?'

Caroline raised her head. Tears filling the hazel eyes, she nodded.

'Yes, please.'

Fiona popped her head out the door and asked a PC outside to bring two coffees before taking a seat in the interview room opposite Caroline.

'I'm going to need a decent lawyer, aren't I?'

'I think so, yes.'

'Our lawyer's in Edinburgh. I'm not sure he'd be any good at this sort of thing, I wouldn't know where to start. Why did they send someone so young? Not that I'd mind if he showed the slightest interest in defending me. I didn't do this, Sergeant. I just want to go home.'

The coffees arrived and the two women were left alone.

'Do you know Colonel Webb very well?' Fiona asked.

'Not really. He was good to Matthew growing up, used to help him with his bike when he got it and things like that. Come to think of it, it might have been him who bought the bike in the first place, not my grandparents. I asked Mother about it and she said it was brought round on Matthew's birthday from an anonymous donor – she thought it was from the vicar and his wife. Doreen – the vicar's wife – has been kind to Mother over the years. When she was allowed to, that is.

'Harold didn't like the colonel at all. I now know why. Mother tells me he persistently asked her out when they were teenagers. She says he warned her that Harold was a nasty piece of work.'

'I see. Do you know if Matthew was involved in a bicycle accident before he disappeared?'

'You're referring to the state the bike was in in the garage. No, I don't. When I saw it, I thought perhaps Harold had wrecked it in a temper to spite Matthew. He was never happy about the gift, but he too thought it had come from the vicar, according to Mother, and wanted to keep in with him.'

'Why did you get rid of it?' *Might as well ask the question*, thought Fiona.

Caroline cupped the mug of coffee in her hands, trying to stop them trembling.

'I was shocked at the state it was in,' she whispered. 'I didn't want Mum seeing what he'd done.'

Bingo!

'What did you do with the bike?'

'I took it to the tip in Chesterfield.' Caroline suddenly looked up at

Fiona. 'Why are you asking about the bike?'

'It could give us important evidence about your brother's death. He may have been run over.'

Caroline gasped as her hand flew to her mouth. Tears ran freely down her face. Fiona pushed a box of tissues towards her.

'You didn't suspect?'

'Of course not. Surely you don't think I had anything to do with my brother's death as well?' Caroline stiffened. 'I need to be alone now, Sergeant.'

Fiona finished her coffee and stood. She pressed a hand on Caroline's shoulder, but it was shrugged away. Sighing, Fiona left the room.

'Where's DCI Masters?' she asked a young PC.

'He's been called to a meeting with the Chief Super. He said for you to wait till he gets back. You're not in his good books.'

She giggled. Fiona glared at the girl whose subordination now had her attention. Tall, pretty, bright blue eyes, heavy makeup.

Yep, just his type. Another notch in his post of conquests, no doubt. Or soon will be.

'I need the pathologist's report on the Matthew Sissons case. Get hold of him, will you?'

The smirk left the officer's face and she opened her lipsticked mouth to protest, but obviously thought better of it. Instead, she moved to a hot desk and picked up the phone. Moments later, she called over to Fiona.

'Putting you through to the pathologist, Sergeant.'

Fiona's phone rang. She sat at her desk and answered.

'Just a minute,' she said, putting her hand over the mouthpiece. 'PC Blythe?' she called. The female officer turned her head from a whispered conversation with a colleague.

'Yes?'

Fiona handed her a £10 note. 'Get me a ham sandwich and a cappuccino from next door.'

The officer scowled as Fiona turned her attention back to the phone.

Who's smirking now? she thought.

It was just as Carlos had thought. The multiple fractures and mangled bike pointed to a road traffic accident. All they needed to know now was whether Harold Sissons had run over his son, and was it accidental or deliberate? The latter, she decided, they might never find out.

She called Carlos and told him what the pathologist had discovered.

'So it was an RTA. Interesting. Have you managed to track down the bike?'

'Caroline dumped it at the tip. Can you give me a description and I'll get one of our PCs to retrieve it if it's still there. I have just the person for the job.'

'Is someone stoking your fire?'

'Nothing I can't handle.'

Carlos gave her the description, then she whispered, 'I don't think Masters has any intention of letting Caroline go. He's determined it's her. Has a meeting with the Chief Super. The local brief is worse than useless. Do you think you can ask Caroline's husband to track down a decent solicitor?'

'I'll go and see him now, but it may be a problem this close to Christmas. Speaking of defence lawyers, I forgot to ask. What did you decide to do about your brother?'

She exhaled sharply. 'That's a problem for another day.'

'I understand. Have you interviewed our psychotic colonel yet?'

Fiona laughed. 'Is your head hurting?'

'You could say that,' he chuckled.

'Poor Carlos. I'm just pleased the shot missed you. In answer to your question – no. I'm waiting for Masters to get back and we'll do it together. It seems he had nothing to do with the bike in the garage so is unlikely to have known about the boy's death. I still have him down for Harold, though. Either that, or he's obsessive about his privacy. Maybe he's got something else to hide.'

'As long as it's not another body,' laughed Carlos.

'Have you spoken to Meg yet?'

'I was just about to go next door when you phoned. I fell asleep, would you believe? Sophie's only just up.'

'Must have been a good night, lucky beggars. You watch that head of yours and stay out of trouble. We'll talk later.'

Fiona polished off her sandwich and slurped back a gulp of the coffee that had been slapped begrudgingly on her desk. She checked her change. Turning around to see PC Blythe giggling again, she sighed.

Where do we get these people from?

'PC Blythe.'

The woman rolled her eyes and cocked her head.

'That's me.'

Fiona handed her a piece of paper with the description of the bicycle.

'I need you to pop to the tip this afternoon and find that bike.'

'But...'

'But what?' Fiona snapped.

'Nothing.' PC Blythe stood with more attitude than a stroppy teenager and stomped out of the office just as Masters appeared.

'What's the matter with PC Blythe?'

'Who?' Fiona pretended not to recall and noticed a few chuckles from other officers.

Masters shook his head, marching excitedly towards her. The triumphant entrance suggested she would need the calories she'd just devoured. He pulled a chair up next to her, a smug grin on his face. She couldn't help but respond in kind.

'Good news, sir?' she asked.

'Excellent news, Sergeant. I've been right all along. Jacobi's an idiot. She did it.'

Feeling a sudden desire to slap him round the head, she squeezed the sandwich wrapper and dropped it in the bin.

'Who did what, sir?'

'Caroline Winslow killed her father. Can't wait to see Jacobi's face when I tell him.'

'We have evidence of that now, then?'

A flash of doubt crossed the DCI's face, but he dismissed it.

'We have evidence that Webb's spade has never been near Harold Sissons. No DNA of the dead man whatsoever.'

Fiona's heart sank, eyes widening. 'That does surprise me. I was pretty certain from his attack on Mr Jacobi and myself that he was involved.'

'Even if he was, he wasn't the killer. Caroline Winslow's our killer. We need to find the murder weapon or some other evidence that she was in the woods. She denies ever being there. We've got her, Cook, I know it. I've got permission to conduct a search of the woods. It might turn something up. I need you out there to head it up. Let me know the minute you find anything.'

Fiona was relieved about the search. She'd been suggesting it for days, but Masters had told her it was a waste of money when he was convinced it was a local thug, and then he'd believed he could harangue Caroline into a confession.

'It's her, I'm telling you,' he raised his voice. 'You still don't seem convinced, Cook. Do you have another theory? If so, I'm listening.'

'No, sir, I don't – I guess I'm just surprised at Webb's attack on Jacobi yesterday, and his pointing a gun at me. I was convinced he was our man and that Caroline Winslow was where she said she was at the time.'

'No. He's a retired colonel, probably going a bit senile. These country types are very precious about intruders. You were lucky. He might have shot you both.'

'That's what I was afraid of. It can hardly be classed as reasonable force to bash Jacobi over the head with a spade. Twice.'

'It wouldn't surprise me if the idiot didn't provoke him. Jacobi's an interfering no-good pretend detective. He was never a good soldier and now he's showing he's an incompetent private eye. I don't want him knowing about this search. Got that?'

Fiona grabbed her mac off the back of the chair. 'He'll find out, sir, I'm sure of it. Small village – people talk.'

She darted out the door, texting Carlos as she jumped in her Mini. Concern for Caroline Winslow filled her with dread as she started up the engine. That so-called solicitor was going to be of no use to Caroline; the DCI was determined to pin the murder on her, with or without evidence.

He must really hate you, Carlos.

The fear that Masters might be capable of manufacturing evidence to prove he was right sent shivers down her spine. Then the seed of an idea bubbled through her head.

'That's a really bad move,' she told herself, but still, as she sat in the car, she made the call.

Chapter 29

Meg was alone when Carlos called round and appeared to be in one of her more compos mentis frames of mind.

'Carlos. Good to see you, I was just making tea. Would you like to join me?'

After following the tea routine and precise placement of tray, pot, cups and saucers, Carlos waited for Meg to sit down before starting. They were back to tea leaves; no sign of tea bags or mugs this time.

'I was wondering if you could describe to me again what happened the day your husband disappeared. You said he went to the community centre in the afternoon as usual. That's been confirmed by the vicar and several people who were at the same meeting. It gets a bit hazy after that. Did Harold come home at all?'

'Harold was angry. He'd argued with someone.' Meg pursed her lips. 'He was often angry, now I think of it.'

'So he did come home after the meeting that afternoon?'

Meg's brow creased. 'He must have, if you say he did.'

Ignoring the confusion, Carlos persisted. 'Did he tell you who he argued with?'

'It might have been Martin. Yes, it was Martin. What have you done to your head?'

'Oh, it's nothing,' Carlos automatically stroked the wound. 'He argued with Martin. Martin's your friend, I gather.'

'I haven't seen him in years, except at a distance. Harold told him to stay away after Matthew died. Martin liked Matthew, treated him like a son. He never had children of his own, apparently. I didn't know he also went to the community centre for those meetings until Harold came home ranting one time. He was never kind when in that sort of mood. I made him some tea.'

'I see. And that one time was the day Harold disappeared?'

'It could have been.'

'And when he went out again, did he say where he was going?'

'I think he said he was going out. Yes. That's what he said.'

'He didn't say where he was going?'

'I expect he did. I... it's all a blur. I'm not certain he came home at all. Is Martin all right? He was supposed to call yesterday, but didn't come.'

Carlos was struggling to keep up with the muddled picture.

'Meg, Martin Webb's been arrested.'

'Will he call today, do you think? He's an old friend. We knew each other at school, you know. He's always been soft on me, or so he says. It would be nice to have a friend again.'

Meg started the humming routine and Carlos felt he'd got all he was going to get from her today.

'I'm not sure if he'll be round today, Meg.' His hand went to his head. He glanced at his phone as a text message came through from Fiona.

'I'd better go now, Meg. Thank you for your time.'

'Was there something to tell me about Martin?'

'Yes. He's been arrested for aggravated assault. He attacked two people, but he may get bail. I'm sure he'll visit when he comes home. Now, I really had better go.'

Carlos rushed next door, told Sophie where he was going and jumped in the car, more confused than ever. He texted Fiona and asked her to send him a photo of Caroline. There was something he needed to do before it was too late.

***

Carlos traipsed the streets of Bakewell, going in and out of every café, showing as many staff as he could the photo of Caroline. It was highly unlikely that anyone would remember seeing her, but he had to try. He was almost at the end of his search. There were only three more places on his list to get to.

Entering a small patisserie, he ordered a Bakewell tart and tea after drawing a blank with the owner over the picture. He hadn't eaten lunch, so sat down for a break before he headed off to the final two cafés.

514

A customer came in, a young woman, and the owner chatted easily with her. Then Carlos heard her cry out and saw her hand go to her head.

'I'll be blessed!' she exclaimed. 'Betsy, you worked on Thursday a couple of weeks back, didn't you...? Hey Mister, show Betsy that photo. This gentleman's looking for someone who might have come in that day.'

Carlos joined the women at the counter and showed the picture to younger one.

'Yeah. She was in here.'

'Can you be sure of the date?' Carlos asked.

'Yeah, I covered for Mrs Browning. You had an appointment, din't ya?' the girl called Betsy said to the café owner. 'She hardly takes any time off, you see, so I remember. Could do with taking more time off, mind.'

'Betsy, the photo,' Mrs Browning encouraged.

'Oh yeah. That woman,' she nodded to the photo, 'came in twice. Place was empty 'cos we'd run out of cake, but I kept it open for drinks and stuff just like Mrs Browning said I had to.'

'And you are sure it was this woman?'

'Yeah, it was her. Stressed out, she was. Looked like she was going to burst into tears any minute. Ordered black coffee so I knew she was upset, like. I mean, you wouldn't drink black coffee unless you were stressed, would ya? By the shape of her, she could have done with some of Mrs Browning's cake. She wore a business suit. We don't get many of them business types in here. When she came back the second time, she'd been bawling. Eyes were red and swollen. She asked if she could use the ladies. I know you say it's customer use only, Mrs Browning, but I figured as she'd been in earlier, it would be okay.'

'Yes, that's fine, Betsy.'

'Can you remember what time she left?' Carlos asked, crossing his fingers.

'Five fifty-nine. I was watching the clock. We close at six. I ended up closing twelve minutes late 'cos she took so long in the loo and I had to check everything after she'd gone and wipe down. When she did come out, she had fresh makeup on. Taking the mick, I thought at the time, but as she was upset, I didn't say anything. I din't mention it, Mrs

Browning. Sorry.' The girl's eyes widened.

'That's all right, Betsy. You get off now or you'll be late home. I'll let this gentleman have your details if he needs to contact you again. He's a private detective.'

Betsy's eyes popped out of her head as she turned and scuttled quickly out of the shop.

'Not the brightest, but she's good with numbers, so she covers for me if I take time off.'

'Good with faces, too. Thank you. If I could take her name and contact details in case the police want to get in touch. She's been a great help – please tell her that, will you?'

'I'll be sure to mention it.'

'One more question: where would the lady have parked to come here?'

'Turn right outside and the car park's a few minutes' walk. That's why we get so many tourists in here. Ideal for people after a long drive.'

Carlos thanked Mrs Browning. After tucking Betsy's details in his wallet, he found the car park easily and scanned the area. Just as he'd hoped: CCTV cameras!

He walked south to the car park where he'd left his own car and drove in the direction of Shady Woods.

***

Carlos spotted Fiona's distinctive pale blue mac from a distance and headed that way. An officer tried to stop him, but he showed his ID and told him he needed to speak with

Fiona. It was almost dark and the police looked to be winding down their search.

'Have you found anything?'

'Not yet, just the old boy's wallet,' she said loud enough to be heard by a few officers packing up a car.

Carlos raised an eyebrow.

'Don't say anything. Remember, I was sent on a wasted journey to Edinburgh. Things haven't stopped since,' she muttered.

'So no planted evidence, then?' He also lowered his voice.

She frowned. 'I felt terrible thinking the DCI would stoop to it, but he really hates your guts. Caroline Winslow has found herself in the firing line because of whatever it is between you two. I couldn't have that.'

Before Carlos had the opportunity to ask what she meant by the comment, an irate Masters yelled, 'COOK!'

'Looks like I'm in the doghouse.' She shrugged, walking over to her boss. Carlos had no problem hearing the DCI's loud voice because all the officers scattered for fear they might be next.

'What's he doing here? I gave specific instructions...'

Carlos crept closer so he could hear more of the conversation.

'He's just arrived, sir. I told you it's a small village. Word gets around.'

'Damn woman's been released. Some fancy lawyer from Edinburgh called the Chief Super. No idea what was said, but we had to let her go. Not for long, though.' He smirked.

Carlos saw him eyeing the woods. 'Did you find it… erm… anything?'

'Yes, sir.'

Carlos had crept up to within a few feet now and both he and Fiona observed a cynical smile cross Masters's face.

'Where is it?'

'You haven't asked what it is we found,' said Fiona pointedly.

'Well? What is it?'

'The dead man's wallet, sir.'

Carlos saw the redness rising from Masters's neck and the jugular vein swelling. For a brief moment, he thought of how he'd love to stop the blood flowing through that man's body. He shook his head violently, causing pain to shoot through it back to front.

'Is that all?'

'That's all for now, sir. The search leader's just called it off until after the weekend. Says we don't have the manpower to work over the bank holidays.'

'Then I'll continue the search myself. You can come with me. That woman's guilty and there's evidence here somewhere...'

Carlos interrupted, 'Actually, she's not guilty.'

'Just because you say it doesn't make it true, Jacobi!' Masters yelled. He tried to march into the woods. Carlos blocked his path.

'Get out of my way,' Masters pushed Carlos, but he held firm.

'Mrs Winslow's alibi checks out.'

Both Fiona and Masters stared at him, Fiona fighting to ward off a smile.

'Really? What have you got?'

'I found a witness who places her in a café in Bakewell at the time of Harold Sissons's disappearance. Swears to it and would be happy to say so in court.' He didn't know that was the case, but added it for effect. 'There's also CCTV cameras in the car park where Mrs Winslow parked, a few minutes away from the patisserie,' he added. 'You can request footage, or I can.'

'We'll do that, Mr Jacobi,' said Fiona. 'Let's hope the search gives us a lead on whoever did this, sir. Shall we get on and finish it together now?'

Masters's face had turned purple. Carlos could see from the tension he was incandescent with rage, but he controlled himself.

'No, Cook. That won't be necessary, it's Christmas Eve. You'd better take a statement from Jacobi here and confirm details. I'll have a quick look around myself. You go.'

'Happy to stay and help, sir.'

'Go, Cook!'

'Right, sir. Mr Jacobi, is it okay if I take a statement at your sister's house? Its freezing out here – looks like rain.' She grinned at Carlos as Masters stomped off into the woods.

'I guess he's gone to retrieve that planted evidence, judging by the look on your face.'

'He won't find it.' She pulled a scarf from her pocket. 'What's the betting this belongs to Caroline Winslow?'

'He'll know you've got it,' he warned. 'Watch your back.'

'And he'd better watch his from now on. He won't dare challenge me on it. Anyone could have picked it up

– even you. I'm satisfied, for now, he won't know who he can trust.'

'You're right. Nice one, Fiona.'

'I wish I had enough evidence to report him to internal affairs; I wouldn't normally rat on fellow officers, but I could make an exception in his case. I'll be watching him closely from now on, and if I find anything else, he's gone. That's if I don't need a favour.'

'What do you mean by that?'

'I'll tell you over dinner.'

They drove separately back to Sophie's and pulled up just as Caroline arrived next door with Aiden.

'Good to see you home,' said Carlos.

'Thank you. Apparently, a renowned defence lawyer from

Edinburgh heard about my case. I don't know how he found out, but he called Aiden to ask if he could represent me. They faxed a form to the station, which I signed. The next thing I know, I'm free.'

Caroline grinned widely. Aiden took her hand.

'What's more, he's representing my wife for free. I offered to pay, although I've now looked him up and he usually represents corporate clients, so would cost a fortune. There are rumours he gets people off who should be in jail.'

'Well, let's just be thankful he's got a philanthropic side to him,' said Caroline.

As Carlos turned back to Fiona, he whispered, 'That's going to cost you big someday. You realise that, don't you?'

She smiled grimly. 'I knew the terms. Masters would have stopped at nothing.'

Carlos took her hand. 'I wish I'd verified the alibi sooner.'

'Not nearly as much as I do.'

'When it does come back to bite, know that I'm here. I'll help in whatever way I can.'

'Thanks, Carlos. As I said, I accepted the terms. Steve tried to talk me out of it.'

That fact worried Carlos more than anything else he'd heard since his unlucky reintroduction to Masters. Fiona had done this for him. Now he would do whatever it took not to let her pay. Any elation he'd felt over confirming the alibi and rubbing Masters's nose in it was lost in fear over what the involvement of a

dodgy lawyer could cost Fiona
further down the road.

Chapter 30

Cooking aromas came from the kitchen as Carlos and Fiona let themselves in to Sophie's. Lady threw herself at him before enthusiastically greeting Fiona.

'Just so you don't feel left out,' Carlos laughed.

He found Sophie in the kitchen, checking the oven.

'Smells delicious.' He kissed his sister when she stood up.

'Lasagne. Hello, Fiona – come in, I'll pour some coffee. Have you two solved the case yet?'

Sophie's bubbly demeanour made Carlos feel better. He grinned.

'Not quite, but the good news is Caroline's been released. We just saw her on our way in.'

'Meg will be pleased, as will Caroline's husband. He was asking where you were earlier, Fiona. Would you like to stay for dinner? There's plenty to go round.'

'I'd love to. We've got work to do, so that would be great. I love lasagne.'

You love anything edible, Carlos wanted to say, but refrained.

'How did the search in the woods go?' asked Sophie. 'Don't give me one of your looks, Carlos. This is a small community. I happened to be in the store this afternoon. It was the main topic of conversation, along with the arrest of Colonel Webb. The villagers are worried it will mar the reputation of their tranquil home. Which reminds me: a reporter was here this afternoon, asking questions. I sent her next door to speak to Aiden.'

Carlos frowned. 'Was it the vicar's daughter?'

'Why would it be the Milnthorpes' daughter?' Sophie enquired.

'She's a reporter and she knew Matthew. They went to school together. Barney warned me she had a personal interest in the case and would be up here. It was too much to expect her to leave it alone, I suppose. I'd be interested to talk to her, because she's the only one who thought Matthew's disappearance was suspicious all those years ago. Odd that no-one else challenged Harold's story.'

Carlos sat at the kitchen table with his coffee. Fiona joined him.

'You've just reminded me, I pulled Matthew's case files. I was going to look at them before the DCI sent me down here. Hang on, I'll get them from the car.' Fiona got up and headed for the door. 'Did I tell you he died from multiple fractures and a crush injury?' she called back on her way out.

'You did,' he replied.

'Poor boy,' said Sophie. 'And poor Meg having to go through the loss of a son and a husband. Whatever we may think of Harold Sissons, she was devoted to him.'

'That's questionable. "Shackled" would be the word I'd use.' Carlos frowned. 'I hate bullies.' His anger with Masters bubbled up, never far from the surface over the past few days. 'When I saw Masters this afternoon, I wanted to kill him, Soph. The strength of feeling frightened me.'

Sophie sat down next to him and put her arm around his shoulder. 'But you didn't. And you wouldn't. However, whatever happened between you two, you need to talk to someone about it.'

'You're right. I will. When this case is over.'

The door slammed. Sophie raised her eyebrows.

'Heavy-handed, your friend.'

'Sorry.' He smiled.

'Here they are.' Fiona put the files down on the kitchen table. Sophie stayed put as they pored through the documents.

'There's not much here, is there?' Carlos scowled. 'A twelve-year-old boy goes missing and they don't do a search or anything. They took Sissons's word about the argument and assumed the boy would turn up in Edinburgh, or be found making his way there.'

Fiona read through the interviews. 'Now this one's interesting. Just when I'd concluded Colonel Webb wasn't involved, look at this statement:

'"Colonel Martin Webb says he met Matthew at the bus stop on the afternoon of his disappearance." It says here: "Matthew seemed angry and upset and told the colonel he was going to stay with his sister".' Fiona looked up.

'So Webb was mixed up in the boy's death after all. Let's think about this. Say Matthew did have an argument with Harold and stormed out. Webb's place is on the way out of the village. What if it was him who ran the boy over. Panicked. Hid the body somewhere to decompose, and later, when things got bad between him and Harold, he got access to the house and placed the holdall under the floorboards.'

'What a horrible thing to do,' gasped Sophie. 'I can't believe it of the colonel. He's abrupt, even rude at times, but I can't imagine him ever doing such a thing. Surely, if it was an accident, he would have just called the police or an ambulance?'

'He's not a harmless old man, though, is he? I bet you wouldn't have believed he would slam a spade into my head. Twice.'

The conversation was interrupted as the front door opened. A waft of air blew through the open-plan lounge-diner into the kitchen.

Sophie jumped up. 'Put those away. No talk of murder over dinner, okay? *Tesoro*!' She ran to greet her husband.

Fiona obediently packed the papers back in the file and surveyed the kitchen.

'I love this kitchen. Big, but not too big. The boat's not ideal for entertaining, but I can stretch to the occasional meal for one.'

Carlos smiled at his friend. 'When the takeaways are closed, you mean?'

She laughed. 'Yeah. You're right. Domestic goddess I'm not, but I have other talents.'

'Such as protecting those you care about.' He eyed her seriously.

'Not so much a talent as a weakness. Let's put work aside for tonight, shall we?'

Carlos was happy to do so. Even he was shocked that Masters would plant evidence. But then again, Masters hadn't owned up to failing in his duty on that fateful day. Carlos's hand went to the back of his head. Every time he thought about it, a pain shot through his head.

'Are you okay?' asked Fiona. 'That bump causing you trouble?'

'It's nothing.'

Sophie burst into the kitchen with Gary on her arm.

'Let the festivities begin!'

Gary grinned adoringly down at his wife. 'Here's an early Christmas present for us from Rolls Royce.'

Sophie took the piece of paper from his hands and her mouth dropped open.

'What's this?'

'My bonus for finishing the project on time.' Gary laughed. 'Hello, Carlos. Hello again, Sergeant.'

'Fiona, please. Carlos and I are old friends. Anyway, I'm eating with you, so best not to be formal.'

'What are you doing tomorrow, Fiona?' Sophie asked, a concerned expression on her face.

'I'm officially on call, so I'll be home.'

'On a boat,' added Carlos.

'That's settled, then. Why don't you join us for Christmas dinner?

You and Carlos can talk shop beforehand while Gary helps me.'

'I wouldn't want to intrude,' Fiona eyed Carlos for help.

'Great idea,' he concurred.

'Okay, thank you. I will,' Fiona beamed from ear to ear.

The doorbell took away any awkwardness Fiona might have been feeling. Gary went to answer.

'Carlos, it's for you.'

Carlos found Caroline waiting in the hallway. 'I just wanted to let you know we're driving up to Edinburgh this evening. I need to see my children and don't want to stay here any longer. We're taking Mother with us. Please, Mr Jacobi... Carlos, find out who did this. I want this nightmare over.'

'I'll do everything I can. And don't worry, you won't be taken in again. I managed to track down your alibi this afternoon. Sorry I didn't tell you before. I found a girl who remembers seeing you in the café on the day your father disappeared, and if needed, we can get CCTV footage from the car park.'

'I can't believe it. So it's over? Thank you so much. Car park, did you say?'

'Yes, there are cameras overlooking it if you were in the one north of the patisserie.'

'That's right. It was a patisserie with a few eat-in tables. I remember the girl. I'm amazed she remembers me, though. Seemed a bit scatty.'

He laughed. 'Scatty perhaps, but observant with it. You left quite an impression.'

Caroline put her hand out and shook Carlos's firmly. 'So there'll be no further need for my new best friend solicitor. I wonder what prompted the man to come to my rescue? I must thank him.'

'Sometimes good things happen. Give Meg my love and enjoy your Christmas. I'll be in touch with any news.'

'Thank you. And a happy Christmas to you and your family. If you need anything from my mother, please let me know. We can always fly down if necessary. Oh, I almost forgot. Your sister has a key to my mother's house. Feel free to use it if you need to look for anything. I think we can trust you.'

'Thanks. I'll return the key Fiona borrowed yesterday when I go round.'

Caroline produced a warm smile, causing her eyes to sparkle. *Maybe her luck will change*, he thought as he closed the door.

Chapter 31

Fiona woke at 5am. Noise from the pothole-ridden towpath outside had startled her. The moonlight revealed a man's shadow standing just outside her kitchen window.

With heart rate quickening, she reached for the truncheon she'd held on to from her days on the beat. The shadow moved and the boat tilted under the weight of someone boarding at the side. The door handles turned, rattling as someone attempted entry.

Standing next to the doors, she slid the lock just as the person pulled hard. The doors flew open and the man fell back on to the hull. She leapt out, standing over him and wielding the truncheon high, ready to bring it down hard.

'What the...?' the man cursed.

'Sir? What are you doing here?'

A crumpled DCI Masters stared back at her through bloodshot eyes, the moonlight making them seem eerily devilish. She held out her hand to assist him on to his feet.

'You could've killed me with that thing.'

'You were creeping around my boat at five in the morning, sir. Did you expect tea and a mince pie?'

Masters rolled over, laughing a deep belly laugh. Fiona saw the light flick on in her neighbour's boat.

'You'd better come inside before he reports you to the police.'

Masters belly laughed again. 'You're so funny, Cook,' he spluttered. 'Do you know what they call you down at the nick?'

'I'd rather not.' Fiona took the drunken man's arm and hustled him through the narrow space into her living room. He almost banged his head, bending to get in through the low entrance. *Shame it missed*, she thought. 'I'll put the kettle on.'

Masters fell on to her settee, trying to sit up straight, but landing to one side. It would have been comical if she knew what the heck he was doing here.

'You do realise it's Christmas Day? I thought you were staying with the in-laws.'

'It was all a ruse, Cook. She's left me.' He was spluttering and slurring. 'Taken my kids and left me. Can you believe it?'

Yeah, I sure can, she thought, but asked, 'What happened?'

'I left the woods not long after you and that...'

'Private investigator, sir.'

'Him, yes. I went round to the in-laws. Her brother was there. Told me to beat it. Said Shirley had had enough and that I needed to find somewhere else to live. I smacked him one in the face, but her dad came out and threatened me with a rifle. Told me to get the hell off his property.'

Carlos is going to love this, was all Fiona could think. She had no sympathy for the wayward DCI, particularly after finding the planted evidence yesterday. Her eyes automatically shot to her mac.

Damn! I didn't take it out of the pocket. She handed Masters a cup of tea and made sure she sat where he wouldn't have a view of the mac.

'Must have been quite a shock?'

'Damned right it was. I drove home and things got worse.'

Fiona couldn't wait to hear the next bit. 'I wouldn't have thought they could get worse than your wife leaving you.' She tried to sound as though she cared, but struggled.

'She's changed the damn locks.' He spat the words out.

Fiona turned back to the kettle to pour more tea and suppress the giggle forming in her throat.

'Oh dear.'

'Oh dear? Is that all you can say? Oh dear? Twelve years of marriage and she does this to me. Trouble with women today; you've got no respect.'

Fiona's hackles rose. 'Perhaps she didn't get any respect herself, sir.'

Masters slurped back his tea. 'Go on. Defend her. Women sticking together, is that what this is? What about sticking with your superiors? Hey? What about that, eh?' He tried to get up, but fell back.

'You're my senior, sir, *not* my superior.'

Her retort was wasted. Masters lay unconscious, snoring on his back,

dribble forming at the side of his
mouth.

'Don't you dare be sick when you
wake up,' she snarled.

She went to the bedroom to collect
clothes before taking a wash,
determined not to meet Terry
Masters in her thermal underwear
again. She heard a loud thud as she
turned the shower off.

Blimey! He's fallen over.

Pulling on her clothes, she went
out to the living room to find the
galley doors banging open and shut
against the boat. No sign of Masters.
Her mac lay on the floor, scarf
missing.

She'd been outwitted.

Was the story about his wife
leaving a lie? She hoped not, but
she imagined that having lost his
family, he wouldn't want to lose his

job as well. She should have known he would have worked out who took the plant.

Oh well. He can't very well accuse me publicly. They would both have to live with the knowledge that she knew he was dirty.

Fiona locked the doors and cooked a fry-up breakfast, her own special Christmas treat. She'd savour this story later, a Christmas present for Carlos.

After breakfast, she felt a chill in the air and watched the heavy clouds drop their snow. A white Christmas – what more could you ask for? She hummed the famous tune. The snow was settling fast, but she wasn't due to go to Carlos's for a few hours.

Perhaps I'd better drive to the edge of the village and wait there.

I'm not missing out on Sophie's cooking today. She put her mac on and stepped off the boat.

'Good morning, Miss Fiona. Happy Christmas to ya.'

'Happy Christmas to you, too, Pete.'

'Did you know you had a leak in your roof, gal?'

'Blimey, I forgot about it. Yeah, I noticed it the other night.'

'Well you don't have it any longer. Fixed it yesterday, I did.'

She beamed at her elderly neighbour. 'I owe you one.'

'Aye, that you do. I'll have a wee dram next time I see you.'

'You're on.'

'Who was that big bloke giving you trouble in the early hours? I almost called the police, but remembered that's you.' He laughed loudly.

'It was my boss. He was drunk and daren't go home to the wife until he'd sobered up a bit. He's gone now.'

'Aye, I watched him scarpering off like a bat out of hell – all over the place, he was. I thought he was going to end up in the cut. Are you sure he didn't steal anything?'

'Quite sure. See you around, Pete.'

Fiona chuckled at the image of her boss trying to run down the towpath, hoping he had fallen over a few times on the way. She arrived at her beloved Mini just as her phone rang. She didn't recognise the number.

'Hello, DS Cook here.'

'Good morning, Sergeant Cook. It's DCI Matlock here. Just to let you know I'm heading up the Sissons cases now. Report to me if there's anything new. I don't expect you to work on it till after the holiday, unless you catch a break.'

'Erm... Right, sir. What about DCI Masters, sir?'

'Off the case. That's all you need to know for now.'

'Thank you for letting me know. Is this the number I call you on, sir?'

'Yes, it is. I'm home with the family if you need me. As I said, I don't expect you will need me today or tomorrow, Sergeant.'

'Understood, sir.' *Take that for 'Don't you dare disturb me over the holidays.'* Climbing down into her Mini, she grinned happily. Could this day get any better? It might just have been worth contacting her brother for the short-term reward – she had no doubt this was also the work of the hotshot lawyer. Her smile turned into a frown – *the bigger the favour, the bigger the payback.*

***

Carlos and Lady returned from their run as the snow started to fall. He stayed outside and watched in wonder as the road turned white. Lady rolled around in it, trying to catch some of the larger flakes as they trickled down. Before long, everything was a beautiful white.

'Your coat is dirty in comparison, girl.' He stroked the excited dog and crouched down next to her, hugging her neck. 'It's like one of those fairy-tale films Sophie loves,' he said.

Shaking the snow from his shoes and coat and removing both, he went upstairs for a shower. By the time he arrived back downstairs, Lady was lying by a coal effect gas fire, drying off.

Sophie hugged him. 'Happy Christmas, Carlos.'

'Happy Christmas, Sis.' He noticed the turkey already out in the open. 'Can I help you with anything?'

'No thanks. It's all under control. Gary promised, as it's our first Christmas in our new home, he'd help prepare dinner.'

'In that case, I'll make myself scarce. I'm going to phone Fiona and get her to come early in case we get snowed in.'

'Great idea. Feel free to use the snug when she comes.'

Fiona was already driving when Carlos called and arrived within minutes. He opened the door and hugged her.

'You left early, then? Good thinking.'

'I didn't want to miss out on your sister's amazing cooking. I've got news for you. You're going to love it.'

Carlos's interest was piqued. 'Let's get you a hot coffee. You can tell me in the warm.'

Fiona removed her mac and Carlos hung it up for her. She also removed her boots. Carlos collected two coffees and, after Sophie had called a polite greeting and happy Christmas to Fiona, they left her to concentrate on the task in hand.

'Come on, Fiona, we've been banished to the snug,' Carlos announced, loud enough for Sophie to hear, ducking as a piece of broccoli was hurtled his way. 'Hey! Remember I've got a sore head.'

'Don't be such a wuss. It's hardly death by broccoli,' his sister retorted.

Still giggling, he and Fiona retired to the snug. Lady reluctantly left the fireside, where she'd settled back down after greeting Fiona, to follow them and park herself at Carlos's feet.

'Come on, then. Tell me this great news,' he said, patting his faithful dog's head.

'The not so great news is that Masters was lurking around my boat at five o'clock this morning. He only just escaped being bashed over the head with my truncheon.'

'Shame he wasn't.'

'He was sloshed as hell, but still had the wherewithal to retrieve the planted evidence from my mac pocket while I was in the shower. He'd collapsed in a heap, so I thought he was asleep. Anyway, it doesn't matter, because I wouldn't have done anything with it.'

Carlos frowned. 'I'm not happy he was snooping around your boat. Sometimes I think he's unhinged. You don't know what he might do if he feels threatened.'

'Nah, I'm not worried about him. Now for the good news. I shouldn't be happy about the first thing, but I am. His wife's left him and changed the locks to their house. I guess there was one affair too many – I'm sure he's fraternising with a PC at the station. She wound me up big time yesterday, but I put her in her place.'

'I bet you did. As much as I like the idea of him being locked out of his own house, is that it?'

'Nope. The best bit is he's been taken off the case.'

'Courtesy of your brother's employer, no doubt?'

'I expect so. I'd have loved to have seen his face when he got the call. I don't think he knew about it when he was with me. Although he was so drunk, you wouldn't know.'

'Yet sober enough to get what he came for,' said Carlos. 'Are you certain he wasn't putting it on?'

'He might have been a bit. Obviously when he collapsed unconscious – that could have been an act. Nevertheless, any awkwardness I would have felt about the scarf is no longer an issue.'

Carlos drained his coffee mug, still concerned about what might hit Fiona further down the road because of her deal with her brother's boss.

'Who's in charge now?'

'A regular bloke. DCI Matlock, family man. He called me this morning and more or less told me to leave it alone over the bank holidays, which is fine by me.'

'Interesting name for a Derbyshire policeman,' chuckled Carlos.

'Changing the subject, have you heard from Rachel?'

'Yes. She phoned this morning before going to bed. She sounded exhausted. I'm taking her out to dinner on Saturday.'

'I remember those days. Pounding the beat on Christmas Eve is no picnic.'

'I've been thinking about this note.' Carlos placed the piece of paper on the coffee table and spread it out. 'If we could find the person who wrote it, we might have the answer to the Matthew Sissons case and why the colonel covered it up, or whether it was all down to him. It would be good to wrap up one of the cases. I don't believe for one minute he's going to tell us what happened himself.'

Fiona sighed. 'The only thing that stands out is it's fancy paper, and a distinctly darker than usual shade for manila.'

Sophie knocked and entered. 'Would you like a sherry?'

Carlos glanced at his watch. The time had flown since he and Fiona came into the snug. It was almost one o'clock.

'I won't say no,' said Fiona.

Gary appeared behind her carrying a bottle and four glasses on a tray. He poured, then they all lifted their glasses.

'Happy Christmas!' Gary announced.

'Happy Christmas,' they replied in unison.

'Dinner's under control, so we have time for a game.' Sophie started clearing the table and saw the note. 'What have you got to do with Peaks Rest Home?'

'What do you mean?' asked Carlos.

'That paper. I recognise it from the care home just outside the village, Peaks Rest Home for the Elderly. We've been defending them in a negligence claim. The firm I work for works in medical negligence,' Sophie clarified for Fiona, who nodded. 'The home's owned by a local GP and his wife.'

Carlos couldn't believe their luck. He leaned over and kissed his sister.

'Thank you, Sis. Do you recognise the writing?' He showed her the note.

'Oh. Interesting. I take it this was anonymous. It's difficult to say from the few words, and they're all in block capitals. You need to speak to Josie Reynolds. She's the manager and head nurse.'

'Josie Reynolds who I met at the community centre on Friday, the church on Sunday and spoke to on Monday? Now it's starting to make sense. There's friction between her and the colonel. I wonder what she knows.'

'Unless she's playing you for some mischievous reason of her own,' said Fiona.

Sophie stuck her chin out. 'Well you can wonder on for a while longer. It's Christmas Day and I'm playing a game before dinner.'

Carlos poured them all more sherry. 'You've got it. Game it is. Cheers.'

Chapter 32

Carlos pulled his Capri up outside the Peaks Rest Home. Five miles away from the village, the home was set back from the road in a beautiful part of the countryside. He and Fiona climbed out.

'Wow, some building,' she remarked.

Carlos agreed. Sophie had informed him the building was a converted convent. Ideal for a care home for the elderly. The familiar sandstone walls made it even more impressive.

An elderly woman stared out of one of the large bay windows as they made their way to the arched entrance revealing a pair of double doors. Carlos rang the bell.

'Solid oak,' he remarked.

They had to ring twice before anyone came. 'It is Boxing Day,' said Fiona. 'Probably working on a skeleton staff.'

A middle-aged woman in a grey uniform eventually opened one of the doors. Fiona showed her detective ID.

'DS Fiona Cook, and this is PI Carlos Jacobi. We'd like a word with Josie Reynolds. I understand she's working today.'

They had called Josie's home after getting the number from the ever-helpful vicar, Barney Milnthorpe. Josie's daughter told them she was at work.

'Come in. Please wait there.' The woman hurried off.

Bells rang continually, demanding attention, and care home staff rushed back and forth. Carlos and Fiona stood in a huge hallway with high ceilings and freshly polished dark oak panels. A table with a visitors' book was set to one side; two armchairs in the waiting area nearby and plush carpet lining the floor.

'Smells fresh as a daisy,' said Fiona.

'What did you expect?'

'Pee, if you must know. Some of the homes I've been in stink. Mind you, they were in less salubrious parts of London. This one's well-maintained. I'm surprised there's a negligence claim against them.'

'Looks can be deceiving, although I agree with you.'

Fiona was becoming impatient when five minutes had passed and still there was no sign of Josie Reynolds.

'I'm going to be ringing one of those call bells if she doesn't hurry up.'

Carlos smiled. 'She's probably dealing with a resident.'

'In that case, I'm going to take a seat.' Fiona plonked herself down in one of the armchairs.

Carlos walked slowly around, reading notices and getting a feel for the place and the woman in charge. Highly efficient and professional, was his conclusion. After fifteen minutes, he was beginning to wonder if Josie was playing mind games with them, but didn't mention it to Fiona. She was impatiently flicking through a magazine, huffing and puffing.

'You'll give yourself high blood pressure,' he said.

'I hate waiting. Never been any good at it. One of the reasons I'm always late. At least that way, you don't have to wait for anyone else.'

He laughed. 'I'll remember that next time I arrange a meeting with you.'

As they joked around amicably, the woman who'd let them in earlier joined them.

'Sorry, I was called to help someone to the toilet and got waylaid. Follow me, I'll take you to matron's office.'

They followed the bustling woman along a wide corridor and up an even wider spiral staircase covered with thick maroon carpet, exposed polished wood at both ends of the steps. Eventually they arrived at the end of the first-floor corridor outside an office labelled simply: 'Matron'. The door was closed. The nurse knocked and waited.

Josie opened. 'Thank you, Sheila, I'll take over now. Mr Jacobi, good to see you again, although I don't know what I can do to help you.'

Josie wasn't fooling Carlos for a moment. The flushed face, wide eyes and cautious tone told him she knew exactly why they were there.

'Call me Carlos.'

'DS Cook.' Fiona introduced herself. 'We're here about a note

Carlos received, but I think you know that, don't you?'

Cut to the chase, why don't you? Carlos thought.

Josie reddened more. 'You'd better come in. Take a seat,' she said and positioned herself behind a large polished ebony desk. Carlos and Fiona took the seats opposite.

'I received this note a few days ago. I was hoping you could explain what it means and why you sent it?' Carlos placed the note on the desk.

Josie cleared her throat. 'What makes you think I sent it?'

'Please don't play games, Mrs Reynolds. We know you sent it, we just need to know why.' Fiona was playing bad cop.

'Okay. Look, I read about Matthew Sissons's remains being found and thought it might be helpful for you to speak to Colonel Webb about them. He can tell you what happened. I didn't want to get involved. That's why I sent it anonymously.' She glared at Fiona.

'I'm afraid Colonel Webb has been difficult to speak to,' Carlos countered.

'You can say that again,' she snapped. 'I heard what happened, but you should be able to speak to him now. He'll be at home.'

Fiona's head shot up. 'What? When?'

'He was released on bail on Christmas Eve. Called to tell me, not that I was interested. He's a pest.'

'How well do you know the colonel?' Carlos tried a different tack.

The blush that had all but disappeared returned. 'I cared for his wife when she was dying, that's all.'

'Look,' Carlos persisted, 'we're not here to judge you about past or present relationships, and you're not going to be reported for any professional indiscretions, but we do need to know the facts.'

Josie sighed heavily. 'I used to do sleepovers to care for Mrs Webb when she was dying. She was a lovely woman – suffered terribly. Martin was a ladies' man, I'm sure you've heard. One thing led to another, and yes, against my better judgement, we had a brief affair.'

'While you were staying in the woman's house as a nurse?' Fiona's disgust was evident.

'It wasn't like that. I still did my job. I liked her. I feel guilty enough about the whole sordid affair, and I thought you weren't going to judge.'

Josie glared at Carlos, who intervened before Fiona said something else that might close Josie down.

'Did Martin tell you what happened to Matthew?'

'Goodness, no! He never spoke of it. He doesn't speak much, to be honest. Our relationship was passion, nothing else. As I said, rather sordid, but the sex was good. I'd been divorced for a few years and he could be charming until he got his way.' A bitterness surfaced in the green eyes.

'So he ended it?' suggested Fiona.

'Not really. It fizzled out. After his wife, Valerie, died, he became obsessed with Meg Sissons. He went through the motions with me. Not that I was the only one. Once the sex was no longer satisfying, we gradually drifted apart. Every so often he tries to rekindle what we had, but I'm not interested. He's as cold as an ice cream in winter, if I'm honest. Except with Meg. I came to my senses and now I detest the man.'

'Is there any truth in the note or is this just revenge?' asked Fiona.

Josie stiffened. 'Of course there's truth in the note. He knows what happened, I tell you.'

'I'm sorry, Josie, I'm not following,' said Carlos. 'You say he never mentioned Matthew Sissons.'

'He didn't. She did.'

Carlos leaned forward. 'Are you saying Valerie Webb knew something?'

'She had drug-crazed dreams and murmured during her sleep. Occasionally I could make out what she was saying. I used to sit with her, mopping her brow, trying to settle her.' Josie frowned at Fiona.

'And?' Carlos pressed.

'There was one topic that became a regular feature of the nightmares. She would rail about a boy; she never said his name. I thought it was the delirium. Again and again, though, she would say, "He shouldn't have got rid of the boy. Martin shouldn't have got rid of the boy." That's what she said.'

'So why didn't you come forward earlier?' asked Fiona.

'It didn't make any sense; I believed it to be drug-induced psychosis. That was until you found Matthew's remains. It was only then

I realised with horror that Martin may have had something to do with the death of Matthew Sissons. I swear, I had no idea up until that point. If I had, I would have asked Valerie about it when she was awake. What I assumed was end-of-life delirium turned out to be deathbed turmoil. Almost a confession. She never mentioned it, except in her sleep or near-sleep.'

'Thank you, Josie. You've been most helpful. We won't take up any more of your time.'

***

'Well that's a turnup,' said Fiona as they climbed into Carlos's car. 'So he was the one who killed Matthew after all.'

'It's still hard to imagine why Harold Sissons and Martin Webb worked together on this, unless the theory of Webb hiding the body and later planting it in the house is right.'

'That's making more sense to me.'

'I suggest it's time to interview Martin Webb,' Carlos said. 'Do you think we need backup?'

'I'm under instructions not to disturb the DCI. I daren't contact him on the hearsay of a delirious woman implicating Webb in a murder that happened twenty years ago. The rifle's been removed from the property. I doubt the spade's been returned yet, so we should be able to defend ourselves against an old man unless he's got a house full of garden implements. A scythe, perhaps.'

Carlos rubbed his head. 'If so, you're on it.'

He pulled up outside Webb's house fifteen minutes later, deliberately leaving the car on the road for anyone to see, just in case. This time, he wasn't going to be lured round the back; he hammered on the front door.

The door opened almost immediately and a pale and drawn Martin Webb left it ajar, walking back inside. They followed.

'Now what do you want?' Webb snapped.

'We'd like to ask you a few questions about the death of Matthew Sissons, Colonel,' said Fiona.

Enough of a flinch crossed Webb's face for Carlos to notice, informing him Josie Reynolds had been telling the truth.

'Such as?'

'Such as, did you kill him?' Fiona pressed.

The colonel remained standing and leaned on his mantelpiece in front of a coal fire. Carlos scanned for anything that might be used as a weapon while Fiona engaged the man, who was distinctly frailer than the one he'd been accosted by a few days before.

Webb laughed cynically. 'You people don't know anything, do you? You didn't investigate when he died and now you're like blind men scrabbling in the dark.'

'Why don't you enlighten us?' suggested Carlos.

'Why should I?'

'Because your wife believed you killed the boy.'

The colonel stiffened. Pulse visible in his neck, he swallowed hard.

'What are you saying?'

'That your wife took a terrible secret to the grave. She confessed it to someone.'

The colonel was visibly shaken. He reached for a chair arm and lowered himself down into it.

'She remembered?'

'Yes,' said Carlos.

'The truth always comes out. That's what they say, isn't it?' The haughty demeanour cracked and a haunted look followed.

'Tell us how it happened. Was it an accident? Why don't you fill in the gaps?' Fiona's voice was gentler, and she sat close to the colonel. Carlos remained standing, prepared to ward off any sudden attack.

'My wife had attended the hospital that afternoon. I was with someone else – a woman.' The doctors gave Valerie some strong painkillers. On her way back from the hospital, she got one of her spasms.' The colonel choked back tears. 'She called home from a phone box to ask me to collect her, but I wasn't there. Then she called again, left a message to say not to worry, she was not far away and would take some of the morphine the doctor had prescribed.'

He put his head in his hands. 'If only I'd been home.'

Carlos and Fiona waited for him to regain his calm.

'Matthew was always flying up and down the road on his bike. He careered out of the Sissons' drive just as my wife passed in the car. I was walking home; I'd waved as she passed, but she didn't see me. There was an almighty loud crash, but she carried on towards our home. I didn't think she knew what she'd done.

'I raced over to find Matthew lying there on the road, crushed. I could see straight away he was gone. Killed outright. Sissons came out. I yelled at him to call for an ambulance. He stood there as if it was a dead sparrow lying on the ground, not his son. The man had a heart of stone. I tried to run into his house to use the phone. He stopped me, told me my wife would go to prison for a hit and run. I didn't have the full story then, but Sissons said he'd seen everything.

'Then, right there, with his son lying dead in the road, he came up with a proposition. He would deal with the body as long as I paid him £5,000 to keep quiet.'

Carlos's jaw dropped open. 'And you agreed?'

'My wife was a sick woman. What would you have done?'

Carlos didn't answer. *Not that,* he thought.

'I got home and found Valerie asleep on the couch. Even then, I was going to call the police until I saw the answerphone machine light flashing. I listened to the messages and her desperate call for help, and realised it was all my fault. Guilt overwhelmed me and I knew I could never let her pay for my indiscretion.

'I didn't know what Sissons did with the body. I never asked. I paid him the money, deleted the answerphone messages and Valerie never said a word about it to me. I didn't think she remembered or even knew what had happened – Sissons must have told her in some sick, twisted moment of retribution. He was always jealous, knowing how much I had loved Meg.

'The blackmail didn't end there. There were numerous payments over the years. If I hadn't loved Meg so much, I would have told the police after my wife died, but I didn't want to see her suffer any more than she already had.'

'You mean you didn't want her to hate you,' accused Fiona.

'No, I didn't, Sergeant. I thought we could make a fresh start once Sissons was out of the way.'

'You were the one skulking in the garage that day, weren't you?' asked Carlos.

'I remembered that Sissons had mentioned a few times how he'd kept evidence in case he needed it. I saw the bike and was going to dispose of it. You disturbed me and I ran. I suppose you've got it now?'

Carlos looked at Fiona who shook her head.

'We'll need you to make a statement and sign the confession,' she said. 'And did you also kill Harold Sissons?'

'I'd love to answer yes to that question, my dear, but no, I did not kill Sissons.'

Fiona beamed at Carlos. 'Perhaps you can accompany me to the station in the morning?'

Chapter 33

The next morning, there was a knock at Sophie's door. Carlos answered to find an attractive brunette on the doorstep.

'Mr Jacobi?'

'Carlos. I assume you're Lorna Milnthorpe?'

'Can we take a walk?' she asked.

'Why not?' He grabbed his coat and whistled for Lady to join him.

'I just want to ask about Matthew. My father told you I'm a journalist, but that's not why I'm here. Matthew was my friend. I never believed he ran away, although no-one at school would have blamed him. He showed me the bruises.'

Carlos gasped. 'So Harold Sissons *was* violent?'

'Yes. Didn't you know?'

'No, I didn't. Did Matthew tell you about it?'

'He swore me to secrecy. He was scared of being taken away and leaving his mother alone with his father. I kept his secret out of respect. He would never have left his mother. He adored her.'

'Did Harold hit his wife?'

'Not as far as I know. Matt – that's what I called him – said his father hit him whenever he could. I don't think Meg knew about it.' Lorna grabbed Carlos's arm, tears brimming over. 'I've carried this for over twenty years, and now I feel so ashamed. Could I have prevented Harold from killing him?'

Carlos stopped and turned to face her, laid his hands on her shoulders. 'Harold didn't kill him. It was a tragic accident. Nothing you could have done would have changed the outcome. All you did was be a loyal friend.'

Lorna stood back and stared up at Carlos. 'But I heard Matt's remains were found in the house. How could it have been an accident?'

Carlos explained what had actually happened on the fateful day. This woman deserved to know. How many more lives had Harold Sissons damaged?

'I can't tell you how much it means to me to know the truth after all these years. I was terrified something awful had happened at the hands of his father, but I was a twelve-year-old girl, and shy to boot. I didn't have anyone I could talk to about it. When I heard about the remains, I was physically sick, thinking I could have saved my friend if I'd been braver.'

They turned back towards the village in comfortable silence.

'I'm pleased Matthew had a friend like you,' Carlos said eventually.

She smiled for the first time since their meeting, a sparkle lightening up the dark lines beneath her eyes.

'You'll be pleased to know I have no interest in the murder of that evil man. There will be no press intrusion from me.'

***

After breakfast, Carlos took the door key to Sophie's house back around to Meg's. He let himself in and hung the key back in its allotted space. Next to it was a small bunch of keys labelled: 'Allotment'.

He reached into his pocket and pulled out his phone, dialling Caroline's number.

'Have you discovered anything?'

Carlos hesitated before explaining about Colonel Webb's part in covering up the death of Matthew all those years ago.

'There was a statement in Matthew's file, taken from Martin Webb, confirming your father's story. It seemed to validate that he'd run away and threw the police off the scent. Colonel Webb was a well-respected pillar of the community. No-one would have suspected him of lying. Harold blackmailed the colonel to cover up what had happened, although Webb only did it to protect his wife. As for Harold, I'm afraid he didn't seem to have a conscience.'

'You don't need to tell me that, I know. Poor Matthew. At least it's comforting to know that he died instantly. For all these years, I imagined he'd been abducted and feared all sorts of dreadful things had happened to him. I'm sorry the colonel colluded with the hateful man, but I can understand how he'd want to protect his wife in her condition.'

'That's very forgiving of you.'

'It was a tragedy of errors. What's the point now? I'm sure the colonel's suffered enough. Will he be charged?'

'That's down to the police.'

'Not that I care, but have you found out who killed Harold?'

Carlos turned over the allotment key in his hand, weighing up his options.

'I fear it wouldn't be in Meg's interest for me to pursue the case any further. Your mother's suffered enough.'

There was a pause at the other end of the phone.

'You know who did it then?'

'I believe I do. Yes.'

'And it's someone you don't think should pay for the crime?'

Carlos drew in a deep breath, wrestling with his conscience.

'I feel the person has suffered enough and justice has been served.

I'd rather not pursue this any further.'

'And what about the police? Do they suspect this person?'

'No. There's no reason for them to do so. As far as they're concerned, it was a robbery gone wrong. The Peak District has thousands of visitors every year. Anyone could have killed him. The trail's gone cold. A new man's on the case who's likely to put it to bed sooner rather than later. I think your new lawyer has connections in high places.'

'I see. You will please send me your bill for the work you've carried out. You'll be happy to know that my mother's decided to sell up and move up here. She's had far too many years away from me and the grandchildren.'

'I wish you and her every happiness, Caroline. It might be better if you deal with the sale and clearing yourself, though. In particular, I believe you might want to clear your father's allotment shed. I found a key on the hook when returning Sophie's key.'

'I'll do as you say. And Carlos?'

'Yes?'

'Thank you for your understanding throughout this horrible business.'

'You and your mother deserve some luck, Caroline. I hope you find peace.'

'Thanks again. Goodbye.'

On that note, it's time for me to see Barney Milnthorpe.

Carlos returned the bunch of keys to their rightful place and made his way towards the vicarage.

Epilogue

Caroline Winslow unlocked and opened the shed door. The allotment was a mile away from Peaks Hollow and it had taken time to find out the address without reminding people of the demise of Harold Sissons the previous Christmas. Eventually she had discovered it from a conversation between the woman in the grocery store and a villager when they were chatting about local produce.

The vegetables on the plot had long gone to seed and weeds were taking over. It had taken six months to sell the cottage, but now the sale was agreed, Caroline was down with the whole family, clearing and packing. Aiden wasn't aware of the allotment; she had pocketed the keys on one of the visits to help her mother gather personal things.

The shed was dark and dingy inside, and musty. The light from the opened door reflected off the front of a polished spade, lying on the floor as if it had been thrown down in a hurry. Traces of mud remained on the spade, which would never have been left that way by Harold. When Caroline turned the implement around, dried brown blood covered the rear.

'I bet that hurt.' She couldn't help smiling, but then shuddered. Her mother's wellington boots stood next to the spade. They were muddy and also bloodstained, as was an old coat her mother must have been wearing.

She wrapped the spade in a black plastic bin bag and put it in the car. It was still dark and no-one was around. She scrunched up newspaper and poured white spirit over the rest of the contents of the shed before throwing a match inside.

Caroline remained in the car at a distance, watching the bonfire until there was nothing left but ash. It would be blamed on kids, most likely, as it was obvious the plot had been abandoned.

Following a bumpy drive, Caroline approached an isolated marina she used to visit with school friends. There was a towpath where the boys would fish while the girls walked the banks, searching for kingfishers. Moving away from the boats that were moored beside the canal, Caroline walked along the towpath and removed the spade from the plastic bag, tossing it into the canal.

***

Fiona Cook had arrived home late. She was still puzzled about the Harold Sissons case; she couldn't understand why Carlos had packed it in so suddenly six months earlier. It was out of character. He wouldn't discuss it, so she trusted his reasons, and suspected they had something to do with whatever had happened between him and Terry Masters.

Carlos had stayed in the area for the week after Christmas seeing the local vicar for counselling. She hoped it had helped, but didn't pry. Personally, she hated having an unsolved case on her books. The police had left the case of the boy, Matthew Sissons, unsolved for twenty years, and she feared history was repeating itself. DCI Matlock had been happy to let it go cold. He didn't want any run-ins with the top brass after the big shot lawyer had rattled their cage.

That also gave her sleepless nights. What did Steve's boss have on the Chief Superintendent that caused him to take Masters off the case? These questions would have to be answered one day.

Masters had requested and been granted a transfer soon after he was removed from the investigation. She suspected he was ordered to put in the request, but would never know if that were the case.

Sleep eventually came, blocking out the questions.

She woke in the early hours, hearing heeled footsteps walking along the towpath past her boat. *You really shouldn't be out walking alone in the dark, dear*, she thought as she closed her eyes again. Just as she drifted back into sleep, she heard a loud splash.

'Damn fly tippers, always throwing stuff in the canal.' She pulled the duvet over her head. 'That's a job for uniform.'

THE END

Author's Note

Thank you for reading *Body in the Woods*, the first book in my Carlos Jacobi series. If you have enjoyed it, **please leave an honest review on Amazon** and/or any other platform you may use. I love receiving feedback from readers and can assure you that I read every review.

Look out for the next in the series. *The Bradgate Park Murders* will be released in 2021.

Why not check out my Rachel Prince Mystery series?

Keep in touch:

Sign up for my no-spam newsletter for news of new releases, offers and competitions at: www.dawnbrookespublishing.com

Follow me on Facebook: www.facebook.com/dawnbrookespublishing

Follow me on Twitter: www.twitter.com/dawnbrookes1

Follow me on Pinterest: www.pinterest.co.uk/dawnbrookespublishing

Books by Dawn Brookes

Rachel Prince Mysteries

A Cruise to Murder

Deadly Cruise

Killer Cruise

Dying to Cruise

A Christmas Cruise Murder

Murderous Cruise Habit

Honeymoon Cruise Murder

A Murder Mystery Cruise

Carlos Jacobi

Body in the Woods

The Bradgate Park Murders

Memoirs

Hurry up Nurse: memoirs of nurse training in the 1970s

Hurry up Nurse 2: London calling

Hurry up Nurse 3: More adventures in the life of a student nurse

Picture Books for Children

Ava & Oliver's Bonfire Night Adventure

Ava & Oliver's Christmas Nativity Adventure

Danny the Caterpillar

Gerry the One-Eared Cat

Suki Seal and the Plastic Ring

Acknowledgements

Thank you to my editor Alison Jack, as always, for her kind comments about the book and for suggestions, corrections and amendments that make it a more polished read. Thanks to Alex Davis for the final proofread, corrections and suggestions.

Thank you to lecturers and fellow students on the MA Creative Writing course who went through the early chapters with me. In particular, thanks to Elle, Amber, Ven, Matt Clegg, Laura, Victoria and Simon for their comments.

A huge thanks to Moy McCrory who offered expert guidance, and who understood what I was trying to get across in the story as a whole. I enjoyed our discussions around coercive control and ethical writing immensely. It was challenging weaving in aspects of traumatic amnesia into Meg's role in the story, whilst gradually revealing small steps of her recovery from decades of control. For Carlos; the challenge was how to give him permission to walk away without his desire to see justice done ending in failure. I think we managed to pull it off!

Thanks to my beta readers for comments and suggestions, and for their time given to reading the early drafts.

Thanks to my immediate circle of friends who are so patient with me when I'm absorbed in my fictional world and for your continued support in all my endeavours.

About the Author

Dawn Brookes holds an MA in creative writing and is author of the *Rachel Prince Mystery* series, combining a unique blend of murder, cruising and medicine with a touch of romance. Her latest venture is the Carlos Jacobi series involving a tenacious PI who is joined by Fiona Cook, a troubled, but likeable detective sergeant.

Dawn has a 39-year nursing pedigree and takes regular cruise holidays, which she says are for research purposes! She brings these passions together with a love of clean crime to her writing.

Dawn is also author of a series of nursing memoirs: The *Hurry up Nurse* series. Dawn worked as a hospital nurse, a midwife, district nurse and community matron across her career. Before turning her hand to writing for a living, she had multiple articles published in professional journals and co-edited a nursing textbook.

She grew up in Leicester, later moved to London and Berkshire, but now lives in Derbyshire. Dawn holds a Bachelor's degree with Honours and a Master's degree in education. Writing across genres, she also writes for children. Dawn has a passion for nature and loves animals, especially dogs. Animals will continue to feature in her children's books, as she believes caring for animals and nature helps children to become kinder human beings.

Printed in Great Britain
by Amazon